UNKINDNESS
OF
CRIMSON QUEEN

ARYA SLOANE

Unkindness of Crimson Queen

Table of Contents

Content Warning

This book contains content that might be triggering to some readers, included, but not limited to, mentions of sexual assault, murder and death, explicit language, sexual content, alcohol usage, blood play, violence, panic attacks, grief, self harm, and eating disorder.

Reader discretion advised. Your mental health matters.

Author's Note to Em Dash Critics

I know I used a lot of em dashes in chapter two. Funny enough, if you look at the top right of your keyboard, you will find humans can use them too—crazy, isn't it?

Chapter 1. Forgive Me If You Can.

Francis.

Her screams echoed through the castle, willing my barely awake body to jerk upwards: off the floor by her room. My head spun in every direction as I scanned the empty hallways, until my eyes landed on the door my Princess hid behind.

I yanked the door wide open, ready to save her from whatever danger she'd found herself in; yet my eyes were met with her peaceful silhouette.

My eyelids heavied as I listened to her calm breathing—a lullaby to my ears. I shook my head, scaring away the exhaustion: I had to keep watch, make sure when she woke she was not alone. All the same, any sleep I'd managed made me more tired than before.

Reluctantly, I closed the door, depriving my mind of the only view that brought me the slightest peace.

My hands shook as I took my designated place by her door; my back screamed in protest, begging for a stretch or perhaps a short break. I ignored my body's demands, determined to stay put: guarding her until she'd eventually order me away. Like the guard dog that she'd called me.

Although, I wouldn't be truthful if I said only altruism ruled me, for if my eyes were deprived of a mere glimpse of her I would surely go mad.

Perhaps I *was* mad, for I could not remember anyone having such power over me before. How masterfully she trapped me in a web of my own feelings without so much as trying. And how lucky I was to be in that trap; how lucky I was to be granted a mere glance into her wondrous, brown eyes, the smell of lavender on her smooth, soft skin; how lucky I was to witness her stubborn yet determined mind.

Even if I was no longer worthy of those things, I still prayed there was a chance of forgiveness. Thus, I sat by her door night and day, listening to her even breathing, guarding her rest from any monsters nearby.

She hadn't woken in days—save for the few times Florence had forced her to feed—and I began to worry. I knew she needed rest after what she'd been through, yet every time she drifted away, I worried her eyes would never open again.

I closed my eyes, regretting it in an instant, for her pained face invaded my mind. The disappointment that had shone upon her features when I'd told her the truth—the truth that made her run from me, run straight into the open arms of our enemy.

The memory of her lips turning into the saddest of smiles shot an arrow straight through my heart. The memory of her eyes filling with tears that threatened to destroy me from within—

The door at the end of the hall creaked open: the red-headed woman appeared at its threshold.

With a silk pillow in her hands, Rox took a small step towards me.

A sigh escaped me as I braced myself for another one of her lectures, yet she spared me the misery, shoving the pillow at my head before shutting the door to her and Florence's room.

"Thank you," I mumbled at the closed door, settling the pillow down on the floor.

Rox hadn't acknowledged me since Simon brought us the note—a few nights after Cordelia went missing—with handwriting I'd immediately recognized as Caleb's.

Royal palace. Forgive me if you can. The note had read, and I'd known it then: Caleb betrayed us. He betrayed us and couldn't even face it—sending poor Simon to relay the message. A traitor and a coward. Though I supposed I was no better.

The parchment crumbled in my fist. "You were right." I glanced at my found sister before dropping onto the chair in our study; guilt crippled inside of me.

Ever since I'd brought Cordelia into the castle, Rox had been voicing her concerns with Caleb's odd behavior that only worsened as nights passed on. I had my suspicions too, yet disregarded Roxanne's controversies, refusing to believe someone I owed my life to could betray me this way.

Royal palace. I reread the note again and again as if the message would change, revealing something I was clearly missing, until Florence ripped the parchment from my hands, disposing of it in the fireplace. "What do we do now?" her voice full of determination.

I watched the paper catch aflame, turning into ash as my mind rushed through every possible solution.

"I must go," I announced to my family, already reaching for my dagger as though my throw could reach the Royal palace from our study.

"No." Simon shook his head, his hand gripped onto my forearm. "It's a trap, we can't trust him."

"Cordelia is there. I must go." I charged toward the exit.

"Not without a plan." Roxanne jerked the sleeve of my cloak, stopping me in place.

"There's no time for a plan," I argued, but stayed put.

"You can't get yourself killed simply because you are emotional." She threw the words I'd used when she tried to go after Issac all those years ago. We never spoke of it, but if I'd let her go that night they would share a grave today. I often wondered if she blamed me for not granting her the peace she longed for. Though, after Florence had joined us, she seemed happy with her cursed eternity.

"Sit down." Roxanne commanded me, her finger pointing at a cushion. "Do you remember the layout of the palace?" She asked, handing me a piece of parchment, a quill, and ink.

Roxanne's plan had been plain and simple, though it required a dozen skilled vampires willing to risk their lives for a royal princess that they had mostly disliked purely for her upbringing: which certainly had complicated the situation and delayed our rescue.

Their deaths would forever be the shadows of my consciousness.

Now I wondered if I'd made a mistake listening to my sister that night.

Perhaps if I'd gone alone I could have saved Cordelia and brought her family home. Perhaps I would have been lucky enough to save her sister before the tragedy occurred. Or perhaps Roxanne had saved my life that day.

My head hit the pillow on the cold marble floor; my eyes studied the ceiling as I battled against the exhaustion slowly winning over my strong will.

The black widow worked along its web on the ceiling, and I watched the creature as my eyelids heavied—

"Where is Cordelia?" Florence's voice brought me out of my swift slumber. "Wake up!" She shook my shoulders with strength I had not expected from her. "Cordelia is gone."

I rubbed my eyes, willing myself awake. How long had I slept—

"What do you mean *gone*?" My voice cracked as I rushed to my feet, pushing through the threshold of Cordelia's room. My eyes scanned the painfully empty space until they landed on a wide open window. "Gods damned me."

Chapter 2. This Must End Now.

Cordelia.

The sunlight played on her golden locks as my fingers worked through her long, soft braid. She asked me to arrange her hair into a crown like all the women in the court did. *"You are so beautiful."* I smiled at her reflection in the mirror.

"So are you." Sandra smiled back, her gaze traveling to the window. *"Where are they going?"* The crease between her brows deepened.

I followed her gaze until my eyes landed on our brother, Brian, and his friend, Gabriel—proudly walking by his side—before they disappeared behind the gates of the palace's citadel.

"Somewhere they will find trouble." I rolled my eyes, pinning the braid the way Sandra wished. *"All done!"* My fingers adjusted a few stray strands before handing her a smaller mirror.

"Thank you, Lia, I love it!" Sandra studied the hairstyle: her smile grew bigger. *"Your hands are magic!"* She beamed.

"It wasn't hard, Sunshine." I shrugged before placing a small kiss on the top of her head, the familiar aroma hitting my nostrils—

"Spare me, Cordelia," my sister cried, reaching for my—covered in blood—hands. *"Please—"* she croaked: my crimson fingers coiled around her throat.

The room darkened. The sunshine disappeared as though it was never there. My gaze met Sandra's: tears filled her eyes, her skin paled.

"I must kill you!" My voice did not belong to me. "I cannot." The tears streamed down my face. "You must die!"

"You are like her!" Sandra screeched; her body went limp underneath mine. "You are just like her," she whispered and her eyes closed.

She died and I could not remember why it mattered.

I stared at her fair skin—that was now a shade darker than her usual color—her golden locks that were now raven-black, and a scar right below her collarbone that painted her skin light pink.

Blood spilled from the woman's mouth when a sinister smile stretched her lips—

My body jerked upwards, struggling to free myself from the web that choked me from within. My heart squeezed in panic as I fought with the invisible barrier that kept me in place until my thoughts gained some clarity; my eyes searched the room I'd learned to call mine.

I forced my lungs to expand, leaving nothing but the dreadful emptiness.

My hands clung to the wrinkled sheets underneath my body—the evidence of my never-ending, restless nights. *This must end now.*

My mind fought through the black widow's web of my thoughts as I forced myself out of the bed—

I glanced out the window. The Moon was barely visible in the snowstorm.

Cold. The window was cold to the touch.

I put on the trousers—that Roxanne had gifted me all those weeks ago—atop the woolen stockings I found in my drawer: the winter was in its full glory, bestowing us with its cruel, cold spells, making my upcoming trip a lot less tolerant.

I placed a dagger in my boot; another at the belt of my trousers. *I will die before I get the chance to use them.*

I would die.

He would die.

He would die and I would find peace I did not deserve. Perhaps the Moon would show me kindness for once and reunite me with my family—

The window frame stood unmoving under my struggles as if it hadn't been opened for centuries. I fought against the rusty latch until it jerked free with a horrible screech.

Third story.

My hands stretched for the closest tree branch. I could only hope it was as strong as it looked.

The last time I had climbed trees, before Mother had prohibited me from such an *outrageous act,* was lost in my memory—

The branch slipped through my hand, sending my heart to my heels.

My skin throbbed as my hold tightened around the end of the branch. The snowstorm sang its serenade—

Several minutes and a few scratches later, my feet felt the ground.

The snow scrunched underneath my steps, though the sound was lost in the hum of the wind. The white snow turned black in the darkness of the night—

The stables were dark and cold. I forced my mind to calm and allow my vision to adjust, remembering Francis' words of our kind's ability to see in the darkness. *Our kind. Our curse.* The curse that made me kill—

Annabelle nickered in greeting as I prepared her for the trip she might have to come back from alone.

Once the saddle was in its place, I yanked on each strap until it sat secure.

Last time I'd found myself in this position, Francis had caught me before I'd managed to escape the stables. Only this time, if he found me, he would chain me to my bed for the rest of my days.

Still and all that wouldn't stop me from keeping the promise I had given to *her*. Still and all, nothing would have stopped me from ordering Annabelle towards the Royal palace.

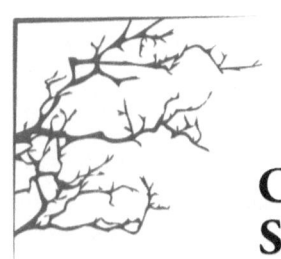

Chapter 3.
Surrender.

The once clear trail to the palace was now hidden underneath a white blanket, stealing Annabelle's every step. I tightened the cloak around myself, covering my face as much as was possible, though even that wouldn't stop dozens of needles–like snowflakes from scraping my cheeks.

It didn't take long for the cold to sneak into my bones, sending shivers through my already weakened body.

"You show me no mercy," I spat at the Moon that surely laughed at me stopless.

Annabelle balked when the wind worsened its blows, almost sending us backwards.

Mother never allowed me to ride in such conditions. How could she not know that one night I might need such a skill? She wished me to fail. She wished me death—

The ache in my throat erupted like a forest catching aflame in the middle of summer. My knuckles whitened as I squeezed the reins harder, refusing to succumb to the wind's blows.

I closed my eyes, willing my mind present, though it did nothing for my inevitably growing hunger.

Florence had forced me to feed two nights ago while I was in and out of consciousness—I couldn't protest.

Though, I won't need to worry about that for long: I walked towards my end.

Weightless—

My body flew forward as my hands dug into the saddle—desperate to keep myself atop—when Annabelle balked against an invisible barrier on the path. She bucked again and again, until my hands surrendered their struggle and the snow caught me in its cruel, cold embrace.

The reins remained wrapped around my right wrist, digging into my flesh; my shoulder screamed in protest. The back of my eyes prickled as tears of pain threatened to escape.

"I despise you!" I shouted at the Moon. "I wish my soul to never be yours!" My voice echoed in the sudden silence of the forest.

Princess knows composure, my mother's voice exclaimed.

Annabelle quieted.

Princess knows forethought. Mother persisted.

I mounted Annabelle once more.

Princess knows consideration.

"Enough." I whispered.

You are to be Queen, act like it.

"Enough!" The roar that erupted from my throat silenced her at once.

The snowstorm calmed.

UNKINDNESS OF CRIMSON QUEEN

After the night in the woods I still struggled to navigate, and the cold spells of winter's strikes, Annabelle was happy to stay behind once I'd said my goodbyes to her. I could only hope a kind soul would untie her reins were I to never return.

The air around me changed when the familiar battlements peered from a line of dense spruce that shielded me from the guards' view. The snow melted through my trousers as I sat on the cold soil; the tips of my fingers now wore a grayish tint. My eyes scanned the now foreign grounds, unable to find a single familiar face.

I couldn't remember the last time so many warriors had surrounded the palace from the outside. Mother had always been against such dangerous theatrics: giving away information as intimate as the size of the Royal army was foolish, thus the guarding outposts had always remained hidden behind the stone walls. It seemed Kane cared not to keep his numbers unknown. Was it arrogance or ignorance? I did not know. Perhaps both.

I moved an inch closer, searching for the entrance to Mother's passage. It'd been years since I last used it... And that day I surely hoped to never have to again.

The day before the Crimson War ended—the only day in the history of our Kingdom when the Royal palace had been invaded and nearly occupied.

Sleep wouldn't reach me on that night, as though my consciousness knew the danger about to crash upon our home.

Gabriel barged into my room when the Moon was still bright: dressed in his armor, he commanded me to vacate the palace. I hadn't seen him in months: he'd been at the front lines alongside my brother.

I couldn't help but to notice the changes in his appearance. His bronze hair was now cut short, his usual cool–toned skin now wore a tan; his green—full of life eyes—were now vacant.

"My brother?" I asked, my hands wrapping around his neck.

He shook his head.

My world broke apart.

The rest of the night crumbled into a blur.

The fire, the cries, the blood...

The world swept past me as my family ran from the palace through my Mother's passage. Royal guards surrounded us, their weapons drawn; we left our home, believing we would never come back.

Even when Mother went into labor in the depths of the forest, I couldn't bring myself out of the trance. Stunned, I watched her bleed onto the grounds, surrounded by our most trusted guards and my younger sister. None of them knew Brian was no longer walking beside us in the Moon's realm.

Now I couldn't remember how we'd returned to the palace; I couldn't remember the faces of my newborn twin siblings, or who had told me my father hadn't survived the war either.

My father's face became a blur in my mind.

Would I forget *her* face too? Would *she* only come to me in my nightmares—

A cold hand wrapped around my waist.

Another fell onto my mouth, drowning my growing scream.

I kicked the air when my feet no longer felt the snow.

The choking panic pushed up my throat.

The dawn was upon my struggles.

My back collided against the stranger's chest, their body towering above mine. I was being carried away from my hiding spot. Away from the palace's grounds...

"Shut it, before you get us both executed." The familiar male voice hissed into my ear. Dozens of goosebumps pierced down my neck; my nails scratched and scraped at his skin. "It's me!" He whispered, turning me against the tree to face him. "Calm down, it's me!" Caleb said, his hand still atop my mouth.

A new wave of panic stole my heart for a moment before the corners of my eyes darkened.

My hand reached for the dagger at my waist.

My mind calmed despite being cornered by the enemy, despite knowing my end neared.

My fingers wrapped around the hilt—

Before I managed to deliver my blow, his hand caught my dagger by the blade, avoiding the intended attack.

His eyes locked on mine; his body—unmoving as a statue.

Fear. Fear—something I never saw Caleb wear—flashed across his face.

My body stilled.

The crunch of snow reached my ears as countless steps shortened their distance. Dozens of Wurdulacs' guards moved in our direction.

This was my end.

An end far worse than death.

Caleb let go off my blade, planting the bloody finger on his lips, gesturing for me to keep quiet. I wouldn't be able to make a sound if I wished to: his other hand was still atop my mouth.

His body pushed mine against the oak tree, covering me from the view.

I squeezed the dagger tighter, drawing a small, silent breath through my nose. Sweat prickled my skin despite the cold air caressing every uncovered inch of my flesh.

The steps heavied as they neared, every bone in my body froze.

Dear Moon, take me to my family.

Dear Moon, spare me the struggle on my way to rest.

I beg of you, show me your kindness this once.

I clenched my jaw, readying for the attack. Readying for my inevitable end—

The snow crunched as the Wurdulacs' steps... marched past us, along the perimeter of the palace's grounds.

The forest quieted; my heart fought for its freedom.

I counted every bang in my chest. Once I reached two hundred Caleb whispered, "They're gone." His hand freed me as he took one step backwards. "You are lucky I found you before the guards went on patrol—"

My fingers squeezed the dagger in my hand before I planted it into Caleb's side—exactly as he taught me. Rage squeezed my throat when his eyes met mine.

No longer could I see the person in front of me—only the blurry silhouette of a man that haunted my nightmares, the silhouette of a man who'd witnessed my soul torn apart.

UNKINDNESS OF CRIMSON QUEEN

The fresh blood reached my nostrils and the familiar smell spun my head into an endless dance. Nausea crept inside my stomach.

Strong hands dug into my shoulders, shoving me onto the bloody snow.

The air escaped my lungs, fire erupted in my chest.

I gulped, rolling onto my back. The pale, morning Moon stared down at me as I struggled for my next breath.

A pair of boots moved my direction. "Do you feel better now that you've made me bleed?" Caleb offered me a hand I ignored. My hands searched for my weapon.

Every breath was as good as ash to my lungs. I stumbled to my knees when Caleb's accusatory gaze met mine.

"I just saved your life: if anyone else saw you here you wouldn't live to see another moonrise." He assessed the injury I'd given him. "And this is what I get in return."

"You deserve far more than that." I seethed through clenched teeth when the first rays of sunshine appeared in the distance.

I retrieved my lost dagger from the crimson snow before turning back toward the palace—I was running out of time.

"Where are you going?" Caleb's hands caught my armed wrist, pulling me back.

"Let go of me, Caleb!" I hissed.

"You are not serious." His hold only hardened. "Where is Francis?"

"What do I know of his whereabouts?" I fought with his grasp.

"Does he know you are here?" Caleb added softer. When the silence spoke for me, he sighed. "Why are you here,

Cordelia?" His eyes filled with a pity I never saw them possess.

Pity. *He pitied me!*

"I am here to kill him." I spat out, forcefully freeing my wrist. How dare he *pity* me?

"Cordelia..." Caleb stared at me and I couldn't help but to study his features back. The resemblance he shared with my long resting brother was astonishing and terrifying. Same dark brown eyes, dark raven hair and light skin. There was no doubt we were blood related.

I averted my gaze, the sickness twisting my stomach.

"You can't stay here." Caleb broke our silence. "Unless you want to burn." He started towards the palace.

I turned towards the palace; my eyes searching Mother's passage in the distance.

"Go to the cabin, Cordelia." Caleb pushed past me without sparing a glance. "Wait for me there." He said over his shoulder before stepping out of the sanctuary of the forest.

"I'm not—" The words deflated on my tongue: the perimeter of the palace caught aflame.

Chapter 4. Brother.

The warmth of the fire reached my skin as my eyes adjusted to the brightness.

"What in the Kingdom?" I stumbled backwards, my back meeting the bark of a willow tree.

A wall of flame surrounded the palace, keeping Wurdulacs safe within the stone walls: forcing intruders away from their sanctuary.

Despite the frustration that spread through my veins, I couldn't help but marvel at the effort the Wurdulacs put into keeping the palace secured during the daylight. Though my appreciation was short-lived, for the rays of sunshine grew from the horizon, ushering me towards the only nearby shelter.

The woods ended its dance with the snowstorm long before I turned onto the small path towards my sanctuary.

My heart galloped inside my chest when the old, beaten down cabin appeared from its hidden spot in the meadow. Seeking shelter in the one place Caleb expected me was foolish no doubt.

If I wanted a chance to finish what I'd come here for, I needed to escape the cabin before Caleb arrived.

The wooden steps by the door's threshold creaked as I retrieved the hidden key from the slit in between the door frame.

I supposed Francis worried not for the intrusion on his family's home when it held nothing of value but his memories. Though the guilt of being here without permission still left a sour taste in my mouth.

I yanked the lock open.

The house seemed to have aged at least a hundred years since the time I was here last. The floors creaked with every step I took, the quiet whispers of the walls silenced.

A strong smell of sandalwood hit my senses when I entered the room I'd resided in before.

Children's old paintings and books with worn out covers still occupied every corner of the room, yet... As though a hurricane went through the room, it felt more disorganized than usual; it felt odd, it felt empty.

It felt empty despite the small bed that almost took up the entirety of the room, despite the wooden chest of drawers in the corner, overflowing with dozens of trinkets.

A painting of two people laid atop the chest. The oil canvas cracked and yellowed with age, dust covered the faces of a couple. A man and a woman sat in an embrace, their smiles shone through the painting.

The woman's features were similar to Francis': brown curly hair, warm, tawny skin, sharp cheekbones, her eyes the color of onyx. She was a true beauty as she leaned against the man in their embrace.

The man was the exact opposite: white as snow hair, nearly translucent, ivory skin, his eyes' rims carried the color of ruby. He shared his smile and the shape of his eyes with Francis.

I laid the painting back down when my legs sunk onto the bed: exhaustion and hunger arising from the shadows.

My eyelids heavied on the small opening of the window where the paint had fallen off with age. Shy rays of sunshine peered into the room; their thin lines shone bright in the darkness.

My hand stretched towards the light until my fingers felt the burning warmth. My hand shook from the sensation, yet I dared not to move away. The dust waltzed under the beam. My skin burned.

I waited, and waited until the pain was unbearable, and then some more.

My skin turned the color of a rich burgundy before I moved from the sunshine flame.

My heart raced as I assessed the injury; my lungs filled for the first time since *she'd* left me.

I closed my eyes, letting the pain spread through my body, reaching every corner of my mind, until my soul quieted from its cries. The pain felt good. I was broken.

I sat on the bed, my eyes watching the light move inch by inch, until it disappeared and the room had become gloomy once again.

Taking my boots off, I made my way into the sheets that Francis and I had shared that night. His pillow still smelled like jasmine, and I let myself drown in his aroma, hoping it would deter the nightmares that were inevitable companions to my sleep.

Grotesque visions invaded my slumber; the rustle of the cabin overwhelmed my rest, shielding me from the nightmares that patiently awaited my failure—

My eyes flew open at the sound of heavy boots behind the black painted window.

My heart raced before I could register the danger, panic squeezing my chest in its strong fist. My hands reached for the dagger attached to my belt.

The main door to the cabin creaked open as I hurried to my feet, ready for whatever was to come.

Everything in my body rebelled against the impending danger; my mind screamed at me to flee, yet my legs stood frozen, waiting to face the disruption.

After what seemed eternity, the door to the room opened. Caleb stood at the threshold: his hands up in surrender.

My brows furrowed as I pointed my dagger at his chest. The dagger that surely couldn't stand against Caleb's skill and the sword—my sword—strapped to his back.

"You stayed." He broke the growing silence between us.

"What do you want?" I rasped, my voice still hoarse from sleep.

When Caleb didn't reply I raised the dagger higher: pointing the blade at his exposed neck.

"I—" His jaw flexed before averting his gaze.

"Don't waste my time." My fingers tightened around the hilt.

"I need your help." Caleb sighed. "I know how to deal with Kane and his loyalists."

The dagger nearly fell from my grasp: surely I was asleep. "Get out." I rolled my eyes, pointing towards the door with my blade.

"I need your help." Caleb repeated with the same calmness as before. "Cordelia—"

"Unbelievable," I hissed. "For years you've been betraying the people that loved you, choosing the monster instead, and now you want to *deal* with him." I seethed. "And you expect *my* help after everything you have done to me." My body trembled as the corners of my vision darkened. "Am I supposed to believe you?"

Caleb staggered backwards. "I am telling you the truth."

"Supposedly." I shrugged. "What in the Kingdom do you want from me?"

Hope shone through his eyes when they met mine as though I had already agreed to whatever he would ask of me. "I need the instructions to create Royal steel." He started. "Perhaps you know where your mother kept the archives..."

A bright laughter—foreign to my ears—broke through me. "Why in the Kingdom would I tell you?" An odd, unnatural, smile spread across my face. "So you could run to your father and destroy all of us at once? I might be a fool for coming here, but I am not mad, Caleb." I rolled my eyes. "If that's all, you should run back to Kane before he starts suspecting your disloyalty." I choked when *his* name left my lips.

Goosebumps traveled through my skin when Caleb took a step forward. I raised my weapon once again.

"You *are* a fool for coming here, Cordelia." His voice dropped a few octaves; my hands trembled as I squeezed the hilt of my dagger harder at his sudden change. "You are delusional if you think you can kill him yourself. You need my help as much as I need yours." Caleb chuckled, taking another step forward until the point of my blade touched his skin. "Next time Kane sees you, you will be begging for death."

Little did Caleb know, I already begged for such an outcome in my prayers. "I am not afraid of him or you."

A sinister smile spread across Caleb's face. "You should be."

"And you dare to wonder why I refuse to help." I seethed. "Get out, Caleb."

His lips turned into a thin line before he retreated a step. I wondered whether he was following my orders, yet his voice reached my ears anew. "After what Kane has done to you and Mories—"

"Mories?" My heart stopped at the sound of my childhood nurse's name.

"She is alive." Caleb swallowed, his eyes staring into the distance. "Barely, but she will live."

I forced a breath in, trying to calm my galloping heart.

"I couldn't take it anymore." Caleb continued. "Not when he hurt someone I know as my true mother." The lighting of the room must have been playing tricks, for the tears filling Caleb's eyes could not have been genuine. "I know there is no redemption for my actions." He whispered.

"You are right, you don't deserve redemption." I spat out. How dare he cry over what he'd brought upon us all? How dare he feel sorry for himself when the dead wouldn't take another breath?

"I want to make things right, even if it's the last thing I ever do, Cordelia." Caleb sighed. "You were right." He nodded. "I am a coward who could not stand against evil. But I am ready to change for my true family."

Claps sounded through the room followed by a low laughter. The man with amber eyes leaned on the doorframe, a familiar smirk spreading across his face. "Such a great speech." Francis clapped once more. "You should write it down."

Chapter 5. I Have No Home.

F rancis took a step inside the room, his eyes fixated on Caleb.

"Francis." Caleb cleared his throat.

"What did I say about seeing you next to her again?" Francis' voice dropped, not a hint of a smile remained. "I can see that you have healed from the wound I gave you, perhaps you need another." He pointed his finger at Caleb's chest. "Right here. What do you say, *brother*?"

"I am not here to fight." Caleb moved closer to the exit, away from me. His left leg dragged behind him—the leg I stabbed the night before.

"I see I am not your only foe." Francis snickered, glancing at Caleb's injury.

Caleb merely shook his head when his gaze fell upon me. "You are not," he sighed. "Please believe me, Cordelia," he said at last without sparing Francis a glance. "We need each other. If you tell me where the archives are, I will—"

"You will go to hell." Francis unsheathed his silver dagger, stepping in between Caleb and I. "And I will personally send you there."

"Please." Caleb put his hands up in surrender. "I am merely trying to help—"

"You will help by leaving and never showing your face here or at the castle ever again." Francis raised his dagger.

"You are making a mistake." Caleb retreated.

"The only mistake I made was trusting you." Francis cornered him, until Caleb's back met the door frame. "Leave before this dagger finds its place in your heart." He growled.

Caleb drew a small breath, reaching for the hilt of my sword strapped to his back.

I swallowed at the sight of the gift my long resting father had left me. The only memory of Father was held by the one who contributed to the deaths of his wife and children. The only memory of him was now a threat to my life.

Francis moved in an instant. His hands visibly shook as he brought the dagger to Caleb's throat, yet it was me who spoke, "How dare you threaten me with my own sword?" I moved to Francis' side.

"I was merely returning what is rightfully yours." Caleb froze.

"How generous of you." Francis rolled his eyes, reluctantly retreating his dagger so slightly.

In one smooth motion, Caleb unsheathed my sword, holding out the hilt towards me. "Please consider my offer."

"Out." Francis pointed the dagger at the door. "Now."

"You know where to find me." Caleb threw over the shoulder, showing himself out.

When the main door slammed shut Francis' eyes found mine. His features relaxed as he put his dagger into the scabbard; his amber eyes filled with relief. "Cordelia," he whispered.

Dark brown curls fell around his face, his soft, bronze jaw now wore a scar; my fingers itched for a touch.

I took a step backwards when his hands reached for mine. "I have to go." I mumbled, attaching the sword to my belt.

I didn't know you. I wasn't in love with you, Cordelia.

"I was worried." His hands dropped to his sides. "I woke and you were gone."

"You needn't worry yourself." I shrugged, moving towards the door.

Did he get the scar while rescuing me from the palace? Was he injured with Royal steel?

I wasn't in love—

"Where are you going?" Francis' charged after me. "Cordelia!" He yelled when I escaped the cabin and broke into a run.

The piercing frost bit my bare feet; the cool wind brushed through my tousled braid—

The horses were only a few yards away when Francis' hand caught my waist. "Cordelia!"

"Let go of me, Francis!" I fought his strong hold—in vain. "I must go!"

"Tell me where you are going and I might consider it." His grip tightened.

"Let go!" A roar broke through my throat as I freed myself, charging towards the forest; Annabelle long forgotten.

"Cordelia!"

The frost embraced my bare feet, the cold snow pricked my flesh with dozens of needles; I ran faster.

"Cordelia!" Francis raced after me.

I unsheathed the dagger Francis had gifted me so long ago when his steps shortened the distance.

Could I hurt him?

Would I hurt him?

"Where are you going, Princess?" He pulled on the end of my tunic, his other hand wrapping around me anew.

"Let go!" I screamed when my feet stumbled upon themselves, dragging us both to the ground. "You won't stop me!" I struggled against Francis' body atop mine.

"Stop you from what?" His face was mere inches from mine.

Without a second thought I brought my dagger to his throat. My hand shook, yet I held it firmly near his exposed skin.

Francis' brows rose as he assessed the threat before he asked again, "Stop you from what, Princess?"

His amber eyes showed no bother by the weapon at his neck. *Was he doubting my skill?*

"Let go." I whispered, my hand moving the blade closer.

"The sun has set, we must go home." Francis' voice turned stern.

Home. Kane has taken my home.

"I have no home."

"You do." Francis moved a stray strand of hair behind my ear. "Now put the dagger down and let's go."

I shook my head; my lips trembled, my grasp on the hilt hardened.

In a swift motion Francis disarmed me, pinning my hands above my head.

"If I have to drag you back to the castle, I will."

"I am staying here." I seethed.

Francis sighed. "All right then." He reached for my waist. "Some might think you just like being carried around by me."

I wrestled with his hold, the words spilling before I could stop them. "I am going to kill Kane."

Francis froze, his knees still pressing against my hips. The silence stretched in between us as Francis' eyes studied mine. "Cordelia..." He shook his head.

"Don't." I croaked. "Save your pity for someone else."

Snow surrounded every inch of my flesh, its cold grasp pulling me under.

Francis pinched the bridge of his nose. "What are you even going to kill him with?" He leaned closer. "With a silver dagger? Come now, Cordelia, it's not safe here."

"I am going to kill him with fire." My jaw clenched.

Would fire burn the same as sunshine?

I would find out soon enough, for Kane would not allow me to walk away unharmed; I would gladly burn alongside him.

"I suppose fire is better than a dagger, yet still not good enough. Let's go." Francis gathered to his feet, pulling me alongside him.

"I am not your responsibility." I freed my hand from his grasp.

"You are now." He brushed the snow off my head. "You are part of the family." He took a step towards the horses. When I didn't move he sighed, "Please, Cordelia, I am so sorry for what I had done to you, and I am so sorry—"

"You did what you had to do," I interrupted. "I understand."

Francis' amber eyes bored into mine as though contemplating his next words. "Charlotte has been waiting for you at the castle," he whispered. "She was very worried about you." My lips turned into a thin line at what he said next. "I promise you that we will come back here if within a week I'm unable to come up with a better plan. I swear it to you."

I closed my eyes, thinking of little Charlotte. The memory turned into my little siblings.

The last thing I'd ever told them was a promise I could not have kept.

We will dance all day tomorrow.

Tomorrow... The day they had turned seven.

I promised Charlotte I would see her again. I should say my goodbyes to her, I owe her at least that. "All right." I gave up. "One week."

Chapter 6.
Mother's Eyes.

The snow shone bright under the Moon's magical gaze; our horses' even steps calmed my racing mind—my eyelids fought to stay open.

"Have you rested at all?" Francis offered me a glance. Despite the cold and fatigue from our trip, he looked flawless as usual. He held the reins in one hand, effortlessly controlling his horse; in the other he clung onto the book—with a navy blue cover—he'd retrieved from his childhood room before we left. "Cordelia?" He crooked his head, frowning.

"Pardon me?"

"Have you slept at all?" Francis asked, reaching for the canteen in his inside pocket.

I shrugged as fatigue washed over me with new force.

"Here." He offered me the drink.

"What is this?" I asked, nodding at the canteen.

"Blood. I figured you were starving: your hands still shake—"

"I am well." I stared at the invisible point in the distance. The back of my eyes prickled, reminding me of the last time I'd felt this screeching pain: back underneath the Royal palace, back in the dungeons that I'd spent every day in my nightmares. The pain I would never mistake for anything else: the pain of hunger. "How did you know I would be at the cabin?"

Francis' brows furrowed, but he put the canteen back into his pocket. "It wasn't hard to guess where you were going in such a rush." He pocketed the blue-covered book. "I made it to the palace right before sunrise, but it was engulfed in flames. I had to spend the day at the Royal lodge—thankfully it was abandoned."

"Once the sun went down, I returned to the palace. That's when I saw Caleb sneaking off the grounds—towards the cabin." Francis met my gaze.

I nodded as though satisfied with his answer, though the question that bothered me most was left unasked. How had he found me at the Royal palace all those nights ago? Why had he even bothered saving me after all the inconveniences I'd caused him?

I ordered Annabelle faster, leaving Francis behind, when his probing eyes kept landing on me with so many questions I was unable to answer.

The castle gleamed even in the darkness of night, covered in snow and ice just like in the fairytales I'd read as a child. The window to my room was now closed, a few candles appeared on its windowsill.

"Don't worry, you can use the door on your way up." Francis winked, though his expression fell once his eyes landed on my features. He cleared his throat before taking our horses to the stables.

I walked through the main doors, heading straight for my room. Perhaps if I was quick enough I wouldn't meet anyone on my way—

Three pairs of eyes waited for me by the door to my room.

"Cordelia." Florence sighed as she took a careful step forward, looking at me as though I was a spooked, wild animal. A single tear fell down her cheek when she offered me an odd smile. She, Roxanne, and Simon all stood by my door, refusing me entrance. "I am so, so glad you are back." Florence offered me a smile that felt forced compared to her usual sunshine glee.

Florence had been the one to feed me on the nights my body was recovering from Kane's assault. In and out of my consciousness, I hadn't been able to separate the nightmare from reality. I supposed they didn't differ much all the same.

Florence had sat patiently by my side, her soft voice had been the only thing that kept my mind from shattering.

I wished I could remember her words now, yet every time I tried to retrace the happenings of those long nights, I was left with nothing.

"Charlotte refused to sleep anywhere else but in your room." Florence looked at me apologetically, bringing me back from my thoughts.

I nodded, glancing at the company behind her. Simon and Roxanne stared shameless. Roxanne's usually schooled expression was now translucent, the horror underneath her eyes bled dry.

An awkward silence stretched as we all stared into each other's eyes. I wondered what they saw in mine.

"All right." Francis appeared behind me, his hand landing on my lower back, ushering me forward. "You need rest." He walked me past the three glowing pairs of eyes, opening the door to my room. "Spare me the trouble and use the stairs next time, will you?"

"One week." I mumbled before slipping inside.

My lungs expanded yet every breath hurt as though I was breathing in fire. I scanned the room I ran from the night before until my eyes landed on a small body resting in the center of my bed; with three blankets wrapped around her, her peaceful features made my heart swell.

Her dark brown curls splattered on the silken pillow, her olive skin reddened underneath her eyes. Silver took his designated spot by her feet.

I reached for the woolen blanket, fixing it around her small frame when my eyes caught a small piece of parchment resting atop the bedside table. My name written at the top made my heart race.

What if...

The curvy and slightly awkward handwriting did not match the one of anyone in my family.

I swallowed the embarrassment and anger, breaking the seal. How foolish of me to think the letter could have been from my family.

Cordelia, I missed you greatly, the letter read. *Florence said you were ill, but I know our kind is safe from any human sickness. Please don't leave again. I missed you dearly. We all did. Charlotte.*

My stomach ached as I reread the words Charlotte had written to me; my eyes prickled as though the tears were about to come, yet there were none left.

"The Princess of Raven Kingdom wished to protect her beloved subjects no matter the cost. She walked into the Onyx castle with bravery the strongest of her Kingdom did not possess." Charlotte flipped through the page of the navy-blue book she'd been reading me for the last few nights. "No one could stop her from breaking the curse the evil King put on her home."

Charlotte's green eyes glowed in the gloom of the room, a delighted smile appeared on her face when she continued to read. "The floors of the Onyx castle creaked under her steps, scaring away the spiders at her feet..."

Silver purred, sleeping by Charlotte's boots atop the windowsill, guarding the child. Occasionally, Charlotte stopped reading to pet him, and ensure I was still listening to the story.

She was young... so young and innocent in a world filled with violence and tragedy. Dread enveloped me whole at the thought of her compromised safety.

Her lips turned into a grin, her bright laughter erupted in the room. Charlotte glanced at me, rereading a sentence that brought her so much joy; I forced a smile to my face.

"You don't like this story, do you?" Charlotte put the book down on the cushion, making her way to me.

"Of course I do," I whispered, my hands reaching for her brown braids. "It's a great story."

She crooked her head to one side, studying me. For a moment I forgot a child was looking at me: her eyes knew struggle, her eyes knew pain and despair.

"I can read you another story if you wish." She smiled. "Francis brought me many books to choose from." She told me, her hands feeling the stray strand of my hair.

"No need," I reassured her. "I want to know how the Princess of Raven Kingdom breaks the curse—"

Charlotte's hands wrapped around my neck. "I missed you," she said.

"I missed you too."

The smile on her face faded once her eyes fell onto my chest. "What a curious stone." Charlotte's hand reached for my necklace, her fingers brushing over the metal lock wrapped around the emerald. "Just like my mother's eyes," she whispered, her voice dreamy.

"Do you remember her?" I dared ask. Charlotte's eyes found mine, the crease between her brows deepened. "Your mother?" I added. "Do you remember her?"

Charlotte dropped the necklace as if it was fire itself. She hurried away from me in an instant, her hands reaching for her book. She found the page she had left off, her eyes scanning the words.

Guilt scratched at my heart. "I'm sorry," I whispered. An odd silence stretched between us: my apology was left unnoticed.

I lay back on my bed, fatigue from starvation making its way through my body. I did not remember the last time I'd fed: it must have been at least a week. Curiously enough, I did not feel the same anguish I had when starvation was forced upon me. Still and all, the lack of blood drained my strength, leaving me with nothing but a void.

A long while passed before Charlotte spoke again. I started to fade away into my nightmares when her voice traveled through the room. "This used to be mama's room." Her fingers traced the fabric of the curtains.

"Pardon me?" I glanced up at her. Her green eyes glowed brighter.

"This room." Charlotte gestured around herself. "It used to be mama's. This whole castle was hers." She hummed as a quiet, soft knock on the door echoed.

The door gave way, revealing the silhouette at its threshold. Florence took a shy step into the room, her eyes jumping between Charlotte's and mine. She fixed her dark green dress that complimented her soft complexion, before a sunshine smile returned to her face. "What have you two been up to?"

"I was reading for Cordelia!" Charlotte skipped towards Florence. "Do you think Francis would let me keep this book for a while? I know my friend, Lucy, would love this story."

"Of course he would." Florence's brows furrowed at the book. "Besides, he is too old for reading children's stories." She picked the girl up, spinning her in a dance.

Charlotte's giggles brightened the room. "Put me down, Florence!" She laughed. "I am too old to be carried around!"

"Are you now?" Florence spun her once more before lowering the child to her feet. Florence's eyes met mine before she addressed Charlotte, "We need to take you back to

Faris, precious." Her voice dropped when she added, "It's not safe for you to stay here long."

Charlotte's gaze dropped to the floor. "All right," she sighed. "Will you both come visit soon?" Hope filled her eyes.

"Of course." I said before I could stop myself.

How could I promise such things when I knew nothing of what tomorrow would bring. Would I even be alive next week?

Something about my features gave away my uncertainty, for Charlotte's—filled with betrayal—eyes burned into mine. She walked towards me, her hands wrapped around my neck in the tightest embrace. "Swear it to me, Cordelia."

The child I came to love was gone: an old spirit now glared at me, demanding my oath. "I swear." I breathed, not believing my own ears when the words spilled.

Charlotte nodded, slowly her features relaxed until a smile spread on her face anew. "Florence said after the war I can go traveling with her and Roxanne, and then stay here at the castle if I wish to."

"After the war." I nodded.

Chapter 7.
Whispered
Horrors.

The room felt utterly empty once Charlotte and Florence had left. I wished I could appreciate the silence, yet nothing but pure rage invaded my mind.

How could I promise her things I knew I could not keep? Why would she make me swear the impossible? How could I allow another child to get hurt by me...

My hands turned into fists, my nails dug into my skin.

The Moon would never claim my soul after all the innocent spirits' pain I'd caused.

I was cursed.

Cursed—

The knock on the door interrupted my racing thoughts. "May I come in?" Francis' muffled voice carried through the door.

I swallowed, staring at my bleeding palms.

"Cordelia?" The door opened ajar.

"Have you reached a plan?" I stood from the bed, caring not how indecent my attire must have looked.

"Yes." Francis said, walking towards my bathchamber.

"Well, what is it?" I followed after him, wiping the blood against my trousers.

"We will talk tomorrow." He set a goblet of crimson down on the small table by the bathtub, his hands reaching for the water basket attached to the fireplace.

"What are you doing?" I eyed the crimson goblet; my throat burned with anticipation. "I don't wish for blood."

"I'm drawing you a bath." He merely stated, filling the tub with water.

"I need no bath." I rolled my eyes. "Tell me what the plan is," I demanded.

"Forgive my boldness, Cordelia, but you do." He looked me up and down.

"You are wasting my time." I seethed.

"Bathe, feed, and then we'll talk." Francis finished up with different oils and petals that hid in the drawer by the sink. "I need you to look presentable for the plan to work." Francis smirked.

"Your rudeness knows no limit." I shook my head, though warm water truly tempted my sore flesh. The blood teased my restraint.

"Would you rather me pity you?" Francis' eyebrows rose. "We will talk of the plan tomorrow, I have some important business to attend to before then." Francis laid the flint he'd used atop my drawer before charging towards the door.

"What business can be more important than—" The door to my room closed shut.

Francis had left before I could finish my question. He'd left me all alone with a bath and a bewitching drink that my hands refused to empty onto the floor.

A sudden sheen layer of sweat covered every inch of my body; a quiet shriek scratched the insides of my throat. My stomach turned upside down as I bent, trying to keep my insides in place.

My eyes burned into the blood as my hands brought it to my lips. It was a lost battle I had no strength to fight: and what for? Were it to happen now or later, eventually my sickness would make me so ill I would be forced to feed. This way I could pretend I was in control.

A small drop slipped into my throat. I wished I could hate the drink for being a necessity to my survival, I wished I could hate Francis for bringing it to me, tempting me against my will. In the end I could only hate myself.

Another drop reached my throat; the corners of my eyes filled with tears I refused to let free. Then another drop. And one more. And one—

My hands trembled when I forced the goblet away from my lips, provoking the rage of the beast. My body shook when I emptied the rest into the fire, ignoring the beast's demands.

My head spun from fatigue, yet I paid it no attention as I sat in the bath that I certainly did not deserve: my skin pleased in the warmth of it.

A week of starvation compromised by a few drops of the treacherous drink. A week of agonizing pain draining into the abyss as the fog in my mind cleared slightly.

How could I ensure anyone's safety when I was so easily controlled? My ill restraint had already killed one, and I couldn't even last for longer than a week in her memory.

Worthless.

Dangerous.

Pathetic.

My eyes locked on the candle Francis had lit by the bathtub, enchanted by it. Everything around me blurred as I watched the flame dance in the darkness, inviting me to join.

I closed my eyes, listening for any sign of life behind my door, for I could not explain to whoever might come in, the horrors my mind whispered for me to act upon.

When I was convinced of my privacy, my trembling fingers reached for the dance.

The flame caressed my skin in a way I hadn't known before.

Pain.

Pain erupted through my twisted mind. I jerked my hand away from the fire in an instant.

I glanced at my injured skin; my eyes widened. Black—as the darkest of nights—painted my skin. I swallowed the lump that grew in my throat, trying to make sense of such abnormality.

My skin cried in unison with the storm outside, yet my mind was quiet: the dreading hole in my stomach ceased as though it was never there.

As though my lost parts had returned to me, I felt whole. How could it be?

Fire was the way to kill a vampire for good, yet it brought me a peace I hadn't known in weeks. The pain that it came with was nothing in comparison to the dread that walked beside me like a shadow.

The black spot on my finger hardened; the skin wailed as I pushed on the abused blotch. Would it stay there forever? I couldn't find it in me to care if it did. It was a small punishment for what I had done.

I glanced at the flame as it kept whispering to me, daring me to try again.

I held my breath when I brought another finger to the flame. It blackened within a moment; I watched the flame dance in victory at my surrender.

My skin melted as though it was snow underneath the spring sun. Slow.

My skin burned as though it was paper. Torturous.

My heart calmed as the flames tormented my flesh.

I studied my injuries, embracing the pain that came with them.

I closed my eyes, imagining the flame taking me whole; the wicked thought brought me comfort—

A piercing pain erupted in my wrist followed by a loud *meow*. My eyes flew open, landing on Silver who leaned against the walls of the bathtub with his front paws.

"Silver..." I gasped, inspecting the two small dots painting my wrist red.

A single *meow* echoed through the bathing chamber in reply.

He had never bitten me before.

No matter my childish refusal, the bath had left me feeling the Moon's paradise.

Her long-dried blood from underneath my nail painted the water red, disappearing into the drain.

I scratched and scraped on my flesh until nothing but the fresh smell of lavender soap was left on my skin. When not a single hair strand carried the remains of that night I reached for the linen cloth Francis had left me.

Bare, I stood before the mirror, my eyes locked on a wicked stranger in the reflection. My Mother's features no longer bothered my soul, for the resemblance—I used to despise—was no longer there: my inherited features now had a new owner.

I stared into Kane's colored eyes, Kane's full lips and his sharply shaped eyebrows. Nothing in the reflection was mine besides the emerald stone, the color of Charlotte's mother's eyes.

My fingers felt its sharp edges, my mind trying to recall the old woman's riddles.

Don't let the sorrow stop you... she'd said, tying the necklace around my neck. *You are our salvation,* she'd declared before disappearing into the void.

The riddle left me confused like the day I'd heard it first. A chill rushed through my bones when I snatched the amulet off my neck, determined to return it to its owner.

Chapter 8. Ghost.

The cool air caressed my still damp hair as I made my way down to the stables. Snowflakes waltzed down my path, crunching under my boots. The thirteenth full Moon was knocking at our doors.

Annabelle nuzzled against me once I was within reach; my hand stretched to pet her when a pair of light-brown glowing eyes planted on me from the depths of the stables.

Roxanne looked me up and down before returning to brush her horse. Her copper hair splattered around her shoulders, reaching her waist; her black cloak contrasted with her light skin, hiding the nightgown underneath: she looked fresh out of bed.

My upcoming trip to Faris need not be a secret—Francis did not specify whether I must stay at the castle after he dragged me back, not that I cared—still and all, I wasn't pleased with an extra pair of eyes and ears upon my departure. Though, Roxanne never seemed to care—

"Where are you going?" she asked as I put my saddle on Annabelle.

"To Faris," I replied, my fingers securing the small belts.

"By yourself?" Roxanne put the brush down.

I merely shrugged, mounting my horse.

"Wait for me." She threw over her shoulder, heading towards the castle.

"You needn't trouble yourself." I called after her, yet the front doors of the castle shut before I finished my sentence.

I supposed it wouldn't make a difference were she to come along. Roxanne wasn't one to indulge in someone's privacy out of curiosity: most of our time together was spent in silence.

"Let's go." She reappeared at the stables a few minutes later. Her nightgown changed into a beautiful forest-green dress, her hair now put into two simple braids, crowning her head. She ordered her horse out of the stables without waiting for me to follow.

As predicted, Roxanne didn't bother me with countless questions along our journey, though her withering gaze fell in my direction more than I preferred.

"Is something wrong?" I dared her to voice her mind after another—rather judging—gaze that was thrown my way.

"You look like a ghost." Roxanne shrugged. "You talk like one too."

She couldn't be serious, could she? I looked at her in disbelief. "Why did you want to come with me?" My brows furrowed. "I didn't ask for company."

Our silent staring was broken by her short, "We need to talk."

Perhaps I underestimated her character. "I don't wish to talk." Since when did Roxanne and I talk anyway?

"It might be a foreign concept to you, but we often have to do things we don't wish to." She spat out.

What in the Kingdom was her problem?

UNKINDNESS OF CRIMSON QUEEN

Roxanne and I were never friends: she barely tolerated me when I'd first arrived at the castle, though the sudden cruelty was still odd. Was our silent truce a pretense?

I almost turned Annabelle back around. Almost.

"Every decision in my life has been against my wishes, Roxanne," I said instead. "What do *you* know of doing as you are told?" I snapped.

Her lips turned into a thin line as we continued on the small path towards Faris. "I'm sorry." Her voice turned dull.

My head flew in her direction: surely I misheard.

"I was not fair to you then, and I am not now." Roxanne continued, her eyes burning into the invisible point ahead. "I wouldn't ask if it wasn't important."

Roxanne needn't voice her question, I knew exactly what she wished to ask. "I know nothing of value."

Unsatisfied with my answer, Roxanne burned her gaze into my flesh. If I didn't know any better I would think she wished to set me on fire herself.

A long while passed before she cleared her throat, addressing me once again. "I was never fond of the Royal family," she offered, earning a judgmental glare from me. "But I know what it's like to lose your loved ones," she added quickly. "I'm sorry you've lost your family."

If it wasn't for the snowdrifts on our path we would already be in Faris, and this conversation would be over. I couldn't help but despise winter's sabotage. "As I said, I know nothing of value."

She shook her head, glancing at me before continuing, "Your silence won't help anyone—"she sighed. "Including yourself."

"What is that supposed to mean?" My hands tightened around the reins. The gloves I put on this evening covered every blackened burn I inflicted upon myself.

"Never mind." Roxanne simply said, making the last turn towards Faris.

Faris was awfully quiet. The faint candlelight flickered behind the windows, fighting to stay alive. As though an old, evil spirit swept through the village, it left nothing but shadows to take the joy's place. Despite the road being filled with people, Faris felt abandoned.

"Where to now?" Roxanne asked in a hushed voice.

"I need to return something." I looked around for the mysterious shop. Surely returning the item wasn't the only reason I'd rushed into this trip, though I felt embarrassed admitting I hoped some cryptic old woman would tell me my future.

"Return what?" Roxanne asked with a dose of annoyance in her tone.

I sighed, preparing for Roxanne's mockery. "There was an old woman that gave me a necklace right before the attack." I showed Roxanne the amulet. "She told me some kind of a prophecy..."

"My dear Moon..." Roxanne rolled her eyes, her fingers feeling the stone. "You are wasting our time."

"Perhaps... perhaps not." I snatched the stone back into my satchel.

"All right." Roxanne shook her head, looking at me as though I went mad. "Lead the way."

We walked up and down the street twice before I gave up. "I swear her shop was here." I pointed at the empty windows. I yanked on the door a few times before admitting defeat. "It's locked."

"Well, that was fun." Roxanne snickered. "Let's go, I still need to get Francis a present."

"A present?" My brows furrowed.

"It's his birthday tomorrow." Roxanne walked across the street without waiting for me to follow. "Maybe you can exchange your cursed necklace for a present for him," she scoffed.

The shop Roxanne had led us into held a large *books* sign on the window; I followed after her.

How could I not know it was Francis' birthday? Even though my mind had wandered elsewhere the last couple of weeks, I realized I actually did not know much about him, despite the proximity we'd shared; despite him being the first man to not hurt me the way they usually had.

It mattered not, I wanted to tell myself. *It was just that—affection, nothing else. I didn't owe him, nor did he owe me.*

Yet something flickered in my heart with refusal.

I walked down the countless rows of bookshelves, filled with different texts—most of them older than myself by hundreds of years—as I followed after Roxanne. She walked down the rows with confidence, as if she owned this place.

"Where are your music books?" she asked the man behind the table in the depths of the shop. He wore a woolen blanket on his shoulders.

"Fifth row, second shelf from the top," he said, eyes stuck to the page of the book in his hands.

Roxanne nodded, leading our way where the man had directed.

"This shop looks a lot smaller from the outside." I noticed, keeping up after Roxanne.

It must have been at least half an hour since we'd gotten here; the strong smell of old parchment made my lungs ache, yet I dared not interrupt Roxanne's hunt for the perfect book. She sat on the floor of the shop, carefully reading through every book's description before putting it down.

I never thought Roxanne would put so much effort into choosing a present—especially for Francis, given every time they were together it ended in a fight of some kind. Though I supposed Brian and I fought a lot too...

"I will be right back," I told her, though she didn't seem to care.

I walked down the row, my eyes scanning the books as I passed by. It seemed this shop carried a collection larger than the Royal library itself. So many to choose from...

They even carried the whole collection of the Forest's Fables—a story my Father had read to my sister and I when we were little. A story I used to read to the twins.

I swallowed down the growing lump in my throat, taking off my gloves before reaching for the latest addition to the tale I never got to read.

UNKINDNESS OF CRIMSON QUEEN

My heart beat faster as I opened the first page. Father had spent years trying to find this volume for us, yet his trips were in vain, as the single edition of the story was apparently here—in the vampire village.

My hands trembled as I flipped through the pages; father's voice filled my mind.

"I'm ready to go." Roxanne appeared at the end of the row, making me slam the book shut in an instant. "What are you reading?" She took a step towards me, her eyes scanning the title in my hands.

"My father used to read it to us." I said quietly before returning the book to its shelf. "Have you heard of it?" I faced Roxanne, but her eyes were planted on my blackened injuries.

I rushed to put the gloves back on, though it did nothing to Roxanne's silent stare; for the first time she seemed speechless.

"It's nothing," I said quietly.

Roxanne stayed silent as her—full of pain—eyes bored into mine.

"It's nothing." I cleared out my throat, walking back towards the exit of the shop. Roxanne's steps followed after.

I pushed on the heavy door, the cold air enveloping me in its embrace. The streets of Faris were quieter than before.

"I will be right back." Roxanne threw over her shoulder, walking in the opposite direction from where our horses stood.

"Where are you going?" I called after her. Roxanne shook her head in reply before turning into a barely visible alley in between the shops.

I made my way towards our horses, my heart banging against my rib cage.

Several minutes passed before Roxanne returned; a jar of light pink liquid in her hands.

"Take off your gloves." She stood before me as she unscrewed the jar.

"I told you, it's nothing." I hid my hands into the pockets of my cloak.

"Take off your gloves."

I rolled my eyes under her withering gaze, yet my hands reached for the gloves, obeying her wishes nevertheless.

The pink liquid spilled onto my burned skin when Roxanne poured out the contents, gentling it into my flesh. A slight burning sensation prickled my injuries, followed by an immediate relief. A sigh escaped my lips when Roxanne moved onto my left hand.

"This will help with the burns." She massaged the elixir into my skin.

"What is it?"

"A medicine." She put the cork back onto the jar, hiding the remains into her pocket.

"What kind of medicine?" I pressed. When Roxanne didn't reply I drew a small breath in. "May I keep it?" I fought for my voice to sound even.

"Why?" Roxanne eyed me, mounting her horse.

"In case I need it again." I shrugged, following her lead.

"Why would you need it again?" Accusation shone bright in her voice. The implication was as bright as day.

My teeth clenched. "It was an accident." I squeezed the reins, ordering Annabelle forward.

"Sure it was," Roxanne murmured. "I'm afraid you will have to find me were *an accident* to happen again." She emphasized the word, leaving me no hope of winning this battle.

My heart banged against my rib cage, anger and fear and... embarrassment filling my chest. "Will you tell anyone?" My voice broke as I avoided Roxanne's gaze.

Moments of silence stretched in between us before she replied, "No, I won't."

Deep in thought, Roxanne paid me little to no attention as we slowly made our way back towards the castle. The wind sang its lullabies, snowflakes landed on my lashes after their dance.

The woods were peaceful, save for my galloping heart. Chains wrapped around my neck, pulling in every direction, with each breath I took.

"I am his daughter." The words broke free without my permission: the words that shattered my soul from within all these nights. I filled my lungs before repeating, "I am Kane's daughter, Caleb is of Royal blood and my brother."

Once the words left my lips, the chains loosened their grip so slightly.

Roxanne's eyes found mine as she studied me in complete silence.

"I know nothing of his plans, or anything useful for that matter..." I continued. "All I know is that he is my father, and I will only know peace when my sword is buried deep in his heart."

"No." Roxanne shook her head; a sad smile appeared on her face. "No, you won't know peace then."

ARYA SLOANE

My brows furrowed when I met Roxanne's expression.

"Kill him to bring peace to all the innocent people," She sighed. "Find your own peace through grief."

Chapter 9. The Last Queen.

Roxanne's words lingered in my mind through the rest of the trip. Her saddened expression left me with countless questions.

She hadn't said a single word for the remainder of our journey, nor had she spared me a glance once we'd arrived at the castle's stables.

"Where have you two been?" Francis' voice dropped a few octaves, his eyes flickered with panic, as he stood at the threshold of the stables.

"None of your business." Roxanne pushed past him towards the castle.

Francis shook his head until his eyes landed on me; he looked me up and down, surveying for injuries. "We went to Faris," I sighed, putting Annabelle's reins in their designated place. "Nothing of danger."

Francis' lips turned into a thin line as he chose his words carefully. "Please tell someone of your whereabouts next time. Florence and I lost our minds worrying for you two."

"Why?" I started past him. "You don't tell me of your whereabouts or your mysterious business that is apparently more important than working on a plan."

Francis sighed before replying, "I went to the human village near Faris to help with the rebuilding after the attack." He walked beside me. "I promise to always tell you my whereabouts if you promise me the same." He reached for the door, holding it open for me.

"I don't actually care what you do with your spare time, Francis." I walked into the castle, guilt spreading through my blood. How could I be mad at him after his candidness? "I am not a child that needs constant supervision."

The bright luminance of candlelight gleamed in the hallways of the castle, the paintings on the walls stared at me with curiosity.

"I was worried you were in danger, Cordelia. Surely you can understand that." Francis' hand brushed mine as we made our way through the hall. "Despite what you like to tell yourself, I care for your safety." He stopped before the door of his study. "Come, we have much to discuss."

The wooden floors creaked as I entered the room, following after Francis.

He sat before the oak table; pieces of parchment covered every inch of the surface, connecting at the corners. They resembled something similar to a map of a construction—a castle, perhaps.

"What is all of this?" I studied the papers Francis had arranged in an order I failed to understand.

"It's the Royal palace's underground paths. Florence stumbled upon it the other day in the library." He raised one brow when I leaned on the table, trying to make sense of the ancient layout. "I didn't even know we carried something like this here," he hummed more to himself than to me.

"It's outdated." I frowned. "By a few centuries at least."

"That is why I needed your help." Francis offered me a quill. "Can you fix what is missing?"

"Why?" I ignored the quill. "What do we need a map for if you have me? I know all the passages."

Francis swallowed, his voice turning gentle. "You shouldn't go back there, Cordelia." Before I could protest he added, "I am not going there to kill Kane, not yet, I am merely looking for the archives Caleb mentioned."

My dear Moon and the Gods... "No."

"No?"

"I cannot believe you wasted three nights coming up with *this*." I shook my head. "Caleb can do this for us, he said so himself."

"You trust him," Francis scoffed, shaking his head.

"I do not. I simply know when it's best to use others for your gain."

"And what do we do when he finds the archives and brings them straight to Kane?"

To that I had nothing to say.

"It's decided. I am going." Francis nodded, offering me the quill once again. "As much as it pains me to admit, Caleb is right. Royal steel is our only chance at survival."

"Then I'm going with you." I shrugged, pushing the quill away—

"What good are those weapons if we have no one to carry them?" Roxanne's voice carried through the study, our heads flew in her direction.

Roxanne and Florence stood at the threshold of the room, their hands in a tight embrace.

"How long have you two been standing there for?" Francis' voice shone with annoyance.

"Long enough," Roxanne said as the women made their way to the settee by the window. A small smile spread across Florence's face when her eyes met mine. I wished I could return the gesture, yet my lips refused.

"Faris is still recovering from its last assault." Roxanne faced Francis. "We lost a dozen vampire warriors trying to free Cordelia from the palace." She glanced at me.

My brows furrowed as my heart beat faster. What was she saying?

"We have no use for the weapons without an army." Roxanne shrugged.

"You didn't come for me alone?" My voice echoed through the study. "Someone else died because of me?"

"The royal family wasn't the only family who died that night." Roxanne's gaze bored into me. "Don't let their deaths be in vain."

"Roxanne!" Florence gasped. "She doesn't mean that."

"I d—" Roxanne started when Florence's hand covered her mouth.

"It's not your fault." Francis held my gaze, breaking his glare at Roxanne.

"As I said, we need an army first, weapons later." Roxanne broke free from Florence.

"Well I don't have an army, Rox!" Francis seethed.

As appealing as the idea of simply walking into the palace and destroying Kane from within was, it wouldn't be possible without the proper preparation. I'd made that mistake once.

"Roxanne is right," I interrupted the looming fight. "We need an army above all else." When Francis' surprised gaze met mine I continued, "For Moon's sake, we got caught breaking in when the palace was filled with humans, not to mention the wall of fire that now surrounds the palace during daytime. We don't even know where Mother kept those archives. This is madness, we should prioritize the army." I looked over my company. "Are there any vampire villages beside Faris?"

"None that would be willing to help." Florence shook her head, disappointment filling her eyes. "All that disagreed with Kane have already made their way to Faris, the rest either joined his forces or chose to simply witness how everything unfolds."

"They plan to do nothing?" I wouldn't give up, unsatisfied with her answer. "Are you sure we cannot change their minds?" When silence followed in reply a wicked thought crossed my mind. "Does Barren's duchy still stand?" Three pairs of eyes buried into mine.

"A human army without Royal Steel is no use to us, we will be sending people for slaughter. Besides, Barren's army is nowhere near big enough." Francis shook his head. "Getting Royal Steel should be our priority."

"Humans can fight with fire." Roxanne protested. "Surely they aren't foolish enough to rid themselves of their Silver weapons either. It's better than nothing." She nodded. "There aren't enough of us here, Francis."

Florence sighed as Roxanne and Francis glared at each other, their silent argument floating in the room.

"Are any other duchies standing?" I asked.

"Not that I know of." Francis sighed, breaking his glare with Roxanne. "All the dukes were gathered for a meeting with the Queen the day of the attack. Barren was the only one to survive, as he was away from the palace with the best of the Royal army looking for Timothy." Francis glanced at the map on his table before adding, "My sources say that one of the Royal commanders currently resides at Barren's estate.

I swallowed before facing Francis. "Barren knows of Timothy."

"Well, yes, they noticed his absence eventually." Francis leaned back on his chair.

I rolled my eyes at his mockery. "Does he know *I* was the one to kill him?" My throat prickled at the thought of human blood. The memory of the crimson pool Timothy was left in tingled on my tongue.

Florence and Roxanne glanced between each other, their brows furrowing; though they withheld the questions they most certainly had.

Francis' lips turned into a thin line. "There's no way of knowing that. Perhaps he blames the Wurdulacs for his death."

"But the Wurdulacs attacked after Timothy's death." I cleared my throat. "His body wasn't far from the palace."

"They didn't find his body." Francis smirked at my puzzled expression. "I went back and got rid of his body the following night, before we left the cabin." Francis sighed before adding, "Don't bother entertaining the idea, Cordelia, William Barren won't help us, he only cares for his own skin in this war."

"I can convince him." I filled my lungs. "I will convince the Royal army commander to combine our forces."

"I'm not sure Barren will let that happen. He claims the Royals army is now his—" Francis started.

"Isn't the army Caleb's now. Given he is the rightful Crown." Roxanne shrugged, picking a piece of lint off her dress.

"What are you talking of." Florence and Francis said in unison.

Before Roxanne managed to explain I replied, "I can convince Barren and anyone who is by his side that this alliance is necessary. We need each other for survival and they know it." I continued before Francis had the chance to interject. "Once the deal is sealed we will figure out how much Royal steel we require and how we can make it." I charged towards the exit. "Write a letter to Barren, Francis," I said over my shoulder, heading back to my only sanctuary in this castle.

Chapter 10.
Birthday.

The soft waltz intruded upon my sleep, scaring away the last remains of my nightmare. My eyes stayed shut as I listened to the melody traveling all the way from the ballroom. Each press of the piano keys filled me with peace I had long forgotten.

I drew a careful breath, so as not to dispel the facade that horrors only haunted me in my sleep and the Moon's realm only knew peace and freedom.

Then my eyes opened.

The reality of my being crashed down on me like an avalanche.

I closed my eyes once again, longing for the peace I was granted a mere moment ago, yet the magic was gone.

No matter the beauty of the piece, it brought me nothing but distress. My heart tore apart at the sound of the piano, my mind filled with memories of her hands over the keyboard. Whoever was playing, I wished for them to stop.

The music persisted when I got out of the bath, the music grew stronger when I braided my hair. Perhaps a ball was happening at the castle tonight, though I cared not to go investigate.

I lay on my unmade bed, my fingers playing with the flint Francis had left in my room last night; the upcoming conversation with William Barren ran through my mind stopless. Confidence left me with each passing moment.

There was only one way of successfully merging our forces: let William believe he was the one giving out orders, while pulling the strings behind closed doors, let him believe he was making the choice in favor of this alliance.

"Cordelia?" A knock on the door echoed through the room before Florence made her appearance at the threshold. "Will you join us?"

I hurried to put my ivory gloves on, sending the flint down my pocket. The burns had not bothered me anymore, yet the dark brown spots were still visible.

"I am not feeling well," I lied, unsuccessfully it seemed, for Florence made her way into my room, her head crooked to one side.

"Come now, it's Francis' birthday." She stood by the footboard of my bed. The dark blue dress sat on her with perfection, small gems reflected the candlelight, glowing as bright as her brown eyes. Dozens of long, small braids reached down her waist, the dark brown ends curled into spirals. "It's a small gathering, he would be happy if you joined," she added.

"I don't have a present." I shrugged, pulling the blanket higher.

"Oh, I'm sure he wouldn't care," Florence chuckled, offering me a hand. "Let's go. You can't stay in your room forever."

When I didn't move, she sat on my bed, her hand wrapping around mine. She eyed my gloves, but refrained from saying anything about my fashion choices. A sad smile stretched her lips. "I meant to apologize for lying to you then—"

"You have nothing to apologize for," I interrupted, averting my gaze; my hand went limp in hers.

"Of course I do." She squeezed my hand, and it took everything in me to hide the discomfort of my healing injuries. "You were right to be upset with me," Florence's voice broke. "I knew of Francis' plan all along and let it happen. I am so sorry."

"You were protecting your family. I understand."

"You are my family too," she whispered as tears filled her eyes. "Will you please forgive me?"

"I am not upset with you, Florence. I would do the same."

"Tell me you forgive me," she wouldn't give up.

"All right." I sighed. "I forgive you."

Her full pink lips stretched into the sunshine smile. "Thank you, I won't let you down again, I promise." Florence let out a sigh. "Now let's go, you can't hide here forever."

"I really don't—"

"No excuses!" She dragged me out of the bed. "I'm not letting you stay alone while all of us are enjoying ourselves."

"I don't—" I trailed off when Florence' hands reached for the unbuttoned part of the dress at my neck. Her fingers swiftly fixed up my appearance until she beamed, looking me up and down.

"Perfect!" she exclaimed, nodding. "Let's go."

"I won't stay for long." I gave up as she pushed me out of the room.

"Of course." She grinned from ear to ear. "I wouldn't expect any more!"

Three—no, four—pairs of eyes landed on me when we entered the ballroom of the castle, which now looked empty compared to the last time I was in here. Francis' fingers still flew across the keys of a grand piano in the center of the room, stumbling only for a moment before he averted his gaze back to the music sheet, smiling.

Roxanne, Simon, and a mysterious guest I had never met before, sat on the settees next to the piano; a circular table held their drinks while they enjoyed the music.

Florence pointed at the settee closest to Francis' bench, gesturing for me to take a seat. It would be pointless to argue with her, so I abided by her demands. She filled my glass with wine, and I thanked all the Gods that it wasn't blood.

Francis stole a few glances at me when the slow and mournful melody turned into a fast and joyful piece. Every time his eyes landed on me, my skin prickled against the tight fabric of my dress.

A few minutes passed before the flow of the piece came to an end; the last note lingered in the air, echoing throughout the ballroom. Francis spun on the bench, facing his small audience as everyone clapped—everyone but Roxanne, who theatrically rolled her eyes, fighting the smile off her face.

When the ovations quieted, Simon cleared his throat. "Cordelia," he addressed me. "Please meet Ash, the blacksmith of Faris." He pointed at the vampire sitting next to him. "They sometimes help me to run the Tavern and—"

"And they clearly have bad taste in men since they chose you as their companion," Francis snickered, to which Simon slipped his shoe off, throwing it straight at Francis' head. The room erupted in laughter.

"Hey! It's my birthday, must I remind you." Francis threw the shoe back at Simon.

Simon shook his head, catching it with one hand. "Ash makes the best caramel fudge, you should definitely come and try it," he continued.

"It is nice to meet you, Ash," I offered them my gloved hand. "I'm excited to try your caramel fudge," I said through the growing ache in my heart.

"It is nice to meet you too." They shook my hand, oblivious to my odd reaction over some dessert. Their hand was warm to the touch, save for all the rings they'd decorated their fingers with. A big red stone shone bright, illuminating with the candlelight; my eyes lingered on Ash's ring, reminding me of a similar stone my mother used to wear.

"Do you like it?" Ash caught my gaze.

"It's beautiful." I nodded.

"Take it." Ash slipped the ring off, handing it to me. At my hesitation they added, "I have at least a dozen in my collection, take it." They slipped the ring onto my index finger over my silky glove.

"It suits you," Florence chimed in.

The red stone sat heavy on my hand, the golden band wrapped around my finger as though it was made for me.

"Thank you," I nodded at Ash.

"All right," Francis finished his drink, setting an empty glass on the table. "I am ready for presents!"

"It's not even midnight." Roxanne shook her head. "You must wait until morning."

"So what if it isn't?" Francis shrugged. "My birthday—my rules."

"Fine." Roxanne reached for the wrapped rectangle underneath her settee, offering it to Francis. "Happy *early* Birthday."

Francis beamed like a child, unfolding the pieces of parchment. Dimples, I'd never noticed before, decorated his bright smile. "Where did you find this?" Francis glanced at Roxanne when her present was freed from the parchment. She shrugged, fighting the smile off her face, though it was clear she was proud of her findings. "This is incredible." Francis flipped through the pages of—what I guessed—was a collection of musical pieces. "This was the very first piano book my mother had brought me to study. I never told you that." Francis' eyes narrowed on Roxanne.

Roxanne shrugged in reply. "A lucky guess, then."

"My turn!" Florence jumped off her settee, rushing to retrieve her oddly shaped present that sat atop one of the tables usually used for the big gatherings.

"What in the Kingdom is that?" Francis' brows furrowed, pulling on the black ribbon.

"I hope you like it." Florence took a sip of her drink.

Francis struggled with the ribbon, turning it into a knot.

"Let me," I teased, unable to hide my amusement at his struggles.

Our hands touched when he passed the present, the thin fabric of my gloves was our only barrier. Though it did nothing to stop the goosebumps from spreading across my arm.

Untying the knot in gloves was more challenging than I'd expected, yet I supposed I needed to get used to my new alterations.

The ribbons fell to the marble floor, revealing the mysterious present Florence had prepared.

"Now you don't have to borrow Roxanne's bow," she beamed as I passed the new, shiny weapon to Francis.

"Thank the Moon." Roxanne rolled her eyes, chuckling.

"Thank you, Florence," Francis said, studying his wooden weapon.

"Happy birthday!" Simon passed the present he hadn't bothered wrapping. An old bottle of wine, with a label that fought to stay in place.

"It's seventy years old." Simon winked. "That was the first bottle I ever sealed."

"All of you decided to spoil me this year, huh." Francis' expression turned serious. "You do know this might not be my last birthday?"

Everyone's face went pale as a dreadful silence fell upon the ballroom.

"Dear Moon," Francis shook his head, laughing. "You should see your faces."

"Stop it, Francis, this isn't funny." Florence huffed; Francis put his hands up in defeat at her annoyed tone.

Ash cleared their throat, breaking the tense spell in the air. "I didn't have time to find you a proper gift." Ash offered a small box to Francis, glaring at Simon. "Because someone forgot to mention your birthday."

"I already apologized." Simon sighed, giving Ash a kiss on their temple.

"You didn't have to bring anything," Francis said. "But I greatly appreciate the thought."

In the box sat a whetstone, its corner decorated with an engraving I couldn't read from where I sat.

"Thank you, I certainly needed one, since Caleb took my fancy whetstone when he ran." Francis put the whetstone into his pocket before opening the bottle of wine Simon gifted him. "I hope we don't get poisoned." He poured everyone a glass.

"We might!" Simon shrugged, finishing his drink in one gulp.

"Oh, Moon..." Florence sighed, studying the contents of her drink.

"May I play?" Ash put the drink aside, pointing at the piano.

"Please!" Francis nodded at them, filling my goblet.

The piece Ash chose to play was foreign to my ears, yet certainly fit the gathering. A playful, yet mysterious melody echoed throughout the room. Their fingers skillfully ran across the keys, a smile spread on their lips.

Roxanne and Florence got up for a dance; Simon watched Ash play with a softness in his eyes I'd never seen before.

UNKINDNESS OF CRIMSON QUEEN

"Sorry I came emptyhanded," I whispered to Francis when he offered me the drink, taking a seat next to me. "I didn't know it was your birthday until last night."

"You being here is the best present." Francis winked.

The wine in my goblet smelled divine. Rich as a forest after the rain, and sweet as spilled honey. It tasted just as fine; soft notes of apples and grapes warmed my throat.

My sister would have loved it.

"I should go," I whispered to Francis, setting the still full goblet on the table. "I'm sorry."

Before he could reply, my legs carried me out of the ballroom, all the way up the stairs.

Up and up, until there was nowhere else to go.

The stairs ended abruptly, turning into a narrow corridor with a small wooden door waiting at the end.

The old floors creaked as my legs carried me towards the opening. The door screeched at my touch.

Blinded by the moonlight, my heart beat faster from its beauty.

Every wall of this tiny room was a window that reached the floor. The ceiling was made out of clear glass, allowing the moonshine to dance in its stained paintings.

I dropped to the floor; my knees crying from the impact, yet the pain was numbed by the beauty of the Moon.

Glorious.

I reached out for the shine to dance on my gloved hands, each color reflecting on the ivory fabric.

The Moon smiled down at me, despite my hatred towards her unkindness.

The music could not be heard from here, yet it still played in my mind, spinning my head drunk.

The skies were clear of storms, the cold winter retreated its spells for the night. I lay on the cold floor, counting the stars. When I reached a hundred, the door creaked open.

"There you are," Francis lay beside me, the moonlight playing upon his sharp cheekbones.

"What are you doing here?" My voice turned hoarse. "You should be celebrating."

"I would rather be here." He glanced at me through his long lashes. "Besides, my dancing partner is up here, and it was decided it was time for dance." When I stayed silent Francis cleared his throat. "I sent the letter to Barren last night," his voice dropped a few octaves. "He usually takes his time with a reply, but expect to go to Silverstone next week." His voice shone with disapproval.

"It's better than breaking into the palace with a map older than the dawn of time," I argued.

"I thought you were desperate to break into the palace just a week ago."

I still was; not without a plan, however.

"I cared not for my own life." I managed a shrug.

"Do you care for your life now?" Francis asked softly.

"Not if it's a necessary death," I admitted.

"Your death can never be necessary." Francis' fingers reached for my cheek. His skin touched mine for a brief moment before he retreated, as though remembering himself.

I swallowed as our small proximity crashed upon me, squeezing my lungs tight.

As though reading my thoughts, Francis sat up, putting some distance in between us. "I brought you some cake."

The dark brown piece of cake sat on a crystal plate, small strawberries decorated its top. The human blood spilling over it spun my head; nausea slowly crept in alongside the demanding, evil beast.

"I don't fancy sweets." I averted my gaze from the dessert, breathing through my mouth.

"Oh, no?" Francis' lips curved. "I will make sure we have no sweets on your birthday, then." He winked, though his eyes darkened, seeing through my weak lies. "When is your birthday?"

"Right after the harvest." I cleared my throat, fighting with the beast that corrupted my thoughts one by one.

"I always fancied autumn's full Moons." Francis nodded, taking a spoonful of cake. "They have this reddish hint to them that reminds me of my father's eyes." Francis' lips tugged into a smile at the memory.

My throat scratched with every breath I took, my eyes kept glancing at the bloody dessert. My hands trembled.

"He always took me to the lake near our cabin on my birthday." Francis took another spoonful, his teeth now wore crimson. "My father," he clarified.

"What happened to him?" I dared to ask, though all I was consumed by was the unbearable sharp pain in my stomach.

Francis merely shook his head. "Not tonight," he whispered, a sad smile tugging on his lips.

I looked out the window, avoiding the sight of blood on Francis' lips.

"Cordelia." Francis put down the plate, blood dripped down onto the floor. "When was the last time you've fed?" He crooked his head to one side.

"I've fed." I swallowed the burn in my throat.

"That wasn't the question." He inched closer. "You haven't had any blood the whole night."

"I've had enough with my bath." I started to my feet, yet Francis' hands caught mine.

"That was yesterday." Francis' eyes bored into mine for answers he'd already had. "You won't be able to kill Kane if you let yourself starve—" The words died on his tongue at my flinch. "Cordelia, I know it's not easy—"

"Don't." I pushed his hands away; gathering to my feet, I charged towards the door. "I am rather tired, I should go."

"No." Francis moved to the threshold, blocking my pathway. "Let me help you." His fingers slipped under my chin, gently pushing my head up to meet his gaze.

"I need no help," I protested, though the beast froze my body into submission. The smell of blood on Francis' breath dared me for a kiss. "No," I told the beast, yet the burning in my throat increased, spreading through my body.

"It's all right." Francis nodded, his free hand started to unbutton the top of his shirt.

"What in the Kingdom are you doing?" My voice turned dreamy at the mercy of the beast's demands.

"If you don't wish for human blood, take mine," Francis whispered.

"Francis—" As though a spell was broken, my body came alive anew. I shook my head; the beast within me rebelled.

"I will keep you safe, remember," Francis spoke, his voice turning soft. "You will always be safe with me, I swear it."

My eyes planted on the open skin. His heartbeat quickened under my gaze when his free hand wrapped around my waist, keeping me upright.

"I cannot." I leaned against his chest, my lips close to his exposed throat.

"It's all right." He ushered me closer. "You can't hurt me."

My body trembled, my eyes shut. *I cannot. I cannot—*

"Look at me." Francis caressed my cheek; my eyes flew open, obeying. "You are safe with me, and you can't hurt me. I will not let anything happen to you, I swear it."

"Francis—" I breathed, my lips feeling the soft skin without my permission.

"Shush, my Princess." His hand crooked around the back of my neck. "You are safe with me," he whispered as my teeth pierced his skin.

The first drop of blood spilled onto my tongue like fine wine, melting into my throat. I wished to protest the beast that had woken within me. I wished to stay in Francis' hands forever.

Francis cradled the small of my back, sending lightning down my spine. His blood spilled into my mouth, calming my aching throat, calming my mind.

My knees weakened as Francis slid down the wall, his hands keeping me from collapsing. "Just like that." A smothered moan pushed past his lips when my hands reached for the collar of his shirt, holding on as though my life depended on it. "Good girl," his voice turned hoarse.

A muffled moan forced its way from the depths of my throat as the flower's thorns—deep in my stomach—wrapped around my insides. His hands tightened their hold around me as I sat between his legs, my teeth buried in his flesh.

"Francis," I drawled against his neck, my tongue catching every drop of blood mixed with my saliva.

"Take more," he commanded; his thumb felt my lips before pressing them back to his injury. "Take more, darling."

My teeth dug into his flesh, my tongue traveled across his skin.

The beast sang triumphant serenades as my body melted into his embrace; my mind quieted like the autumn's skies before a storm.

"Just like that, Princess."

Chapter 11.
Unexpected Guest.

His heartbeat sang in unison with mine. The Moon sparkled in his eyes; the stained glass shone rainbows on his soft cheeks.

We sat on the wooden floors, his hands still wrapped around my waist. Unable to say a word, I rested my head on his shoulder as guilt and shame spread through me like wildfire.

"I despise you," I whispered against Francis' neck for his hand in my lost battle.

He merely chuckled. "I can live with that."

My eyes closed as two forces spun my head into madness.

I didn't hurt a single soul—

Dangerous.

No human suffered for my weakness—

Worthless.

"I must go." I sighed, abandoning our embrace. "Happy birthday, Francis."

"Thank you, Princess."

The stairs spiraled underneath my feet as my legs carried me away from the observation room.

My mind spiraled with a longing for pain.

I haven't hurt a soul. I repeated my mantra, though my heart ached for fire.

Nausea crept in as my gloved hands met the doorknob of my room. My mind screamed at me to enter, to give in to my wicked, broken thoughts.

I haven't hurt a soul—

I swallowed as the need to burn spread across my flesh, my skin prickled in anticipation—

"What is the matter?" A voice at the end of the hallway exclaimed. My head flew in the direction, glowing eyes met mine. "Are you well?" Roxanne eyed my ivory gloves.

"Yes." I dropped the doorknob as clear thoughts crept into my mind, crushing the broken wishes on their way. "I am," I lied as I walked past her, down the stairs, somewhere far from my room; for if I were to enter, the broken thought would eventually win. "I am well," I whispered to myself, pushing against the main door until cold air hit my exposed skin.

"I didn't hurt anyone, I will not hurt myself," I repeated again and again, walking towards a willow tree behind the stables.

My back met the wall of the stables when I slid down onto the cold ground.

"I am safe." I breathed in through my nose. "I didn't hurt Francis." I breathed out through my mouth.

You won't be able to kill Kane if you let yourself starve, his words rang loud through my mind and I nodded as the meaning slowly settled in.

"I needed to feed, and I did not hurt anyone," I whispered to the willow tree.

"Talking to trees now, are we?" The familiar voice made me jump from my spot; my eyes scanned the night forest until they landed on the man. My mind rushed through every possible escape route there was. Would I even be able to outrun him? Would anyone hear me if I screamed?

"I come in peace." Caleb put both of his hands up, stepping out from the shadows of dense spruce.

"There's a first for everything," I scoffed, allowing myself a quick glance towards the only pathway back to the castle.

"I brought Francis a present—" Caleb started, his hands reaching for the small box in his pocket. "Couldn't find the courage to walk in..." He took a step forward. A few more steps, and I would be trapped in the corner.

"He told you he doesn't want to see you, Caleb." If I ran the other direction, I could make it to the small kitchen door on the other side of the castle. What were the odds he'd come alone?

"I also have valuable information," Caleb said. His eyes scanned my features for any sign of interest: I showed him none.

Moon save me, I should stop leaving the castle alone.

Caleb took another step towards me; I didn't dare move. "I found a vault in the hidden passages of the Queen's rooms." He crooked his head to one side.

I schooled my features to the best of my abilities. I knew of that vault. I'd seen it once: the night we ran for our lives. Mother had not allowed anyone in; screaming from labor that night, she'd rushed into the vault, retrieving a small silver casket before hastening out into the forest.

When I stayed silent, Caleb continued, "I can't find the key."

"I don't know of any vault," I told him. "And I don't know of any key."

"Are you certain?" Caleb took another step in my direction. "This could change everything. The archives on Royal steel must be in there."

"Even if I knew, you would be the last person I'd tell, Caleb," I scoffed, yet everything in my body stilled.

He drew a small breath in, his eyes closed in a plea. "I know you have no reason to trust me, but—"

"You gave me no reason to trust you," I seethed. "But you can do something for me and perhaps I will reconsider." The words spilled out before I had time to think through what I was about to demand.

"What can I do?" Caleb's eyes shone with enthusiasm.

"Bring us Royal steel weapons," I dared him.

A frown painted his face. "I can't." He shook his head in disbelief. "You know there is not nearly enough at the palace, they haven't made Royal steel in years." Caleb pinched the bridge of his nose. "That is why we need to get into the vault."

"Surely you can steal a few daggers, Caleb." I rolled my eyes. "You stole a whole person before, you have experience," I sneered. "Bring us the weapons, and then we will talk."

"What you are asking of me is impossible..." Caleb's lips turned into a thin line. "But I will try." He nodded, passing me a small, wrapped box; I didn't move. "Would you give this to Francis?" he asked. "Please."

"He won't accept it."

"Please."

I snatched the box, making sure our fingers didn't touch. "Don't come back without weapons," I spat out when Caleb turned around on one heel, heading towards the woods.

My heart still galloped when I studied the box. My gloved hands trembled; the red stone reflected the moonlight in the darkness—

A gasp pushed past my lips at the memory... Suddenly, I knew where the key to the vault was.

Chapter 12.
Punishable by
Death.

I sprinted up the stairs; my lungs screamed from the lack of air as I barged into Francis' room without knocking.

"I need to find my mother." My voice turned breathless.

"Are you all right?" Francis caught me by my forearms when I stumbled into the candelabra on the floor.

Why in the Kingdom did he have a candelabra on the floor?

"We need to find my mother." I shoved Caleb's present into his hands.

"Cordelia... she is—" His brows furrowed when he looked at me as though I had lost my mind. The crimson still stained his neck.

"I know she is dead." I rolled my eyes. "We need to find where they buried her. Her ring is the key to the vault."

"The vault?" The crease between Francis' eyebrows deepened.

"Caleb believes the archives for Royal steel are in there." I sat on Francis' unmade bed, still catching my breath.

"You spoke to Caleb?" The muscle on his jaw twitched when he glanced at the box.

"We are wasting time, Francis," I groaned.

"I will find her grave, I promise." He nodded, setting the box on the table with his other trinkets. "Do you have any idea where they could've buried her?"

"I am going with you." I rushed to my feet.

"I don't think that's wise—"

"I am going with you."

Francis' lips turned into a thin line. "We will leave the moment the sun sets."

"No, we leave now," I protested. "If Kane finds it before us, we are doomed."

"The sun is to rise in a few hours." Francis shook his head. "We won't make it on time."

"We can't wait—"

His hands fell on my cheeks, gentle thumbs caressing my skin. "We will find the key first, I swear."

I sighed at his touch. "The moment the sun sets."

Sleep didn't find me no matter my fatigue. Silver lay atop my chest as I watched the small opening in the curtains turn darker—the sun was about to set.

My heart fought for its way out with every breath I took; my restless mind spun in a storm. I couldn't face her lifeless eyes, not after what I'd done.

Silver stretched across my chest, deep in his slumber. I allowed myself a small smile at his unbothered muzzle before moving him onto the bed.

"Sorry, friend, I have to go," I whispered when Silver meowed, complaining about the disturbance to his sleep.

The trousers sat comfortably on my body, the warm fabric felt nice to the touch. Mother would be furious were she to see my attire. *Such an insult to our family,* she would say. I contemplated changing, but the growing storm outside made the choice for me.

The walls buzzed with the storm's whispers as I made my way up the stairs to Francis' room. To my surprise, the room was vacant once I walked in after several failed attempts at knocking.

Did he leave without me? My heart galloped. Panic spread through my veins at the thought.

I turned to leave when my eyes caught a piece of parchment resting on his bedside table.

Cordelia. It read, when my hands reached for the letter.

Oh no. No, no, no. How could he leave without me?

"Snooping around, are we?" His voice came from behind me, making me jump. Francis walked into the room, his eyes planted on the parchment in my hands. His brows flew up. "Were you never told theft is punishable by death?"

"Sorry." The heat went up my cheeks as I dropped the letter back onto his table. "I didn't mean to intrude."

"So I see." He grabbed the cloak off the chair, fitting it around his shoulders.

"I thought you left without me."

"As sweet as the thought is, I wouldn't break my promise like that." He showed me out of his room. "Come, we must be on our way if we are to make it on time."

"Of course," I mumbled, averting my gaze as I followed him down the stairs: away from his room, away from the letter he wrote to me.

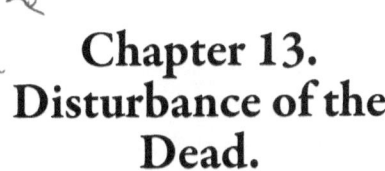

Chapter 13.
Disturbance of the
Dead.

The storm calmed shortly into our trip, yet the drifts of snow were difficult to navigate nevertheless: Annabelle's fatigue traveled through me with every step she took. I squeezed the reins tighter, forgetting of my injuries that ached from the sensation.

The gloves kept the burns away from unwanted eyes, yet my hands cried from having to wear the fabric so much—despite being used to such torture from a young age.

Mother had insisted my hands be covered in public ever since I'd turned five, only letting me go barehanded after the engagement. Was it to show off the ring to the Court and make their new alliance known, or perhaps to ensure my hand would never be taken by another—I would never know. Though, I supposed the latter, since I stopped wearing that ring right after my birthday: no matter her withering gazes at my bare finger.

I sighed, watching the snow fall on Annabelle's mane. How could I be mad at the woman after knowing what I did now?

I'd often wondered whether she'd loved us, but now I wondered whether she'd known love at all? Betrayed by her parents, heartbroken by her lover, her firstborn stolen away from her while still an infant...

She'd become what she'd needed to be in order to survive, and I wondered if that would have been my fate had I stayed at the palace.

No matter what I preferred to believe, I knew the answer.

My mind spiraled, remembering our last conversation at the Royal lodge. She'd told me to stay away from Francis then, told me his family could not be trusted.

They will bring no more than disaster into your life, she'd said and I couldn't agree more...

"Mother said she knew you." I let the words out before I thought better of it.

Francis faced me: his eyes glowing amber under the moonlight, the snow veiled his long, black lashes. "Pardon me?" His brows furrowed.

"My mother—" I swallowed, regretting the question. "When Mother and I spoke last she told me she knew you. She also told me to stay away..."

Francis chuckled, shaking his head. "Of course she did."

"Did she?" I cleared my throat which suddenly felt stuffed. "Did she know you?"

"It's not an easy conversation to have." Francis' face soured. I nodded, ready to leave the discussion when Francis spoke once more. "The Queen was present when my parents were executed."

"What?" A gasp escaped me. "What are you saying?" I swallowed, ready to hear the worst. *Mother couldn't... She couldn't be the reason Francis and Issac were orphaned.*

"We were poor," Francis began and my heart froze in place. "After my father fell ill, my mother's small apothecary shop wasn't enough to feed us all. She began to steal." A sad smile stretched his lips. "My father wasn't aware, but when the royal guards barged into our cabin—" Francis took out the canteen from the inside pocket of his cloak. "He took the blame." His voice dropped a few octaves. "My father thought he was saving us: facing possible execution, and ridding us of the burden he believed he was...

"The guards dragged them both to the royal grounds." Francis' throat bubbled as he took a sip. "Issac and I ran after them barefoot—all the way to the palace's citadel."

The back of my eyes burned as Francis continued.

"They beheaded them both by order of the King. They forced me and Issac to watch." Francis sighed. "The Queen was the one to take us to the orphanage. She gave us a dozen coins each and a pocket full of caramel fudge.

"I remember trying it for the first time, yet it only left a sandy taste in my mouth."

"I am so sorry," I whispered. How could the father I loved so much be capable of such horror? "I am so sorry, Francis."

"It is not your fault." Francis sighed. "I used to blame my mother for disobeying the law," he snorted. "I believed she doomed us to such an end." A sad smile stretched his lips. "It wasn't until I was on my own, responsible for my siblings, that I realized the burdens she had to carry all by herself. I wish I was older when my father fell ill, perhaps I would've been able to work, or..."

"I'm sorry," was all I was able to say.

"It's in the past." Francis shook his head. "Cordelia?" Francis said after taking a sip of his drink. "What did Roxanne mean by Caleb being the rightful heir to the throne?"

My brows rose as my heart sped up. "I assumed Roxanne told you."

"We weren't on speaking terms until last night—though I'm sure that was only a temporary truce." He chuckled. "Will you tell me?"

"There's not much to tell." The lump in my throat grew bigger.

"As a birthday present?" Francis' eyes filled with hope.

"I thought my presence was enough," I teased.

Francis smirked. "Why, Princess, I am getting jealous," he purred. "How come Roxanne gets to know and I don't?"

"There is not much to know." I shrugged.

"And yet?" Francis wouldn't give up.

I sighed. "Mother had Caleb before she married my father." My eyes planted on the point ahead. "She later had an affair with Kane and they had Brian and me. Kane is my blood father."

"Caleb is of royal blood." Francis said under his breath. "Did he know that?"

I nodded. "Since Caleb was born before she was married, they couldn't leave him as one of the Royal children. They got rid of Kane and Caleb to save face in front of the Court. Kane managed to return to the castle a while after... that's when Brian and I were born."

Silence stretched between us; deep in his thoughts, Francis drank from the canteen.

"You believe this story?" He eventually asked.

"It matters not." I squeezed the reins, navigating Annabelle away from the black ice that had formed on the trail. "Though, it certainly sounds like something my mother's parents would do. When I first met Caleb, he reminded me of my brother. And Kane..." I swallowed at the eerie resemblance between him and Brian. "They look identical."

"You and Caleb do look alike," Francis stated, almost disappointed.

"As I said, it matters not," I mumbled, squeezing the reins tighter.

"Do you trust him?" Francis pressed.

"His promises seem sincere." Did I trust him, though? I wasn't sure.

I'd seen the burden he carried, back in the dungeon: the regret that had filled his eyes from what he'd done, the pain he'd tried to hide when I'd called him a coward.

Was that enough to trust him?

Blood brother or not, I did not know a single thing about that man.

"Time will show," I told Francis when the first battlements of the palace peered from the line of dense spruce.

Chapter 14.
Unkindness.

The Royal cemetery was quiet. Empty.

Snow covered every engraved stone, shining under the Moon. We walked along the graves, our boots leaving a trace behind us, as I read every name we passed.

"They are not here," I whispered, the cold cloud lingered on my breath. My lips trembled at the realization once we'd reached the last stone that carried my name. "They didn't bury them at the Royal cemetery," my voice shook.

"We will find them." Francis walked down the rows several times; the shovel in his hand dragged along the snow. "Where else could they be?" He stood before me; his face inches from mine, yet all I could see was my engraved name above the empty casket.

"I don't know." My lungs caught aflame as I forced my next breath. "I don't—"

"Think, Cordelia. We don't have much time." Francis gentled, his hands covering my cheeks. "There must be another cemetery nearby, or perhaps a meadow of some kind. They wouldn't just leave the bodies to rot near the palace."

I shook my head. "I don't know! What if they burned them, or—" I trailed off when the thought clouded my mind. "Oh dear Gods..."

"What is it?" Francis searched my eyes.

"There is only one other cemetery nearby." My voice didn't belong to me when the words escaped my trembling lips.

"Where is it?"

"North."

Burying the Royal family in the cemetery meant for traitors was a stab in the back I hadn't been prepared for.

No stone stood at this graveyard, no names remembered at the empty land. The gate screeched with age when Francis pulled on the lock, snow fell on his uncovered hands.

"We will never find them here." The back of my eyes prickled as I took a step into the cemetery. "Traitors don't get a memorial." I turned to Francis. His hands still held the rusty lock; his eyes shot past me, bewilderment filling them.

I followed his gaze, and my heart stumbled as I took a step backwards, my back hitting Francis' chest.

"What in the Kingdom..." he muttered.

"Ravens." I swallowed, walking towards an unkindness of ravens that circled the patch of fresh fallen snow.

My legs shook as they carried me forward against my better judgment, yet something pulled me towards the birds no matter my fear.

Onyx eyes met mine when I stood before the birds; their quiet stare pierced into my soul as they crooked their heads at once.

"It's here," I whispered to Francis standing beside me.

"I wouldn't be so certain—"

"They are buried here." I nodded without breaking my stare with the ravens.

"Cordelia—" Francis trailed off when a deafening croak filled the cemetery. The ravens squawked at once, their strong wings whistled as the unkindness rose to the black sky. Disappearing into the woods, their song rang in my ears.

My lungs ached when I took my next breath; my eyes closed, welcoming the raven's prayer. "It's here." I swallowed. "I can feel it."

"Moon help me," Fracis muttered, pushing the shovel into the cold soil.

The Moon had faded into the sky by the time Francis' shovel stuck deep inside the pit: the morning twilight was upon us.

"You should probably go." Francis glanced up at me when the big wooden box appeared at the bottom of the pit.

"I need to see them." I swallowed the growing nausea.

"I don't think that's wise, Cordelia," Francis argued. His perfect clothing was now wrinkled and covered in soil as he cleaned the remaining dirt off the box, fidgeting with the cap.

"I need to see them."

I clenched the ends of my sleeves. Nausea clawed at my weak stomach.

Francis sighed, his lips turned into a thin line, yet he obeyed my wishes, opening the cap to the dishonorable casket.

My legs weakened as an invisible force kneeled me before my fallen family.

My ivory gloves turned the color of dirt.

Their bodies were a bloody mess.

I clenched onto the edge of the grave, my fingers digging into the frozen soil.

If it hadn't been for Mother's jewelry that still hung on her broken fingers, if it hadn't been for the two tiny bodies clutching onto each other, I would've never guessed they were my family.

Their limbs rested in the most unnatural of ways, their skin broken apart as long-dried blood sat on every inch of their flesh. Their clothes ripped apart, clinging on their broken ribs, their bruised cheeks shone purple against their pale—covered in blood—skin.

A strong smell of sour-rot and soil hit my nostrils; my jaw clenched shut, nausea making its way through my insides.

Then I saw her.

My dear sister.

She lay beside our mother. Her body was not broken into shreds like the rest of our family's were. Kane had spared her at least that. Her hair still wore crimson, her wrists marked by long cuts.

"It's a gift." She had told me before—

"I do not wish to stay without Frederick and Eleanor," she'd said. *"This is a gift."*

Oh, how I wished for such a gift at that moment. How I wished for the Moon to take my soul, despite my unfulfilled oath.

Had Sandra been there when Fredrick and Eleanor were murdered? Had she been forced to watch such horrors?

Were they together now, in Moon's paradise, safe and sound?

"I am sorry," I whispered to them all. "I am so sorry."

Francis' gaze bored into my flesh before he cleared his throat, his voice as soft as velvet, "Which ring is it?"

"Her ring finger," I replied, staring at Mother's ruby stone that no longer sparkled: covered in blood and soil. Identical to the one Ash had given me. "Her wedding ring," I said, almost laughing.

The irony wasn't lost on me... The woman who surely hadn't loved my father, put so much meaning and purpose into the symbol of their marriage.

Francis moved to my mother, removing the ring from her hand. My gaze was planted on her face.

Mother looked peaceful. The most peaceful I had ever seen her. Her sharp features now softened, her withering gaze now hidden, her edged lips tendered.

I forced air into my lungs, giving a small nod to Francis before he closed the cap.

"I love you," I told my family as the first pile of dirt fell onto the casket.

The trip to the cabin was a dream—a nightmare—brought to life. The faces of my loved ones, engraved in my mind, walked alongside me every step of the way. My eyes closed in an attempt to rid myself of the horrid memories in vain.

Francis fought with the frozen lock of the cabin's door when the darkness crept into my wrecked mind, daring me to act upon its wicked needs.

"Cordelia?" Francis started, opening the door for me. "If you wish to talk—" he trailed off as I rushed into the cabin, walking straight for the ladder next to the black-painted door.

I'd never been in the room on the second level, as it was the residence of Roxanne and Florence. I wished not to indulge in their private space, yet in that moment I could not find it in me to care. I knew what I had to do to be rid of the memories from this vile night; I knew what I had to do to bring slight justice to the pain I'd inflicted upon my sister.

"I wish to be alone," was all I said before climbing the ladder and shutting the door closed.

The room darkened as I walked in. The drawn curtains kept the rising sun at bay. I scanned the space until my eyes landed on the bedside table that carried a candelabra with three unlit candles; my heart skipped a beat in anticipation of the upcoming repose.

I took the bronze flint out of the pocket of my dress as my shaky legs carried me towards my salvation. My lungs squeezed shut.

My trembling hands held the flint as I watched the candle catch flame. An invisible hand squeezed my lungs, refusing to let air in as I stared down the flame: my imminent punishment, my imminent relief.

UNKINDNESS OF CRIMSON QUEEN

The candle chanted, frantically dancing, putting me under a spell I was unable to resist.

I watched her face inside the flame. Her disappointed eyes bored into mine.

"Forgive me, little sister," I told the flame.

The fire sparkled, inviting me to receive what I deserved. My breathing turned frantic.

I set the candle on the bedside table, rolling up the sleeves of my tunic.

"Forgive me."

I brought my exposed skin to the flame, surrendering it to the pain.

My eyes squinted in anticipation until the fire delivered its punishment.

A gasp pushed past my lips, but the pain had yet to bring me relief. I kept my wrist above the flame, yet the pain would not release me, keeping me hostage in the evermore torture.

A muffled cry escaped me as my skin caught aflame. The blackened spot moved inch by inch across my arm until it reached my elbow. And yet, it brought no relief.

Terror clawed at my spine as I moved my hand away from the ever–judging flame.

Nausea crept in at the burning smell of my flesh.

My hands trembled when I felt the hardened skin. My skin wailed from the touch.

Dear Gods!

Dear Gods, and the Moon!

Oh, Moon!

I forced my lungs to expand—they refused.

"Dear Moon." I choked.

My knees weakened as I dropped onto the floor, my eyes never leaving the assault. My vision darkened as I felt my consciousness slip away from my strong grasp.

"Forgive me," I whispered when the dark, cold wave dragged me under.

Chapter 15.
Revelations.

My eyes flew open as a dull knock on the door vibrated through the walls of the cabin.

"Cordelia, are you all right?" Francis' voice hummed through the locked door. "The sun is about to set, we must go."

"I need a moment," my voice rasped; the echo rang in my ears.

My back screamed out in pain at my weak attempt to gather myself from the wooden floor I must have fallen asleep on. I swallowed the growing pain as the back of my eyes burned.

"I will prepare our horses," Francis said. "Come outside when you are ready."

The floors creaked—the sound echoed through my head, accompanied by a terrible ache—when I managed to adjust myself into a seated position. My body caught aflame in an instant.

Chills went through my bones as the pain persisted. Every breath left me trembling. My left arm screamed out in agony as I wiped the cold sweat off my forehead with the end of my cloak.

"Oh no." I stared at my blackened skin that started to turn a shade of blue. "Oh no, no, no."

The injured skin felt rough to the touch, the discoloration moved in every direction, reminding me of the shape of lightning.

"Fuck," I breathed as a new wave of nausea threatened to break through.

Sweat rolled off my temples, falling onto my wrinkled—covered in dirt—trousers. My throat bubbled, my limbs shook.

I must have had a fever.

"Cordelia?" Francis called from down below.

"I am coming!" I rushed to my feet through the shivers, gathering myself as much as possible: the gloves slipped onto my hands, the ends of my cloak tightly tucked inside of them, hiding the sickness.

"Are you well?" Francis looked me up and down when I opened the door. "You look pale."

"I am merely tired," I lied, setting my feet onto the first rung of the ladder.

"Would you like to stay at the cabin for another day?" Concern rang through Francis' voice.

"No!" I blurted. I needed to get to Roxanne and her mysterious medicine as fast as I could. "I would like to sleep in my own bed." Especially since my previous day was spent on the floor...

My head spun senseless on my way down the ladder, my hands gripped onto the rungs for dear life.

"You are shaking." Francis caught me by my waist when my foot slipped off the last rung. "Are you hurt?" His eyes bored into mine as he set me down on the floor.

"I am well, I promise." The words burned on my tongue. "I've had a long day and want to get back to the castle."

"Are you well enough to ride?" The crease between Francis' brows deepened.

"Well enough." I nodded, storming out the main door.

The cold air brushed over my face, soothing the fire that spread through my veins. My legs still shook, making it harder to mount Annabelle, who wouldn't stop swaying from side to side. Was she always like that?

"Do you need help?" The snow crunched behind me. The sound banged on my ears.

"I am all right." I squeezed the horn of the saddle, gathering all of my strength before pushing off the ground, forcing myself atop.

"If you need to stop for a break—"

"I am fine." I ordered Annabelle forward: towards the dark forest, towards the Moon that I prayed to for the strength to reach Roxanne before the inevitable.

Relief washed over me when my eyes caught the proudly standing castle behind the line of dense spruce. My sickness worsened by the time I brought Annabelle to a halt near the stables. It was a miracle I had not fallen off the horse on our journey.

Everything spun and blurred as I walked Annabelle to the stables. I leaned on my horse—mere seconds from collapsing onto the ground. My eyes closed when the darkness of the stables welcomed me into its embrace.

"Cordelia?" Francis' voice carried through the fog in my mind. "Cordelia—"

Cordelia—

My body felt weightless—

"I cannot believe you two left without consulting us!" Roxanne's voice rang in my ears like church bells. I was going to be sick from the sound alone.

I forced my eyes open. His face was inches from mine, his eyes—

"We didn't have time to wait," he told Roxanne without breaking his stare.

"What's wrong with her?"

I drew a small breath in, fighting with the nausea.

"I don't know." Francis shook his head, his hands catching me in an embrace. "Let's get you to bed."

"I am well—" A moan broke through me when Francis' chest pressed against my injured arm. My vision darkened, dozens of stars lingering in front of my closed eyes.

"What's wrong with her arm?" Roxanne's cold fingers reached for my tucked cloak; I had no strength to protest. "Oh Moon, what have you done?"

"What in the Kingdom..." Francis' voice vibrated through me as his hands brought me closer.

"We need to hurry, or she is going to lose her arm."

"I—" I started, yet the sickness traveled faster than moonlight.

"Fuck," Francis grumbled, carrying me towards the castle.

"I didn't mean for this to happen." My lips trembled; my eyes fluttered. "I didn't—"

"Florence!" Roxanne called. "We need your help!" She opened the door to the small study; dozens of differently colored jars sat on each shelf.

Francis carried me in, setting me down on the chair in the corner of the room.

"Find her some moonshine," Roxanne ordered Francis, frantically searching the cabinets of the study. "Florence!"

Francis nodded, rushing out of the room.

The staircase above the room screeched. The darkness drowned me.

"You have to stay awake." Roxanne's fingers squeezed my cheeks, shaking my head left and right. "Stay awake, Cordelia!" She pressed a few Vasyalisk berries against my lips.

The berries slipped into my mouth, the bitterness burned on my tongue. The edges of my eyes watered as the door to the study flew open.

"What is going—" Florence trailed off when her eyes landed on my arm. "Oh Dear Moon."

"We need fresh snow or ice," Roxanne ordered at her. "Preferably ice."

The running boots disappeared into the hallway as Florence rushed to fulfill Roxanne's command.

"This is going to hurt," was my only warning before Roxanne applied a thick layer of paste across my arm.

"Stop!" I yelped against my better judgement. "Stop!"

"I got the moonshine."

My vision darkened when I searched for Francis' face, his eyes lingered on mine before the darkness pulled me under—

"Put it under her nose, we can't let her lose consciousness."

No amount of fire could compare with the flame that spread though my hand, reaching my heart. An excruciating scream fought for freedom, scratching my throat, yet silence captured my mind—

"Cordelia?"

My head shook, my wrist caught aflame.

"Cordelia!"

Cordelia.

Cordelia—

The darkness smiled down at me, dozens of stars dimmed into nothingness.

Nothing—

"What are you doing?" echoed through my mind, each word slowly traveling through the fog.

What are you doing?

What are—

"Bringing her back."

Back.

Back—

The blade fell onto the marble floor. The sound bounced off the walls, ringing in my ears.

My lips numbed when his soft skin brushed over them. Wetness fell onto my tongue. My eyes flew open when the crimson reached my throat.

Francis' bleeding wrist pressed against my lips as the drops of his blood spilled into my mouth. My healthy hand pressing his injury closer. My nails dug into his skin, clinging onto him like a drowning man to a branch.

"Good thinking." Roxanne nodded to Francis whose eyes never left mine as my teeth bored deep into his flesh. "I'm almost done," Roxanne said, setting an empty jar onto the table.

The sickness subsided, leaving nothing but an uncomfortable numbness to take its place. Francis' blood calmed the flame so slightly, or perhaps it was the berries, I cared not.

My throat soothed as the crimson warmed my insides. I closed my eyes, submitting to the weakness.

It wasn't long before my nausea returned anew.

I pushed Francis' wrist away, filling my lungs with air, though the sickness did not step away. As though on a boat, the strong ocean pushed me in every direction, spinning my head drunk.

I'd been on a boat once when Father took me and Brian to see his older brother in a Kingdom across the sea—

A moan pushed past my lips when a new wave dragged me under.

Francis' hand fell onto my sweaty forehead. "She is still burning."

"I know." Roxanne sighed. "We don't have any herbs at the castle to bring down the fever."

"I can go to Faris and get some," Florence's voice appeared out of nowhere. How long had she been standing there for?

"No," Roxanne exclaimed as the ice touched my numb hand. "You are not going to Faris by yourself. Francis will go with you."

"I can't leave her," he protested, pressing a cold cloth against my head.

"You know nothing of burns, it is better I stay with her."

Silence stretched across the room, save for my racing heart echoing in my ears.

"Let's get her to bed first," Francis said at last when my eyes shut, welcoming the peace.

A cloud wrapped around me as I floated through space. Weightless was my body, weightless were my thoughts; my head fell onto the soft pillow, the smell of which brought me comfort.

"I can't believe you knew she'd been burning herself and didn't tell me," Francis hissed. My eyelids were too heavy to open, my lips sealed close.

"I didn't think she would do this!" Roxanne hissed back. "And need I remind you, she burned herself while in the same house as you. How could you not notice?"

"I would have noticed, if you told—"

"This is not the time," Florence hissed at them both. "And I am truly sick of your constant arguments."

"You know I am right—" Francis started.

"Don't." My lips felt like rocks against each other. "Fight." I swallowed the dryness in my throat.

"Cordelia," Francis' voice was so close. "We brought medicine for your fever."

The dream that floated through my mind a mere moment ago shattered as I forced my eyes to open.

"Here." Francis' hand slipped under my shoulders, lifting me into a seated position.

"This should lower your temperature." Florence brought a spoonful of dark brown liquid to my mouth.

The medicine held a surprisingly pleasant taste: sweet, but bitter all the same.

"You should rest," Francis whispered before my eyes closed once again.

The cold wrapped around my arm as my dream fractured into small pieces. My eyes flew open, only to find Roxanne sitting on my bed, tending to my healing injury.

"I didn't mean to wake you," she whispered. "I have to change your band for a fresh one," Roxanne explained, setting the paste on my skin. The numbness was no longer there, yet the pain was bearable.

"How long has it been?" I croaked, looking at the covered window. The sun shone bright through the small opening of the curtains, gilding the floors in shimmer, reminding me of Sandra's golden locks.

"Two nights." Roxanne shrugged, focused on her delicate work.

I filled my lungs, noting the aching burn was no longer there—with it the fatigue faded as well. "How long will it take to fully heal?"

Roxanne's lips turned into a thin line. Her voice turned quiet, "I don't know. I never went this far." Roxanne met my gaze. "The pain should cease rather soon, but the mark..." She shook her head.

I nodded as the realization of what had happened slowly settled. Panic rushed through my veins, my heart beat faster. *I could have lost an arm. I could have died—*

"You are fine now," Roxanne said, as though reading my thoughts, as she wrapped my arm in clean fabric. "You are going to heal." She tightened the ends around my elbow, her expression turning serious. "But if you manage to kill yourself, I swear, I will find you in the next life and murder you myself, do you hear me?"

I chuckled at her expression. "What do you care if I live or die?" I shook my head as the images of her threat floated through my mind.

"Oh, I don't." She shrugged, collecting the old wrap in her hands. "But Francis and Florence will be devastated, and I don't take any insult to them lightly."

I couldn't help but smile. "Surely you would be upset a little too..."

"A little." She nodded, fighting her smile. "It would be rather inconvenient."

"Thank you." I sighed. "For everything."

A mere nod was the reply to my sincerity before Roxanne said, "You cannot keep burning yourself, Cordelia." She stood from the bed. "William Barren replied to our letter, they are waiting for us on the full Moon, and you must be strong for that meeting." With that, she left the room, leaving me all alone with my thoughts.

I stared at the ceiling of my bedroom, counting every black widow I saw, though it did nothing to settle my heart that fought for freedom.

The memories of my family deep in the grave invaded my thoughts, and I longed for the fevered mind I had before I'd woken. I longed for the pain in my arm that distracted me from agony far worse than this. Yet there was none.

No distraction, no salvation.

The empty hole in my stomach filled with desperation. Yet the tears would not come.

I swallowed the growing lumps, forcing myself out of bed. My skin ached at the movement, and I welcomed the discomfort—anything to get rid of the tragedy that was about to occur.

My legs carried me out of the room, towards the pain, towards the agony I had yet to allow.

There was only one place I wanted to be, only one place that would finish up the deed and shatter my soul into small pieces once and for all.

Chapter 16.
Forgotten Waltz.

The doors of the music room creaked open as I stepped in. The polished grand piano stared at me, daring me to join the last battle.

I sat on the stool before the piano, opening its lid. I hadn't played the instrument in years: always preferring the dramatic and passionate violin to gentle and soft piano, but today my mind demanded tranquil melancholia that could reach to the very depths of my soul and make me feel something—anything beyond this utter hollow.

My fingers brushed over the raw keys of the instrument as I tried to remember any piece I'd learned, yet only one came to mind. Only one seemed to fit such circumstances: Sandra's favorite.

She hadn't fancied waltzes as much as I had, but this one she'd asked me to play again and again on my violin, until my fingers would be sore from the instrument, and every bone in my body would beg for rest.

I warmed up my fingers as the empty hole inside of me grew with dread. The burns on my fingers almost faded, leaving me with nothing but emptiness.

I took a deep breath, settling my hands in the proper position. My eyes studied the keys I was so afraid to press. For the last time, I glanced at the closed door, making sure no one was to witness my inevitable shatter.

I wasn't sure why I did this at all, knowing that the music would lead to an unstoppable meltdown. Perhaps I needed it somewhere so deep in my soul that even my consciousness guarded me from the thought. Perhaps I was so tired of the heartbreak, that the pain that would come sounded like salvation.

I hadn't cried since the day I'd lost her, for I'd known if the first tear were to fall, they would never have stopped until my soul had drowned in misery.

I closed my eyes when the first note played; every inch of my skin was covered in bumps. My hands shook as I pressed the keys: slowly, as though the melody would grow claws and end me before my heartache would.

My marked skin screamed in agony, yet my soul screamed louder.

The dread in my stomach shrunk the more I played, yet the tears didn't come. Not yet, though I knew they would.

The melody smelled like Sandra: wildflowers and caramel, fresh dew and old books. The melody painted pictures of dawn that would shimmer in Sandra's hair, and green, as the summer forest, that reminded me of her eyes.

The music continued on its own, my blackened fingers didn't belong to me any longer, sounding harsher than it needed to be, though it perfectly fit the story of Sandra's life in the end. Horror and despair. Excruciation and... Death.

The music carried me away from the castle—somewhere I had no right to be—for Sandra's gentle hands stretched out to me, soothing my crying heart. She was so close: I could hear her strong heartbeat, her bright laughter, and her magical singing.

The ballad she'd written when we were children, about a girl who grew wings which carried her far-far away to a land that only knew happiness and peace, erupted in the room.

Her voice, so strong but so delicate, caressed my ears and forced silent tears to my soul. Her sweet voice stripped me of all the anger that had filled me from the day we'd parted. Bare, I was unsure how to handle the vulnerability. I let the tears fall.

The tears burned my cheeks, falling down onto the keyboard of the piano. My eyes could no longer see the keys; my fingers kept missing the notes, yet it mattered not. If I had to stay here forever, playing the same piece to hear her voice for a mere moment, I was glad to oblige.

I hit the keys as more tears fell; my fingers could no longer move, my eyes could no longer see, my mind could no longer think.

I stared at the keyboard through the glass that covered my vision. The music echoed in my head—

Careful steps moved towards me, and I wiped the evidence of being distraught off my face.

I got up from the stool, ready to flee. Yet, when I saw Francis standing in the center of the room, my mind betrayed me.

My legs gave out as I collapsed onto the marble floor before him, my knees screaming out in protest from the impact.

"I killed her," I whispered before the agony teared up my throat. "Francis—" I bellowed when he dropped beside me, his hands holding me tight from shattering into small pieces.

"I killed her," I kept repeating again and again as my heart fractured. "How can I live—"

"Shhh." Francis' hand fell onto the back of my neck; his cold fingers caressed my skin. "You didn't kill her, Kane did."

"No!" I tried to push him away, yet his hands held me firmly in place. "I could have—I should have—" I choked. "I don't want to hurt anyone, Francis."

"It's not your fault, love." He held my cheeks. "It is not your fault."

I blinked the tears away, filling my lungs as his eyes bored into mine. "It is not your fault," he whispered again. "I am so very sorry I let it happen."

I shook my head. "It isn't your burden to carry." I glanced at the black marble floor before confessing, "I didn't think you would come at all. Not after our conversation."

Pain painted his face as his brows furrowed. "Cordelia..." His voice dropped a few octaves as his arms wrapped around me once more. Jasmine and winter washed over me when I closed my eyes, filling my lungs with his aroma. "I would never leave you, Cordelia." He said against my shoulder. "I would never leave you, even if I am the last person you wish to see. I swear it to you."

I closed my eyes against his shoulder. Hot tears spilled down my cheeks onto his skin. My trembling hands veiled around his neck, and I welcomed the closeness. The ache of my injury ceased the longer we sat in this caress, the warmth spreading through my body, reaching my soul bit by bit.

A sigh pushed past my lips as I brought my face closer to his neck. His heartbeat sang me lullabies, serenity pouring through me like honey: no storm could reach our embrace's ward.

"I love y—" My eyes flew open, disturbed by my own admission. My lips sealed close before the words spilled out without my permission, piercing my heart all around. I swallowed as my galloping heart throbbed against my ribs. *Damnation.*

Blood rushed to my cheeks; the air escaped my lungs at once.

"I didn't mean—" Had I meant it? Did I love— "I—I don't—I don't know—" I stuttered, my lips shaking as embarrassment rushing through my veins. My brows knitted together. "I'm sorry."

A corner of Francis' lips tugged upwards. "It's all right. You had a long few nights, I understand." His hand fell atop my injured one, connecting on the marble. "Don't you worry about it."

"I don't know why I said that," I rasped. "I don't—" I shook my head, my stomach turning in every direction possible.

"It's all right, Cordelia," Francis whispered. "You are tired. Let's get you to bed."

"I'm sorry." I nodded, gathering to my feet. "I am a fool," I said under my breath, charging towards the exit.

"No need to apologize." Francis rushed after me.

My heart still banged against my rib cage when I hurried up the stairs, the tips of my ears burned in shame.

Francis' steps followed. I need not look at him to feel the piercing gaze that prickled the back of my head, and I chided myself for such foolishness. "Have a good rest, Cordelia." He reached to open the door to my room, inviting me in. I froze still in place.

My throat went dry at the threshold to my room. My eyes planted on his hand atop the door's knob, for I could not bear meeting his eyes.

I needed to be alone, needed to straighten everything the storm had wrecked on its way to free me. So many wicked thoughts, so many bewildering feelings that my heart had no business unleashing upon my mind...

Oh, but how afraid I was to stay alone with my monsters for even a moment. "Would you stay with me?" I asked, against my better judgment.

As though my life depended on it, I waited for Francis' answer, hanging onto every breath he took before replying, "Of course."

Chapter 17.
Crimson Petals.

I sank into his embrace as the night moonlight broke through the small opening in the curtains. My lungs finally filled with air that did not burn. I took another breath, and another, stunned by how easy it was—breathing. How had I not noticed the struggle before?

"Good evening," Francis whispered into my ear, and the warmth of his voice enveloped me whole: a small flame growing inside of my heart.

I turned in his embrace until my cheek rested against his chest. He still wore the blouse that carried my dried tears. His hair now reached his chin, splattering on the silk pillow. "Good evening," my voice turned hoarse as my lips tugged into a smile that felt peculiar on my face.

His hands tightened around me, ushering me closer. "Would you like for me to draw you a bath?"

"I much prefer your embrace." I shook my head, breathing in the jasmine and cigars. The warmth erupted deep in my stomach as the long–forgotten flowers freed their thorns.

"Who says you can't have both?" His voice filled with a sudden mischief; his eyes shimmered in anticipation. "If you want, of course," he then added.

My eyes met his as a genuine smile stretched my lips. "Yes, that sounds lovely."

"Wait here." He winked, depriving me of the embrace, though the flame he planted in my chest merely grew bigger.

Hot steam filled the bathing chambers along with the fresh smell of lavender and jasmine. The petals floated in the water in a beautiful rainbow; candles lit up the room, our shadows uniting.

"Would you like for me to leave?" Francis crooked his head to one side, his eyes searching mine.

"Someone promised me a nice embrace along with my bath..." The moment the words left my troublesome mouth, my heart flustered: my tongue had a mind of its own.

"I wanted to be certain you didn't change your mind." Francis' fingers reached for the top button of his shirt.

"I didn't." My mouth went dry as the flowers low in my stomach bloomed.

I swallowed the nervousness before my fingers pulled on the strings, untying my dress. My heart skipped a beat; I took off the top layer of my clothing until nothing but my undergarments were left.

A moment of hesitation stole my breath before I freed myself of the rest of my clothing.

The startling confidence overwhelmed me. I could only hope for regret to never come.

Bare, I stood before the bathtub, every inch of my flesh covered in bumps. I couldn't bear glancing at Francis at that moment... even if my life depended on it.

My breathing heaved when I made my way into the water. The hot bath prickled my skin, enveloping me in its embrace as I sat in the center of it.

The petals brushed over my skin, covering my bare body from view. I took a slow breath in before my hands reached for the hairpin that held my waves hostage—safe from unwanted touch. I swallowed, letting my strands fall into the water, allowing such vulnerability.

My fingers brushed over the petals, grateful for the distraction.

"May I join you?" His sultry voice echoed through the bathing chamber, setting my flesh aflame greater than fire ever could.

I nodded, for if I spoke, my voice would give away the weakness. I dared not look up from the petals in my hands, studying them as though they were my most precious possession.

The water swerved as he sat behind me, my throat ached when our knees touched.

My hands visibly shook as a silent fight with the monsters from my past broke into my mind. Francis didn't move, waiting for me to make up my mind.

Before the panic forced its way onto myself I swallowed the growing fear, embracing the moment I longed for.

Princess knows bravery. If I weren't so anxious, I would have laughed at my own foolishness.

Stop it, Cordelia. I shook my head as my eyes closed. *You are such a fool.* I sighed, closing the distance between us.

His hands wrapped around my waist in an instant as I rested my back against his bare chest, shielding me from my own wicked mind. My chest rose above the water, exposing my bare body, yet the shame I was expecting to break through stayed silent. The fear that threatened to destroy me retreated. My mind calmed.

The warmth caressed me; the centers of my breasts hardened, yet I could not find it in me to care for such exposure.

His hands, softer than velvet, caressed my lower stomach, unraveling the flowers that coiled around my insides, as a welcoming silence fell upon us.

Chapter 18. Means of Survival.

I must have fallen asleep in his arms, for when I opened my eyes, the water was as cold as a winter storm. Yet, I could not be bothered, as his body pressing against mine set my body aflame.

"Sleep well?" Francis murmured against my ear, sending dozens of goosebumps down my flesh.

"I must have been exhausted." I turned to face him.

"As much as I fancy your company, Princess, I now must go." His fingers brushed over my cheekbone before dropping to my hand. "There's lots to do before tomorrow."

"Tomorrow?" My brows furrowed as I stopped myself from grabbing his hand and pressing it against my cheek once more.

"The full Moon," Francis' voice echoed through the chambers. "Barren is waiting for us."

"Of course." I had completely forgotten about the meeting.

"Don't worry, I wouldn't expect you to plan anything, knowing your *cautious* nature." He winked, his lips curling.

My eyes rolled, yet no attempts to fight my smile were successful. "I do have a plan, believe it or not."

"Is that so?" Francis chuckled. "Care to share?" He repeated the same question he'd asked me before our first meeting at the Barren's castle.

"I will convince Barren he is in charge even when we are the ones giving out orders." I shrugged.

"And how will you manage that?" Francis wouldn't give up; his finger brushed a stray strand of hair behind my ear.

"You have to trust me," I teased, my lips stretching into a mischievous smile.

Francis' gaze flickered to mine when the small distance between us suddenly bothered me in all the wrong ways.

His eyes reflected the candlelight as they gazed into the depths of my soul. "Princess?" His sultry voice caressed my flesh.

"Yes?" My voice dropped to a shaken whisper.

Wickedness sparkled in Francis' eyes as they darkened. "May I steal a kiss?" He rasped, his pulse visible on his neck.

"A thief asking for permission to steal," I teased, my heart galloping in my chest. "That is certainly unheard of."

Francis chuckled, averting his gaze to the candle that stood on the rim of the bathtub; wax flowing onto the marble, sliding into the cold water.

A smile tugged on Francis' lips, "Is that a no?"

"I've never said that." I shrugged, allowing myself a glance at his lips.

"Why, Princess, you certainly enjoy torturing me," he tsked, yet he made no attempt at granting his own wish.

"You make it far too easy." My voice cracked, betraying my act.

My lips ached for his kiss, my ribcage could hardly contain my eager heart. My mind screamed at me to not make the same mistakes, though by then it was past due for such warnings.

"Perhaps next time," Francis said at last, and I battled the startling disappointment attempting to break through my schooled features. "When we aren't laying bare in a bath of cold water."

"Next time." I nodded, already wishing for that time to come sooner.

Francis smiled, pushing up from the bath, and I wished to have the bravery to ask for his promised kiss. Alas, I was not as fearless as I hoped to be: not when I had to ask for far worse than a kiss.

I rushed out of the bath, slipping the silky robe atop my shoulders on the way. "Francis," I walked into the room, noting he had already put his trousers on, his hands drying his curls with a cloth.

My lips turned into a thin line as the blood rushed to my cheeks. With a silk robe around myself, I had never felt more exposed than in that moment. "I need—" I swallowed the words, unable to hold Francis' piercing gaze.

"What is it you need, Princess?" His hoarse voice reached my ears, worsening my already fragile body.

"Nothing." I shook my head as shame spread through my body, blood rushing through my troublesome center. "Never mind."

I fought the urge to run when Francis' amber eyes dug into mine. "Tell me" He caught my chin, bringing it higher until our eyes met.

His lips were far too close to mine.

Were someone to ask for my name at that moment, I surely would not remember.

"Cordelia?" His brows rose high, his gaze forcing the words out of me.

"I need to feed," I whispered, before thinking better of it. "Before the meeting."

Francis nodded as realization settled in his eyes. A sinful smile tugged on his lips. "That you do."

I bit my lower lip, holding my breath as the words left without my permission. "I don't want human blood."

Francis chuckled, "You could just say you fancy mine."

My cheeks turned hot against my wishes. "Your arrogance would know no limits were I to say that." I rolled my eyes. "Besides, your blood is no different from others, I merely do not wish to partake in gruesome activities."

Francis laughed, his head flying backwards. "Is that so?" His lips stretched out into a smirk. "And here I thought I was special. Turns out I am merely a means of survival."

"Precicely." I shrugged, though my voice shook nevertheless.

"Lucky for you, I am still happy with my downgraded title," Francis rasped, catching my wrists in his firm grasp as he pressed my hands against his chest. His arm held me in an embrace, another brought my lips to his exposed throat.

My silky robe felt utterly soft on my skin when my lips felt his pulse. My heart beat in unison with his when my teeth dug into his flesh and the eruption of my peaceful mind made itself known.

His blood soothed the monster within me that I learned to respect. My tongue brushed against his skin, catching every drop that followed.

A muffled moan vibrated through Francis' chest, reaching my lower stomach. My own moan followed after, and I didn't bother to hide it.

It wasn't long before my lips were able to escape his hold, as my tongue worked through his injury, satisfying the monster within. My eyes rolled back when the, sweet as honey, blood filled me; my head spun when his hand caressed my lower back.

"And I was told my blood was no better than any other." Francis' sultry voice exclaimed when I pushed away from his throat.

"Precisely," I breathed, noting for the first time that we had somehow made our way onto my unmade sheets.

He smirked in reply, pushing off the bed.

Still splattered before him, I watched him reach for his shirt; his eyes never leaving mine as he worked through the buttons.

My lips caught aflame when my fingers felt the blood that covered my skin.

"Forgive me, I must go." Francis did not bother to wipe the blood from his open injury. "Try to get some rest before tomorrow, it promises to be a rather difficult night." He fondled my chin, forcing the flowers deep in my stomach to collapse all at once, before turning around and taking his leave.

Chapter 19.
Harmless.

Francis' study buzzed with uncertainty when I entered; my sword secured to my belt, a dagger in my boot. Though I supposed, no matter my weaponry, I could not stand against Barren's army were he to order my end. Human or not—their numbers were a threat; we were walking straight into whatever they had prepared for us.

I drew a small breath, my hand playing with the Royal stamp that I'd hid in my pocket before leaving my room, as I settled on the corner of a settee Florence had occupied. She glanced at me, shifting to the side, creating space for me as her lips shook into a smile.

"Are you all right?" I asked, my brows furrowing at her odd expression.

"Yes!" she exclaimed, her fingers toying with the sleeves of her burgundy—a color I had never seen her wear before—dress. "I still don't fancy human Royalty—" Her face turned sour. "Sorry."

"That's all right." I smiled, yet my own fears clawed at my lungs anew.

I wished Florence wouldn't have to go, wouldn't have to struggle. Especially when danger might come because of me. "Perhaps you both could stay behind," I told Roxanne as she entered the study. Her eyes planted on Florence's worried expression when I continued, "Surely Francis and I could meet with William ourselves."

Florence's eyes grew bigger, though she refrained from saying a word. Roxanne's lips turned into a thin line: watching her beloved struggle so much, she certainly considered my offer.

It was Francis who spoke in disagreement, "We are all going. End of discussion." He walked into the study, swiftly packing a stack of parchment into a satchel. "It is too dangerous to split up when the Wurdulacs have gained so much power. And we need numbers entering the Barren's duchy: the more the better." He moved the curtains aside, glancing out the window: the freshly risen Moon glared down into the poorly lit room. "Simon and Ash should be here any moment."

"Simon and Ash are coming as well?" I frowned, hearing of it for the first time.

"As I said, we need numbers for our proposition to be taken seriously." Francis closed his satchel, letting it hang over his shoulder. "Barren will not be alone, given that every survivor of the palace's attack fled there. We will need numbers."

"How many humans will be there?" Florence's voice shook as she swallowed.

"I don't know." Francis' lips turned into a thin line. "But it is safer there with us than staying here alone," he added.

The confidence slipped through my fingers as the realization of what I'd suggested all these nights ago slowly settled. I'd convinced Francis it was safe to enter into a meeting with

Barren, convinced him it was our only choice. Now I wasn't so sure—not when so many people would be at risk by association: not when I'd have to convince not only Barren, but whoever he had by his side.

"Can I have a moment with you? Privately," I asked Francis, exiting the study. He sighed, following after me.

"Did you change your mind about the necessity of this trip?" His brows flew up. "Did you just now realize the madness we are about to walk into?"

"There is no reason for so many people to go," I whispered, glancing back at the study. "I killed Timothy." I faced Francis. "If they know they will set me on fire the moment I set foot onto his estate; all of you will follow in my steps." I swallowed. "I should go by myself."

"Absolutely not. You are not going there by yourself." Francis shook his head. "We either go together, or not at all. You do not stand a chance at this by yourself."

"But—"

"Either all of us, or none of us." Francis shook his head, sheathing his daggers.

"There is no reason for Florence to go," I hissed. "She is shaking like a leaf."

"And she can handle herself," Francis' stern tone reached my ears. "She knows how to fight, and above all, she is a vampire." He sighed. "For the last time, for this to work we need numbers."

I closed my eyes, drawing a deep breath. "I don't want anyone else to die on my behalf."

"No one is going to die." Francis' thumb brushed over my chin. "I would never let that happen. I would never agree to this if I thought the risk was too high."

"As I recall, you were quite against this trip." My eyes met his.

"I was against this because I believe our time is better spent gathering weaponry, not because I was afraid for the safety of my family." Francis sighed. "I would not let us all walk into jeopardy, Cordelia. I do think through my plans, remember?"

"Everyhing will be well." Roxanne rolled her eyes, walking towards us; Francis dropped his hand, his thumb parting from my chin. "The three of you are so dramatic. It's just a bunch of humans playing Royalty. They are harmless," she added, putting a cloak around her shoulders.

I envied her confidence.

"He has the whole Royal army in his possession currently," Francis mumbled, walking towards the window by the main door. "But sure, they are just harmless humans."

"Please stop speaking of it." Florence shook her head. "Before I get ill." Florence followed Roxanne's suit and set the cloak atop her shoulders. "And we won't leave you, Cordelia, even if it means all of us die," she added.

I guessed they'd heard the whole conversation then. So much for privacy...

"Eavesdropping is impolite." Francis passed me a cloak, putting his own on.

"No one is going to die, dear Moon." Roxanne rolled her eyes at Florence, glancing out the window. "Simon and Ash are here, we must be on our way." She opened the main door as we all followed her down to the stables.

Snow veiled the bare branches of the forest, keeping the resting trees warm in its embrace. Bright stars decorated the dark skies; the crescent Moon proudly hung in the center of her realm as we walked through the labyrinth of the night woods.

My hand tightly wrapped around the reins when the frost made its way down the tips of my fingers, my other hand played with the stamp in my pocket. A tremble journeyed down my spine as a few snowflakes landed on my lashes.

"Winter is rather cold this year," Ash noted, riding their horse alongside mine.

"It is indeed," I agreed, watching Francis and Simon ride a few yards in front of us: deep in an argument about wine. "I am sorry we didn't get to properly meet last time." I turned to Ash, remembering my abrupt departure on Francis' birthday.

"No worries." They smiled. "I had to leave shortly after you." Ash shrugged.

Annabelle reached for a nearby branch despite my best attempts at keeping her upright; the branch snapped into two as she chewed on it.

Roxanne and Florence rode past me before I managed to turn Annabelle back onto the path. Shaking my head at such disobedience, I caught up to the rest of my company.

"I hear you play the violin." Ash waited on the path for me and Annabelle, glancing at Francis who shook his head at something that Simon had said. "I hear it is the sound of heaven."

"That is hardly true," I chuckled. "Whoever told you that must be a fool."

"I highly doubt that; Francis rarely praises anyone." Ash winked, the corners of their lips tugging upwards. "I used to play too." They nodded. "But when the Crimson War started in the East, we had to flee, leaving everything behind."

My heart skipped a beat at the reminder of the horrors that erupted in the East, the horrors that took my brother away from me. "Where are you from?" I cleared my throat.

"Here and there." Ash shrugged. "My human father was a sailor, so I am not even sure where I was born," they tittered. "But I spent the final years of my human life in the East—in the city of Vel'mi, that is where my mother was from—until the Wurdulacs came to our home seven years ago."

Vel'mi.

"I am very sorry." I swallowed.

"I'm sorry too." Ash nodded.

"Brian—my older brother—loved Vel'mi." A sad smile tugged on my lips. "His letters were always filled with appreciation for Vel'mi's charm."

Ash sighed, their eyes searching for the crescent Moon. "It is in ruins now," they whispered. "No one cared to rebuild it after the war. Everyone who lived there is either dead or fled that day to places that won't be found on the map."

Annabelle halted, forcing my attention before me. The woods thinned in the distance, the Barren's estate peeked through the forest.

"Let's leave our horses here." Francis pointed at a willow tree peacefully collecting the snowflakes onto its glorious branches. "The rest of the trip we'll make on foot, it's not far," he told us, meeting my gaze for merely a second before dismounting his horse and adjusting the satchel around his shoulder.

I dismounted Annabelle; my boots touched the freshly fallen snow as my fingers rushed to tighten the reins around the willow tree.

"What is in your satchel?" I caught up to Francis, who walked towards the castle with no care in the world.

"Documents." He shrugged, staring straight ahead.

"What kind of documents?" I persisted, fixing the sword at my belt that was there more as an accessory than an actual weapon, given that I hadn't trained in ages—something I had to fix before the Wurdulacs made their way back to Faris.

"The kind that might help us today." Francis looked me in the eyes before averting his gaze to the, growing in the distance, estate.

"Francis." I crooked my head to one side, rolling my eyes. "I need to know."

"So you need to know of my plans, but I can't know yours, huh?" Francis smirked.

"You know I am the only person who can do this." I walked faster to keep up with him. "And I told you my plan."

"Vaguely," Francis countered.

"What is in your satchel?" I grabbed his hand, pulling him to slow down.

"The list of everyone in Faris who wants to fight," he sighed, looking at our joined hands. "Along with the amount of weaponry we possess. As proof of our competence and reliability."

"A scrabble on pieces of parchment without the official stamp is hardly any proof," I scoffed. "But you will be making a mistake by exposing such intimate information. Besides, it won't be needed: William is a coward that always falls for my bluff. I have a plan."

"And what if he learned after your last trick with compromised letters," Francis said. Before I could argue, he added, "But I will let you do what you've planned, Cordelia, because I trust your judgement." He pointed at the satchel. "This is merely a precaution. There will be more than just him we have to convince tonight."

To that I had nothing to say, and I didn't need to, for our company halted at the abrupt end of woods, staring straight at the armed castle.

"Well, they are certainly prepared," Ash noted, glaring at the dozens of guards standing by the gates.

"Let's not waste time." Roxanne charged towards the closed gates; all of us fell into step after her.

The gate opened almost immediately at our arrival, the guards didn't bother asking why we were here: the guards didn't bother treating us as invaders like they had last time.

Barren was desperate indeed. So desperate that he cared not to show otherwise, though I was sure he would give me a run for my coins once we were in private.

I did not expect anyone to bow this time as we walked through the citadel, towards the main doors; I did not expect any recognition at all, yet most still bent their heads in respect that I certainly did not deserve. Their eyes shone with pity and tenderness I was not pleased by. I was not weak as they seemed to think of me. I needed not sympathy.

My chin rose high as I strode through the open area. The mask of indifference—that no longer felt natural—slipped onto my face out of a habit I was glad I still possessed. Without waiting for the guards to open the doors for me, I yanked on the handles, allowing myself entrance.

The strong smell of sweet irises and frost hit my senses as usual, forcing my mind into obedience before my own shadows. Yet there was no pain: not anymore, for I knew the one responsible for my sufferings was long beneath the ground, rotting in soil and dirt. And I was the reason for his deserved end.

Our steps echoed through the empty halls as I led my company to the center of the estate, Barren's favorite room—the courthall he often used as his personal study.

Two guards stood adjacent to the closed doors of our meeting room, their eyes narrowing on me with suspicion.

"Tell His Grace we have arrived." Francis winked at the guards; a familiar smirk stretched his lips.

The guards glanced at each other—their eyes growing bigger—before one of them awkwardly nodded, slipping through the door of the courthall. Simon struggled to contain his laughter at the exchange: covering his mouth, he pretended to cough.

"Stop it, both of you," Roxanne hissed as the doors opened wide, allowing us entrance.

Odd calmness spread through my veins when I took a step into the hall, confidence growing from the depth of my soul.

Little did I know, it wouldn't last long.

Chapter 20.
Pretend Queen.

William Barren sat at the head of the table, his two companions—whom I had the pleasure of never meeting before—sat by his side: I could only hope at least one of them was reasonable.

At least a dozen warriors stood by the wall of the hall, eyeing us like prey.

Barren's eyes flickered with excitement as he watched us emerge into the courthall. His pale lips stretched into a crooked smile when I sat across from him; he fixed the stray strand of greasy hair that fell onto his eyes before the room erupted into a ringing laughter.

"Cordelia, Cordelia..." William laughed, leaning on the back of the chair that looked awfully similar to a throne. "Our dearest Cordelia."

Francis sat in the chair next to mine, gesturing for our friends to follow his lead.

"Oh, Cordelia!" Barren's laughter wouldn't stop. I was sure he was going mad—not that he hadn't been mad already...

The man—with gray hair, blue eyes, and light skin—sitting at Barren's right, picked up the laughter, as though the reason for such an odd reaction was as bright as sunshine. The woman at Barren's left remained quiet.

Our gazes met for a split second before she averted her dark—almost black—eyes. Her coily hair sat in a bun at the nape of her neck. A barely visible blush appeared on her brown cheeks.

I'd seen her before, back at the palace. I wished I could remember on which occasion.

"What is it that amuses you so, *Your Grace*?" Francis' lips stretched into a smirk as he crooked his head, watching the two men laugh.

"Oh, merely the amount of companions you've graced me with." Barren narrowed his eyes at his right hand, silencing the man at once. "Afraid for your safety on human grounds, orphan boy?"

Florence sat by my right side, her knees brushed mine when she glanced at me with concern. Roxanne, Ash, and Simon settled into their seats as well.

"Surely six vampires cannot be that intimidating to your *army*." Francis mimicked William's position, leaning back on his—rather ordinary—chair. "Are you afraid for your safety, given you surrounded yourself with warriors, William?" Francis countered.

I refrained from rolling my eyes at his provocative nature.

"Why, since your letter stated you wished to discuss war plans, I assumed it was only right for the commanders of the last human armies to attend." Barren sipped on his wine, his gaze averting to me. "Cordelia," he tsked. "I've waited for you to make an appearance ever since the attack. What took you so long, dear?"

"War can make one rather busy," I said. "I'm sure you understand."

"Ah! Of course!" Barren chuckled. "Tamira here," he pointed at the woman by his side. "Had her hands *rather busy* after the Wurdulacs murdered her commander and half of the Royal army." William's lips turned into a thin line before he continued, "After your kind failed to come to our aid as you agreed upon with our resting Queen."

I forced my heart to stay put at his provocations, yet the ache still spread through my lungs. "The deal was not yet in place when the palace was attacked." I kept my voice even, remembering the last conversation Mother and I had. "The Queen promised us weapons at the following full Moon, the deal was to be sealed at the exchange." Needless to say, Faris had no way of knowing the palace's walls had been compromised. Yet the guilt of our failure still clawed at my mind. I supposed that was Barren's plan all along. "Let's get to the matter at hand—"

"Have you heard of Timothy's sad end?" William topped off his goblet. "We learned of his disappearance right before the attack, can you believe that?" He emptied the cup in one gulp. "Right after you left." His eyes narrowed on me. "Some might not believe in such coincidences."

The commanders glanced at Barren in unison before their gazes fell on me. A piercing silence broke through the air.

"Are you accusing me, William?" I crooked my head to one side, annoyed that I even allowed him to entertain the topic instead of dominating the conversation as was planned.

A bright laughter bounced off the walls of the courthall as Barren wiped an imaginary tear from his eye. "Of course not, dear," he wouldn't stop laughing. "We both know you aren't capable of hurting your dearest sweetheart, let alone murder him." He glanced at Francis, a smirk coercing his lips. "You were such a lovely couple..." Barren sighed, his eyes locked on Francis—who, surprisingly, kept quiet. "It pained me to learn of your change–of–being, truly." William's hand fell onto his heart before he let the evil words spill. "Though, I must admit, Sandra was a nice replacement."

My mask of indifference slipped for a split second before I managed to gather my racing mind. My teeth pierced the inside of my cheek, letting the blood soak my tongue.

"Such a lovely, innocent soul Sandra was," William murmured. My nails dug into my palms underneath the table. "A little naive, sure, but always so lovely." William's piercing gaze bored into mine. He sat at the head of the table, his head crooked to one side: taunting me, begging for a reaction I refused to let loose. "Alas, the Gods are unfair to us sometimes, aren't they, dear?" Barren sighed. "I hope Sandra and Timothy have reunited in the afterlife. Shame I am not to witness it." He nodded.

"I can fix that for you," Francis seethed before I managed to gather my thoughts.

My heart raced. The back of my throat ached.

I taught you better than this, daughter, my mother's voice swept through my mind. *How could you let him talk to a Roy-*

al daughter in such a manner? She scolded. *How could you fall for his traps so easily?*

"Always so eager to throw out threats, orphan boy," William tsked. "I was merely sharing my appreciation of young love."

Would his army follow my orders were I to murder William right now?

"Did you invite us to waste time, William?" I said instead.

Barren eyed me as though seeing me for the first time. "Why, yes." He looked surprised. "I merely wished to see you, dearest, given I don't see how you can be of any help—"

"Do you always talk so much?" Ash's voice broke through the space, interrupting Barren at once.

Barren eyed his new opponent, looking them up and down. "And who are you?"

"Ash." They stretched their hand towards Barren in greeting before changing their mind as William attempted to grab it; his face reddened with embarrassment when his hand met empty air. I struggled to contain my amusement. "I came here to speak on behalf of Faris' army," Ash added.

"An army!" Barren mused. "You heard them!" He turned to Tamira and the man I still didn't know the name of. "They have an army," William chuckled. "What do you need me for then?"

Every pair of eyes turned to me. I filled my lungs before executing my memorized speech: I only had one chance, and I could not waste it.

Please be the fool I think you are.

"I came to collect what remains of the Royal army, along with what remains of yours." I rested my arms on the table. I learned a long time ago: the only way for Barren to agree to anything, is he must feel as though it was his choice all along. And, oh, how I loved playing that game. "I am the last of Royal blood standing, both armies are now rightfully mine, and I am entitled to take them in a time of need."

Tamira's eyes flickered to mine; the men, however, stayed silent.

I knew I wouldn't be able to convince William of my newly made up title, yet uncertainty still shone bright in his eyes.

Francis bestowed me with a swift glance, mere amusement written on his face that Barren and the commanders were oblivious to.

"Need I repeat myself?" My voice cut through the air before the room erupted in predictable laughter.

"Oh, Cordelia, you are a joy to my ears today," Barren said through his exasperating chuckle.

"As the last of Royal blood, the armies in your current possession are rightfully mine," I stated. "You claim hold of the Royal army, and yet made no progress beyond these walls. You do not stand a chance without our help, and you know it. You saw what happened at the palace," I said just as calmly, facing all three of them. "The human armies are better off in our care." The gray haired man's laugh cut short at my words as he cleared out his throat, facing me.

"And how could we ever trust a vampire leader, such as yourself, after you had left the palace to fend for itself?" the man asked; a small crease appeared in between his brows.

"Where are the guarantees you will not leave us like you left them? Where are the guarantees you are not using the human armies as shields to save your kind?"

"We have explained ourselves already." Roxanne answered before I could. "The deal was not yet sealed."

"Remember that while Wurdulacs are coming for us all, the human fate will be far worse than that of vampires," Simon added.

The grayhaired man paled, glancing at William, whose mouth was finally sealed. It was Tamira who spoke, "Trusting vampires is a pathway to the grave."

"Facing Wurdulacs alone is a pathway to the grave," I countered. "You used to be one of Martin's seconds," I narrowed my eyes on Tamira, remembering where I'd seen her before. "My mother appointed you a few years ago."

"She did." Tamira nodded.

"She spoke highly of your skill and mind," I lied, for Mother had never spoken to me of anything regarding politics, unless it had required my assistance. Though, I was sure those were Tamira's characteristics, given her rather young age at her time of appointment. "You must realize the rationale in our words, then. You do not stand a chance without our assistance: it's best to join our forces. And as the last of the Royal family, I have the right to demand such an outcome."

"Enough begging." Barren topped off his drink once more. If my plan failed, perhaps he would get himself drunk enough to agree to our proposition. "It is rather tiring and, quite frankly, pathetic, dear." He sipped on wine. "I see you are so desperate that you are willing to use a title that you no longer possess to your advantage, despite the disgrace you are putting onto your resting parents." He smirked, walking straight into my trap. "So I will offer you a different deal, since I am feeling rather generous."

"Which is?" Ash rolled their eyes, fed up with his unnecessary speeches.

Barren licked the wine off his lips, staring me down. "I will support you in this war, and the human armies will fight alongside the vampires, but!" He pointed his index finger upwards. "*I* will remain in command, and once this war is over, the Royal army will join mine completely. The crown will have no say in the matter." Barren took a sip of his drink. "You will also supply us with Royal steel weaponry," Barren replied.

Oh, William, you are so predictable.

"Deal," I declared, before Francis had a chance to reject. The smirk of satisfaction at my *desperation*—as William had called it—spread across his face, pride filling his eyes.

"We have a deal," I repeated, meeting the eyes of my companions. "Bring me a piece of parchment and ink," I addressed William, uncovering the Royal stamp from my pocket.

The night was in its full glory as we left the Barren's castle. The dull Moon accompanied us when we walked past the main gate with two guards standing adjacent to it.

"Your Majesty," Francis mocked, offering me a hand.

I rolled my eyes, accepting the hand nevertheless. "I knew if I demand more than Barren is willing to give up, he would offer the *alternative* that we needed," I said, once the guards were out of earshot.

Francis shook his head as a shadow of a smile touched his lips. "You could have at least warned us."

"I didn't want to spoil the show," I teased, mounting Annabelle as I ordered her to follow after everyone else.

"The show was entertaining indeed," Francis chuckled, riding side by side with me as we caught up to the rest of our company. "You have gifted him an entire army to command after the war, though," Francis sighed. "Do you think that was the right thing to do? At the end of the night, someone as ruthless and foolish as William is dangerous for all in a position of true power."

"It was never mine to give away." I shrugged as we reached the pathway leading back to Faris. "It was never Barren's to take," I said, noting all five ears were listening to our conversation. "People are the ones who choose their ruler, offering respect and trust in return for protection. No one will stand by his side when the war is over: certainly not the Royal army." I met Francis' gaze: doubt still written on his face.

"Barren's personal army—that my mother gifted him ages ago—is loyal to him, no doubt," I started. "They are more loyal to him than they were to the Queen herself, even though they all answered to her." I sighed, remembering how I had to pay for her mistakes. "She learned it was harder to control Barren as time passed on. That's when she came to me.

"Mother wanted the support of his army; William wanted to reach higher in the ranks of Royalty." The words spilled, freeing me of the burden, and I cared not who listened. "Therefore, the marriage." I swallowed as the memories of that day shadowed in my mind like nightmares. "As the Queen, Mother could just take his army with no consequence, but she knew better: it would do her no good, not when the people chose Barren as their ruler instead of her.

"Barren can proclaim himself the ruler of all the armies in the Kingdom, and not a single thing will change," I said at last, meeting the five pairs of eyes looking in my direction as we continued on our path home.

The morning twilight spread through the forest when the six of us stood at the crossway by the line of spruce trees that hid Faris from unwanted eyes.

"What do we do now?" Simon asked, reaching for Ash's hand when they turned away from the main path—towards Faris. "What is our plan?"

The trip from Silverstone was surprisingly fast, despite the growing storm nature gifted us with. The triumph of our successful mission spread through my chest, though I knew better than to celebrate when nothing of value had been accomplished. Not yet.

"We must still find a way to make Royal steel," Francis said, brushing off the snow that had fallen on his hair. "That is our priority."

"The ball is next week." Florence reminded him. "We can go to the palace the day after." She wrapped her cloak tighter as a visible shudder swept through her shoulders.

"We don't have time for a ball," Francis argued.

"We must find time, Francis," Simon sighed. The tall spruce tree covered him and Ash from the fallen snow. "Faris is running low on blood: I have people coming to me daily, asking for a meal, for they have nothing left at home."

Ash nodded, agreeing, "And whatever was stored after the last ball is about to spoil." They met Francis' gaze. "You don't want vampires to abandon the treaty with the human village, out of survival, right before the war breaks loose."

"Some told me they haven't had human blood in weeks." Simon's voice quieted. "You know a vampire can't survive on their own kind's blood for long. We need everyone to be strong and ready."

My brows frowned at his words; my stomach twisted in an unnatural way. *What in the Kingdom does he mean?*

"Very well then," Francis said slowly, oblivious to my re-action. "I can go to the palace by myself while all of you tend to the ball."

"You are not going by yourself!" Roxanne groaned. "We have already talked about this."

"It would be foolish for us all to show up at the palace's gates," Francis argued, his knuckles whitened around the reins.

"I'm coming with you." My voice broke through the storm's howl. "I am the only one who knows my way around the palace."

"We are all going." Roxanne rolled her eyes. "This conversation is a waste of time, the sun is about to come up."

"The more people who come, the more likely we are to get caught," Francis countered.

"You don't know what's in the vault!" Roxanne's voice went up a few octaves. She scraped the snow off her horse' mane, throwing it at Francis' face. "We don't even know how many Wurdulacs are currently at the palace."

"We need a proper plan before going," Simon agreed, ignoring Francis, who worked to clean the snow off his face. "Come to the tavern tomorrow and we shall talk about it." He turned his horse towards Faris, Ash followed after, waving us goodbye. "And don't you dare leave by yourself." Simon eyed Francis over his shoulder. "I will not forgive such betrayal," he said, disappearing into the depths of the spruce.

Chapter 21.
Replacement.

S ilver greeted me when I entered my room, his tail wrapping around my ankle as he circled by my feet.

"Hello, friend." I crouched to pet the creature, the tip of my sword scraping the floor. Silver's purrs echoed through the room; his fur warmed my frozen fingers as they slowly regained mobility after the trip. "How was your day?" I brushed the cloak off my shoulders, letting it fall onto the floor.

Silver rushed to the fallen piece of clothing, caring not for my attention any longer. He settled in the middle of the cloak, embracing the warm material.

I shook my head at his betrayal when a smile stretched my lips. "I'm glad you are enjoying yourself," I told the cat, getting up to my feet.

The sword reflected the candlelight when I removed it from my belt, setting it on its designated place atop the drawer.

My back straightened, freed from the additional weight of the blade, and I almost laughed at the ridiculousness of the situation: how could I pretend to be skilled with the weapon when my body screamed in pain from merely wearing it?

I had to get back to training if I wanted a chance at surviving whatever the Wurdulacs would bring upon us, and I had to start soon: right now, perhaps.

I grabbed the hilt of the sword anew, pointing it at an invisible opponent. My legs moved into the correct stance. *Was the sword always this heavy?*

I swung the weapon in every direction until my shoulders ached from the motion. My wrists weakened with every passing second, making me realize the absurdity of my body's lack of strength.

And I thought I was capable of destroying Kane single-handedly...

I charged for another swing of my sword as the force—or rather fragility of my hold—sent the blade flying across the room.

Oh, dear Gods... I rolled my eyes when the sword clanged against the floor, the bang bouncing off the walls.

Silver sprinted under the bed, distraught from the noise, before I could comfort him.

"Sorry, friend!" I searched for his glowing eyes underneath the frame. "I didn't mean to startle you."

Silver stared at me, refusing to accept my apology, getting comfortable in the corner by the wall.

I sighed, retrieving my fallen blade from the floor. The blade stood unscratched despite my clumsiness—a miracle, nevertheless. I laid the blade down onto the drawer and wondered how Father could have ever trusted me with such a weapon. How could he have gifted me a sword that was more likely to be my end rather than salvation?

UNKINDNESS OF CRIMSON QUEEN

At least one thing was abundantly clear—I needed assistance if I wanted to change the inevitable outcome.

The sound of Francis' steps reached my ears, freezing my fist inches away from Francis' door. The door creaked open as Francis stood at the threshold; wet curls were brushed away from his face, his torso completely bare.

"How can I be of service, Your Majesty?" He bowed to his waist, a playful smirk curling his lips.

My eyes traveled down to his loose trousers that hung low around his hips. The candlelight played on his warm-toned skin. "Cease calling me that, Francis." I regained my clarity, meeting his eyes.

"And yet?" He gestured for me to come in. "How can I be of use at this late hour?" He closed the door behind me, walking towards the table that carried many tomes of works I'd never heard of.

The close proximity pressed against my lower stomach; his eyes glowed into my soul.

"Should I put on a shirt?" Francis murmured, crooking his head. "Princess?"

"Yes! No. Yes—" I shook my head as the heat traveled up my cheeks. "I have a favor to ask." I sat on his unmade bed, forcing some distance in between us.

Francis' smirk deepened. "Ask away." He crossed his arms against his bare chest—which certainly did not help my lack of attention.

"I need you to train me." The words left my lips before I could regret them.

"Train you?" Francis' brows rose as he slipped on a linen shirt. The lack of bare skin didn't stop the bothersome feeling from slowly creeping deep in my stomach. I traced the line of his uncovered chest and the shadows of his hands as his fingers worked through the buttons. "Am I a replacement for Caleb?" He chuckled, forcing my gaze back to his.

"I need to learn how to fight." I ignored his remark. "So I can protect myself at the palace."

"If you give the rest of us the directions to the vault you won't need to worry yourself with training." Francis finished buttoning up his shirt. "But even if you decide to go... I will protect you there, you have nothing to worry about."

"I am going, and I don't want your protection." I stood from the bed. "I don't want to rely on others for my safety." My arms crossed at my chest as I shrugged. "I can always ask Roxanne—" Even the idea of that sent a shiver down my spine, though perhaps things wouldn't be disastrous: now that she appeared to dislike me less. Perhaps.

Francis' bright laughter filled the room before a coy smile spread across his face. "You needn't manipulate me, Princess," he mused. "I would love to train you, I am merely stating that you don't need to come back to the palace." He took a few steps forward, depriving me of a clear mind. Surely Francis training me wasn't a great idea, especially considering how things had ended last time... I supposed it was a lost battle.

"So you have said." I rolled my eyes, desperately avoiding his piercing gaze. "I will wait for you in the training hall once the sun sets." I passed Francis, walking towards the door.

"And here I thought I would have the honor of spending the day with you," Francis tsked, walking after me. His face was inches from mine as he stood before me; my mind went mad in an instant. Thankfully, before I had to come up with a reply to such a scandalous—and appealing—remark, he continued, "We will train first thing tomorrow evening." He planted a small kiss on the top of my head, opening the door for me to exit.

"Until tomorrow." I cleared out my throat, rushing out of his room. My stomach twisted in the most satisfying way, the flower caught aflame.

I rushed to my room, locking the door behind me. Stunned, I stared at the ceiling for a long while, unable to make sense of all the things that flew through my mind.

This is a mistake, I kept telling myself.

And yet, I felt no remorse.

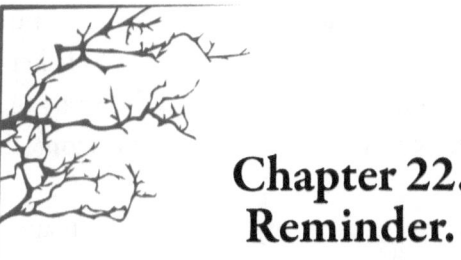

Chapter 22.
Reminder.

A pair of glowing, brown eyes met me in the mirror, the cold water slid down my cheeks, washing off the last bits of my wicked dream—the dream I wished hadn't ended so fast.

My cheeks were the color of crimson, no matter my best attempts at stopping these ridiculous—and certainly inappropriate—thoughts of Francis. My skin heated at a mere touch, my stomach twisted in anticipation.

How was I to train with him if even thoughts were so distracting?

"You are ridiculous," I told the mirror, though it didn't stop the woman in front of me from looking all ecstatic.

The castle's halls were silent: save for the whispering paintings on the walls and the humming statues, whose eyes followed my path to the training hall.

The smell of old lit cigars erupted in the air as I passed Francis' study; my heart fluttered. Every breath left me with an ache in my lower stomach that I wasn't capable of ruling.

"Enough, Cordelia," I whispered, shaking my head in a weak attempt to clear my mind before yanking the door to the hall open.

Francis stood in the middle of the hall. A linen shirt hung on his shoulder: the top few buttons left loose. He held the bow Florence had gifted him, his strong hands setting the arrow free. The visible veins on his hands made my stomach flutter anew.

I would've rolled my eyes at my own folly if Francis hadn't been staring at me from the center of the hall.

"I wasn't expecting for you to wake so early," he said, glancing at the stained glass window by the ceiling: sundown was upon us.

"Couldn't sleep." I shrugged, making my way towards him.

"I hope I wasn't the reason for your restless night." Francis winked, settling his bow back onto its stand.

"Do you ever tire of your arrogance?" My voice betrayed me as I rolled my eyes, unsheathing my sword.

"Is that a blush I see on your cheeks, Princess?" Francis pointed at my face, a smirk growing on his face.

"Possibly." I pointed the sword at the bare area of his chest. "I often find myself feeling flustered when others embarrass themselves."

A bright laughter bounced off the walls of the hall. "Is that so?" Francis' smirk grew bigger.

"Are you here to train me, or mock me?" I pushed the blade closer to his throat, fighting my own smile.

"Can't I do both?" Francis' brows rose when he eyed my weapon with amusement. "You seem to enjoy putting the tip of your blade at one's neck."

"You seem to enjoy having the tip of my blade at your neck."

Francis took a step backwards, forcing me to lower my sword. "Let's see what we are working with then." He walked towards the wall that carried dozens of swords of different kinds.

He grabbed one that seemed fit to his liking, spinning it by the hilt. "Attack me." He took his stance a few yards away from where I stood.

"What if I hurt you?" I mimicked his stance; my fingers wrapping around the hilt of my sword. "This is Royal steel."

"Then you will have to suck the poison out of my wound." Francis winked, gesturing me closer. "Come now, fight me."

"All right." I swung my blade, lunging in his direction.

"Not too bad." Francis' sword met mine: the metal clanking against each other echoed through the hall. "Don't lean forward as much, you are compromising your balance."

I lunged again, trying to follow Francis' advice. Each swing of the sword made my wrists cry out in pain. Every time Francis' sword met mine I was forced to fight to keep the weapon in my grasp.

It didn't take long for me to run out of breath. Sweat rolled down my forehead, my palms becoming slippery.

"Tired already?" Francis moved towards me: each step leaving me less room to maneuver. "We just started," he chuckled.

"I am not tired," I protested, deflating his attacks.

"Oh no?" Francis' sword pushed me into a corner. He seemed entirely unbothered by the extent of our activity. "How come your sword shakes so much?" He pointed at the hilt of my blade.

"I am just not used to it." I swung my sword once again, the blade slipping off my palm, flying past Francis: into the opposite corner of the hall.

Francis retrieved my blade, holding it before himself at a perfect angle. He studied the blade as the metal reflected the candlelight.

"It's too heavy for you," he said at last, spinning my sword in every direction.

"It is not," I choked: my lungs still on fire. "It was made specifically for me." I demanded the blade back.

"Cordelia, it's heavy even for me, and unlike you, I do train often." Francis gave my sword a final spin before passing me the weapon. "With a physique like yours, you shouldn't fight with a sword. Not yet at least." He put his weapon back in its place. "The sword will bring more harm than protection."

"This is the only Royal steel weapon I have." I sat on the floor against a wall, my lungs finally calming.

"You are more likely to get killed by it than to protect yourself." Francis stood by my feet, his boots touching mine.

"I thought you were supposed to be helpful, not call me weak," I mumbled, meeting his gaze.

"I am not calling you weak," Francis chuckled, offering me a hand. "All I am saying is that this weapon is not right for you, but I do have an idea." He pulled me to my feet. "Bring your sword to the dinner tonight, hopefully Ash has worked with Royal steel before." Francis offered me his dagger. "In the meantime, train with these."

My fingers wrapped around the slim hilt of Francis' dagger when he pointed at the target on the wall behind my back.

"Do you remember our last lesson?" He murmured into my ear before taking a step backwards, allowing me space.

I mostly remembered what happened after the lesson... "Yes." I held the dagger by its tip, swinging it for a throw.

The blade spun in the air when I let go, flying straight into my target. To my biggest surprise, the tip of the blade landed close to the center of the painted target. An inch of the tip disappeared into the wooden panel in a smooth motion.

"That was... good." Francis retrieved the blade from the wood, offering me the weapon anew. "Really good," he said, surprise written on his face.

I shrugged, as though it wasn't mere luck that had spared me the embarrassment.

"Go again." Francis stood behind me when I readied to throw. The smell of jasmine and cigars invaded my space.

This time, the blade was nowhere near the painted target, though it did land into the wood—certainly progress from our last lesson.

"The closer to heart the better." Francis retrieved the blade, handing it to me. Our fingers brushed against each other, sending waves of excitement through my bothered body. "If you manage to hit the heart, the poison from the Royal steel will kill your opponent before their next breath." He stood behind me—closer than before—as I swung the blade forward.

"Good," Francis murmured into my ear when the blade split the wood anew. The smell of his flesh spun my head drunk, his heartbeat reaching my ears.

I hadn't fed in days—

"What did Simon mean by *a vampire can't survive on their own kind's blood for long*?" I faced Francis, remembering the unsettling comment Simon made. "Does that mean, eventually, I will have to..." The words died on my tongue.

"You needn't worry yourself." Francis put a stray strand of hair behind my ear. "He was talking of those who feed on vampires that do not have access to human blood themselves," Francis started. "Since I still consume human blood, you get everything you need from me. That is precisely why Faris manages to survive without draining hundreds of humans weekly; even though we still need some of their blood."

The idea of innocents hurting at the hands of someone like me turned my stomach upside down.

"There is no reason to pity them, Cordelia." Francis reassured me as though reading my thoughts. "While what they do is dangerous, it is their own choice. Many come here again and again for pleasure."

"Pleasure?" My cheeks reddened, despite the nausea that settled deep in my stomach.

"Those who did not break the law on human grounds, and come here of their own accord, mostly do it for pleasure, yes." Francis nodded. "Sure, most of them believe they are giving their blood as part of a sacrifice to the divine, but you can't deny the pleasure they get from the act itself." A mischievous smile tugged on his lips. "Just like you did when begging me to take your blood."

"I felt no pleasure," my voice turned into a whisper at my blatant lie. My heart fluttered at his words, my mouth watered.

"Oh, no?" He smirked. "Perhaps you've forgotten." Francis crooked his head to one side, his eyes darkening.

"Perhaps I have." The words spilled without my permission; yet I felt no remorse, no shame. "Perhaps you need to remind me." I had lost my mind.

Francis' brows flew high when the realization of what I had asked him settled. He cleared his throat before a smile unveiled his dimples. "I would be honored to." His hands fell onto my waist, ushering me closer.

My hands fell onto his shoulder, my fingers still wrapped around his dagger.

His lips brushed over my neck, goosebumps covered my whole body. I moved my head to the side, offering him access, my fingers dug in his shoulders as the idea alone made my knees weak.

He planted a tender kiss on my skin, his soft lips stretched into a smile against my flesh before he asked, "Do I have your permission, Princess?"

The flowers bloomed deep in my stomach as my center ached in the most satisfying way possible. "Yes," I breathed, my eyes closing in anticipation—

His teeth pierced my thin skin, a whimper pushing past my lips at the impact. His tongue waltzed across my skin as my blood spilled into his mouth.

My moan echoed though the training hall, and I cared not to stay quiet.

"Please," I whined as my fingers let go of the dagger, letting it fall onto the marble floor—the clang rang in the hall. "Please." My nails dug into his skin, pushing him closer.

His teeth punctured my skin once more, forcing another whine out of me. My limp body soothed into Francis' embrace, his hands holding me from collapsing.

My eyes fluttered when his teeth escaped my flesh.

His tongue traveled across my open wound, catching every drop of blood.

More. I wished to beg, yet the words would not come out under Francis' playful gaze.

His lips carried drops of crimson; his face inches from mine.

"Is it *next time* yet?" His husky voice brushed over my ears.

"Hm?" My eyes struggled to focus through the fog that invaded my mind.

"You said I may steal your kiss next time," Francis murmured, his lips moving closer to mine. "Is this *next time*?"

My stomach dropped to my heels as the flowers bloomed, wrapping around my center. My lips parted when my eyes planted on his lips.

I managed a small nod before finding his lips with my own.

Our tongues collided in a dance.

My teeth punctured his lower lip, his blood blending with mine, spilling onto my tongue.

His hand fell onto my cheek, ushering me closer. He tasted like fine wine—

"Cordelia?" The door to the hall creaked open as I broke our kiss in an instant.

Florence stood at the threshold, her gaze jumping from me to Francis. "Sorry!" She hurried out of the hall.

"No!" I called after her, pushing Francis away. He didn't move an inch. "Wait! Is everything all right?"

Florence peeked through the ajar door. "I merely wondered if you would like to go to Faris earlier, Charlotte has been asking of you."

The warmth traveled up my cheeks when I fought Francis away from me, he didn't budge.

"Yes, of course!" I nodded at Florence, ignoring Francis' smirk.

"Awesome!" Florence beamed, her smile growing bigger and bigger as she eyed Francis' hands on my waist. "We will leave in half an hour then." She closed the door behind herself, her steps fading in the distance.

"Francis!" I hissed, fighting the smile off my face.

"Why, Princess, are you ashamed of me?" He pulled me closer, closing what little distance we shared. "Am I embarrassing you?" His lips brushed over my neck, tracing a pathway all the way to my ear.

"No." A smile stretched on my face; my heart skipped a beat when he reached the corner of my lips.

"Well, good then," he rasped. "Because you kissed me, I still haven't had the chance to kiss you." He teased as his lips found mine once more.

Chapter 23.
Blessings.

The once rainbow-colored stained glass now carried bleak colors, as though a shadow swept through the castle, draining the spirit from the orphanage. Children's laughter still sounded from the main street of Faris, yet it was fainted by the gloom of the broken roads.

"Cordelia!" Charlotte ran towards me from across the foyer: the wooden doll she was playing with long forgotten. "I missed you greatly! Oh, how I missed you! How I missed you!" Her hands wrapped around me, almost knocking me to the ground.

"I missed you too, dear." I returned her tight embrace, my hands brushing over her loose curls.

"Are you feeling better?" Concern swept over her face when she pulled away slightly. "I really hope you are feeling better."

"I am." I smiled at her, fixing a fold on her sleeve. "Much better."

Charlotte's lips stretched into the brightest smile I'd ever seen her wear as she tightened her hands around me once more.

Florence disappeared into the depths of the orphanage, a dozen children following after her. Charlotte and I stood at the threshold of the castle for a long while before the girl let go of our embrace, grabbing my hand into hers. "Come! I have to show you the drawing I made of Silver!" She skipped towards the stairs, her hand pulling me forward.

The room Charlotte resided in carried three beds and a small mirror in the corner. Children's paintings occupied every inch of the light blue walls, each bed had a name carved onto it.

"Here!" Charlotte passed me the parchment from under her pillow. "Do you like it?"

"I love it!" I studied her drawing. Silver sat in the center of parchment, the bright crescent Moon hung above his head, illuminating his gray fur. "It's beautiful." I smiled despite the unease that grew within me the longer I looked at the painting.

The painting was beautiful.

Too beautiful.

No child could replicate such a piece, no matter their talent and skill. The details of each stroke of the brush, the combination of color, and the perfect technique, beamed through the parchment.

"It's perfect." I swallowed, returning the drawing to Charlotte.

Charlotte's smile grew bigger as she put the painting back underneath the pillow. "Would you like to play *dolls* with me?" She crooked her head, waiting for my answer.

"I would love to." I nodded as Charlotte pulled me out of the room, back to the foyer that carried many wooden toys and the spirits of children who will never know mortality.

UNKINDNESS OF CRIMSON QUEEN

Tears had filled Charlotte's eyes when it had been time for Florence and I to leave. I only had myself to blame for her heartache: were I to never allow our closeness, she wouldn't know pain once it was time for our separation.

No matter my sincerest promises of visiting here, we both knew one day I wouldn't be able to fulfill it. One day would be the last time we see each other, and I despised myself for the pain my death might bring her. The pain I was far too familiar with...

"May I ask you a question?" I asked Florence as we walked the empty streets of Faris: not a soul strolled by, making Faris feel abandoned.

"Of course, anything." Florence walked on the brick road, caring not for how disturbing the emptiness was. The snowflakes fell onto her blushed cheeks, her sunshine smile melting the coldness.

"You told me once: you were not bitten, but reborn," I started. "I was wondering if... if..." I sighed as the words wouldn't come out. "If my siblings..."

"There is no way of knowing, Cordelia." Florence met my gaze. "Each soul chooses a different path, and only the Moon is privy to such knowledge."

I nodded as the disappointment spread through my heart, making it ache.

"I am sorry." Florence stopped in the middle of the road, facing me. "It is the greatest pain to endure: losing your loved ones. I wouldn't wish on anyone. There is no salvation but time." She held my hands.

I swallowed the tears that threatened to spill as the back of my eyes burned.

"As much as it pains me to say—" Florence's lips turned into a thin line, her sunshine hands warmed my heart so slightly. "The eternity forced upon small children is not the same as it is for you and me. To be trapped in a young body for centuries can be maddening." Her dark brown eyes stared into my soul. "I see it everyday: the fight between an old spirit and a child's mind. It is truly heartbreaking."

I nodded, though my selfish heart refused to accept her words, despite seeing it firsthand.

A single tear escaped my eyes, sliding down my cheek: Charlotte's unchild-like gaze flashing in my mind. "Charlotte told me the Bloodlake Castle used to be her Mother's?" I remembered our last conversation in my room.

"Perhaps." Florence shrugged. "Charlotte has no reason to lie, but we will never know for certain. There is no record of the owners of the Bloodlake Castle before Kane. And Charlotte doesn't even remember her family name..."

"She doesn't?"

"Reborn children do not remember their parents, do not remember their prior identity. It is merely a shell of their past." Florence sighed. "She has been in this life for a long while, Cordelia. Even for bitten vampires, memories eventually fade."

"Does that mean—" I start, my heart galloping against my chest.

"Yes." A sad smile appeared on Florence's face, the snowflakes freezing on her lashes. "In many years from now, you will forget everything from your human life."

"Do you still remember yours?" I dared ask.

She shook her head, resuming her walk through the Faris' streets. "Only what I have written in my journals after my new life began." The snow crunched under our boots.

"I am so sorry," my voice turned into a whisper.

"Don't be, Cordelia." Florence's voice dropped an octave, a slight crease in between her eyebrows deepened. "I often deemed it a curse—an unfortunate loss. I knew it was coming for me once I started to forget the faces of my dear ones.

"I was mad. I screamed at the Moon for stealing the last from me." Florence sighed. "But now watching you, Roxanne, and Francis struggle so much... I can see it's a blessing. It's a blessing to forget what it's like to lose your loved ones." She caught a snowflake in her palm, her eyes studying the small creation before it melted. "Come, we will be late." Her voice shone bright anew as she held my hand, pulling me towards Simon's tavern.

Chapter 24. Part of The Deal.

The tavern buzzed despite such silence on the streets of Faris; laughter and dancing prevailed in the space. A group of musicians played their fiddles and drums in the corner of the tavern, their harmony reaching every ear within.

"This way." Florence walked me through the dancing bodies, towards the table occupied by Roxanne and Francis.

Drinks in their hands, the pair did not notice us at first. Yet, when Francis' gaze met mine and his lips stretched into a smirk, my body caught aflame. He nodded in greeting, urging the flowers within me to bloom.

"What took you so long?" Roxanne gave Florence a kiss on the cheek when the woman sat by her side, leaving the only available chair to me.

"We went for a little stroll on the way here. You know how much I love snowing Faris." Florence removed her cloak, letting it rest on the back of her chair. "It is truly magical."

"It is indeed." Roxanne pushed a bowl from the center of the table to Florence. Bright red filled the contents. "I thought you might want something warm."

"Mhm." Florence smelled the contents of the bowl. "Pumpkin soup, my favorite!" She beamed. "Thank you, love." She started at her meal.

Despite the delightful aroma coming from her soup, the crimson tint spoiled it for me.

"I didn't know what you would like," Francis explained the lack of a meal in front of me.

"I am not hungry, thank you." I followed Florence's lead and took the snowy cloak off my shoulders, settling onto the chair next to Francis. "What have you two been talking about?" I glanced at Roxanne and Francis, hoping my obvious attempt at changing the subject would be left unmentioned.

"Mostly how foolish Roxanne is." Francis shrugged, pouring crimson from the pitcher into his goblet.

Roxanne's lips turned into a mischievous smile. "Actually," she started. "We were talking about you, Cordelia!" Her voice shone with an unnatural—to her—charm. She brought the drink to her lips, her eyes glowing with larkiness.

"What about me?" I asked, knowing the answer was not meant for my ears, for Francis nervously pulled on the collar of his shirt.

"Roxanne has finally lost her mind tonight, you see." Francis rushed to reply, cutting Roxanne off.

Her smirk grew bigger as she finished her drink, setting the empty goblet down on the table. "Is that a bite on your neck?" She pointed at the collar of my dress.

My brows rose at her boldness—that lacked the unusual venom—as a bright smile stretched her lips.

"You are being childish, Rox." Francis sighed, shaking his head, though a shadow of a smile still brightened his lips.

"I am merely expressing joy for your happiness." Roxanne laughed, taking a spoonful of Florence's soup. "Am I not allowed to feel happiness for you?" She pouted.

Pouted!

"I can't even leave you for an hour it seems," Florence mumbled, demanding her spoon back.

"Cordelia," Roxanne giggled, reaching for my hand. "I meant to tell you how truly glorious you look tonight." She frowned before adding, "And always! You always look glorious!" Roxanne dropped my hand, turning to Florence, though it seemed she was more interested in her soup...

She has *lost her mind, indeed.*

I breathed in the contents of the pitcher by Roxanne's goblet, the smell of moonshine reaching my senses. "Is she drunk?" I faced Francis, pointing at her long empty goblet.

"Very much so." Francis fought the smile off his lips, in vain, as he leaned back in his chair; the back of my neck prickled, his eyes boring into my flesh. He winked at me before his gaze traveled back to Roxanne.

"Perhaps Francis will stop writing sad music for once!" Roxanne's bright laughter traveled with the sounds of the fiddle. "Isn't that thrilling?"

"I don't write sad music," Francis chuckled.

"Yes, you do." Florence nodded, sending another spoonful of soup into her mouth.

"You do!" Roxanne's eyes sparkled. "And I love it! Your music is divine! A talent sent from the Moon!"

I wasn't sure which Roxanne I preferred: the gloomy one or the joyful one—both terrified me equally.

"So many compliments in one day..." Francis's hand reached for mine. "You are doing no good for my *arrogance*, Rox." Francis' eyes flickered to me as his hand wrapped around mine.

Roxanne's delight grew bigger at the scene. "You are not arrogant!" She argued. "You are very humble and..." Roxanne sighed, a bright smile tugging on her lips. "I love all of you so much!" She declared at last.

"All right." Florence moved the pitcher to the edge of the table: away from Roxanne. "You've definitely had enough."

Roxanne merely laughed in reply. "Simon!" Her smile somehow got brighter. "We've missed you so much!"

"We saw each other earlier tonight, remember?" He chuckled at Roxanne, putting a bowl of soup in front of her before turning to me. "What do you fancy on this fine night, Cordelia?" He murmured. "The pumpkin soup is tonight's favorite. The caramel fudge is still hot."

"I am not hungry." I shook my head; my stomach turning upside down with anxiety at the mere idea of human blood. "Thank you."

"Are you certain?" Simon didn't give up. "I made the dessert special for you."

"I—" The words abandoned me, unable to argue with his generosity.

As I was about to agree to the meal, out of guilt for the time Simon spent, Francis spoke on my behalf, "She said, she wasn't hungry, Simon." His voice dropped an octave.

Simon put his hands up in surrender, his brows furrowing at Francis' sudden tone. "Very well then. Next time."

The warmth stretched up my neck, reaching my cheeks. "Thank you, Simon," I added, forcing a small smile onto my face.

"Where is Ash?" Florence chewed on a—soaked in blood—piece of bread, saving me from the embarrassing interaction.

"Oh, Ash is upstairs, working on their new project." Simon pulled a chair from a nearby table, taking his seat at the head of ours. "A set of arrows for Gilbert," he explained. "With Kane gone, Ash's hands are full, given they are the only knowledgeable blacksmith around here."

"Speaking of..." Francis nodded at the weapon attached to my waist. "Can they remold Cordelia's sword into a few daggers?"

Simon eyed the sword, his eyes squinting. "I don't see why not." He shrugged.

"Perfect." Francis nodded for me to take off my sword. "Tell Ash we are very appreciative of their help."

"Actually, I have something for all of you upstairs, why don't you come up? We can discuss our plans there." Simon got up from his chair, ushering everyone to do the same. "And you can thank Ash yourself."

"What is it that you have for us?" Roxanne's eyes filled with excitement.

"Come and see." Simon laughed, gesturing for us to follow.

The musicians skillfully bowed their fiddles as we passed them, each note replacing the former swiftly.

My mind drowned in the bliss of their music, putting a genuine smile on my face.

"This way." Francis rested his hand on my lower back, ushering me towards the back of the tavern, towards the door that carried a *residents only* sign.

I entered after Roxanne who leaned onto the wall for support.

The music echoed through the dark hall when the wooden door closed behind us; a set of stairs stood ahead, each level carrying two doors across from each other.

"Simon," Roxanne groaned, struggling up the stairs: she leaned on the wall as Florence put Roxanne's hand around herself, pulling her upwards. "You should consider moving to the first level."

Simon chortled, "Perhaps I should." He watched Roxanne struggle. "Many of those apartments are now vacant anyway." He continued up the stairs. "A lot of vampires left after the Wurdulacs came back."

"Others will come," Florence's soft voice traveled through the set of stairs despite practically carrying Roxanne. "They always do."

"Oh, finally!" Roxanne groaned as we reached the fourth level. "This is exhausting, how do you do this everyday?"

"I don't drink everyday, despite what you choose to believe, Roxanne." Simon fiddled with the lock of his door that carried the number seven. The door creaked when Simon pushed it open, inviting us in.

Roxanne rushed to the couch that occupied the majority of the guest room, dropping onto it as though she'd run a few miles. "I am staying here tonight." She yawned.

Florence bestowed her with an eye roll, settling on the couch next to her lover. "I hope I won't need to carry you home..."

I took a few steps into the room, gorgeous rugs covered every inch of the flooring and one of the walls. The metal chandelier carried dozens of lit candles, illuminating the detailed woodwork of the bookshelf and doorframes leading into the depths of the apartment.

The apartment was small, yet carried an irreplaceable spirit of love.

"Wait here," Simon told us before disappearing into the room in the back.

"Are you all right?" Francis leaned, whispering into my ear when Roxanne lay onto Florence's lap, demanding a kiss.

"Yes." I averted my gaze from the couple when Florence decided it was useless to argue and obliged with Roxanne's demands. "Why do you ask?"

"You have been awfully quiet." Francis frowned at the couple before turning to me. "I'm sorry if Roxanne made you uncomfortable with her chatter." His gaze fell atop my neck, sending my mind into a hurricane. "I didn't share anything private about us, only confirmed what she already knew. I didn't mean to, but she sees through my lies far too easily... even when she is drunk, apparently."

"No," I breathed, sending a glance to his lips. "It's all right."

The wooden floors squealed under Simon's and Ash's steps as they appeared from the back room. "A present." Simon mumbled, showing off five shining daggers and a letter in his hands.

"You made those?" Roxanne crawled off the sofa, taking one of the daggers. "You made Royal steel." Her eyes grew bigger as she studied Ash: clarity returning to her eyes.

"It's from Caleb, he asked us to give them to you." Ash passed the daggers to Francis, Florence and me.

Caleb stole the daggers for us, the realization settled in my mind. *He fulfilled my long forgotten request.*

"You saw Caleb." Francis glanced at Simon and Ash before moving the dagger under the candlelight.

Simon nodded. "He came in last morning, while everyone was still asleep. Don't worry I didn't tell him of our plans." He handed me the letter. "That's for you."

"To what do we owe such generosity?" Francis crooked his head, glaring at the letter in my hands before his eyes met mine.

"I asked him to." I ripped through the sealing wax, dreading the contents of the letter.

I completed my part of the deal, now is your turn, Caleb wrote.

Only we had no deal. I'd told him I would *consider* helping him were he to steal the weapons for us, no promises were made. *Meet me where we last met during the ball.* I wouldn't be coming.

"What's in the letter?" Francis' voice dropped a few octaves when Caleb's words settled.

I folded the pieces of parchment, dropping it into my pocket. "Nothing of importance." I met Francis' gaze, the playfulness that filled his eyes moments ago long gone.

"What did you promise him?" Francis seethed.

"I promised him nothing." I answered his anger with my own.

"Cordelia..." Francis closed his eyes, sighing. "I swear to the Moon—"

"I owe him nothing," I hissed.

"Cordelia—"

"Oh, let her be." Roxanne rolled her eyes at Francis, putting her newly gained dagger in the scabbard. "She got us the weapons that—if you didn't notice—we desperately needed before our trip to the palace. Now we stand a chance at walking out of there alive."

Francis shook his head, yet scabbarded his Royal steel dagger all the same. His jaw twitched as though he fought to keep his thoughts at bay.

I turned to Ash, unsheathing my sword. "Is there any way for you to remold it into daggers?" I handed my weapon to them, dismissing Francis and his gloom.

Ash took the sword, studying it from every angle. "This is very fine work." They nodded. "I can make three, or perhaps four daggers out of it. It shouldn't take long."

"Thank you." I smiled. "Perhaps you could bring them when we go to the palace?"

"Oh, I am not going." Ash studied the sword. "There's plenty of work here, Faris needs weapons like never before." They set my sword atop the chest in the corner of the room. "Besides, I won't be much help in the palace." Ash shrugged. "Simon can bring the daggers with him."

Florence raised from the couch, taking Roxanne's hand into hers before turning to Ash, "Perhaps I can stay with you and help while they are gone?"

"Of course!" Ash nodded. "I am always happy for company."

"Are you certain?" Roxanne crooked her head, concern flashing in her still dreamy eyes.

"I was only going because you are afraid for me to stay on my own, this way I won't be alone were something to happen."

Roxanne's lips turned into a thin line before she replied, "All right." She nodded. "Perhaps you are right."

"Everything will be well," Florence reassured her. "You know I would be a burden at the palace."

"Promise me you are not going to go anywhere by yourself until I return." Roxanne sighed.

"Promise." Florence whispered, a sad smile tugging on her lips.

"Then it's decided: Florence and Ash will stay here, while the rest of us go to the palace," Simon concluded.

"We will stay the day in the cabin and the moment the sun sets make our move to the palace," Roxanne agreed. "What is the easiest way to get to the vault?" She faced me; nothing of the joyful Roxanne was left on her face.

I cleared my throat before replying, "The vault is in my mother's passage, we will have to go through there." I scabbarded my dagger. "Last time there were two Wurdulacs guarding it; outside of that, it should be rather easy, given that the pathway is far from the main entrance: where the majority of Kane's warriors are gathered." I glanced at Francis whose features still hid under shadows. "If we don't attract any attention, we should get in and out without any trouble."

"Sounds easy enough." Simon brushed over his jaw, though none of this would be easy.

The room fell into silence, yet everyone's thoughts were bright as day: some of us might never come back from the palace, some of us would say their goodbyes one last time.

"We will leave the night after the ball," Roxanne interrupted the growing dread that fought for power with the peaceful spirits of the apartment.

"The night after the ball." Simon's voice grew stronger when he glanced at Francis, who wouldn't take his eyes off me.

Chapter 25.
Bargains.

Roxanne and Florence rode through the night forest—a few yards before me and Francis—deep in a conversation I tried not to listen to, allowing them privacy. Francis and I did not spill a single word.

I knew he wasn't thrilled about me entering into any agreements with Caleb, yet I was not one to apologize for doing what was helpful. Besides, I hadn't sought Caleb on my own accord, and truly had forgotten about my bargain with him to ever mention it.

I glanced at Francis as he lit up a pipe in his mouth. His eyes met mine before averting his gaze to our company.

"Cordelia." Florence turned on her horse to face me. "I have this beautiful purple dress that I think would suit you well. You should try it on when we are home."

"I would love to." A small smile turned the corners of my lips upward.

"Perhaps you could wear it to the ball!" Florence beamed. "If you like it, of course," she added as we rode out of the woods, towards the Bloodlake Castle.

"Thank you, Florence." I nodded. "And I'm sure I will love it."

The sunshine smile stretched on Florence's face before she dismounted her horse, walking into the stables.

I freed Annabelle of the saddle, fighting with the old, rusty belts before carefully setting it at its designated place in the stables. By the time I succeeded, the stables had emptied, leaving Francis as my only company.

He leaned on the threshold, watching my every move. "May I read the letter, Princess?" He murmured.

"No." I tried to walk past him without sparing him a glance.

Francis chuckled at my reply. "I don't appreciate you scheming behind my back, love." He caught my wrist, yanking me to the side until our bodies pressed against each other.

My body caught aflame under his piercing gaze; his eyes darkened, filled with trouble. The kind of trouble my body begged for, the kind of trouble I was eager to entertain.

"I wasn't scheming." My voice filled with an unfamiliar mischief. Our faces were inches from each other. "I didn't think he would actually bring us the daggers."

He crooked his head to one side, a smirk decorating his face. "Then why don't you tell me what's in the letter?" His lips still carried the drops of blood from the tavern. The red tint bothered my body more than I cared to admit.

"Because, while there is nothing of importance, it would still upset you." My fingers toyed with the collar of his shirt against my permission—I cared not to move them away.

Francis' thumb brushed over my chin, lightning erupted in my insides. "I can handle myself," his voice turned sultry.

"Can you now?" I teased. "You have to trust me, Francis. Unless—" My eyes narrowed on his, watching his reaction to what I was about to propose. "You wish to exchange this letter for the one you wrote for me?"

"What letter?" The crease in between his brows deepened.

"The letter I saw in your room." My fingers moved up to his neck, as though they had a mind of their own, caressing his soft skin. "The one addressed to me."

"Ah." Francis threw a glance at my lips, his hands pressing me closer. "Bargaining, are we?" His husky voice swept through me.

I shrugged, "I learned from the best." Our lips were so close, it was a miracle—and my deepest disappointment—they didn't touch.

Francis chuckled, then sighed as his thumb brushed over my lower lip. "The bastard wrote nothing of importance, do you promise me?"

Disappointment at his refusal to show me what he'd written washed over me. "Is that a no?"

"Sorry to disappoint." He shook his head. "So? Do you promise there is nothing I need to know?"

"Hm..." A mischievous smile spread across my lips. "Who knows what is in that letter," I teased. "Perhaps a promise to murder me in my sleep..."

"Cordelia." Francis' voice dropped a few octaves, his thumb freezing under my chin.

I laughed at his expression. "I might have another proposition for our exchange." I couldn't believe the words I was saying.

"Is that so?"

I bit my lower lip before the words spilled. "A kiss?"

Francis chuckled, though his eyes turned darker, giving away his true feelings. "Come now, Princess, your kiss is worth far more than some letter." He moved closer, our lips brushing against each other. "I would give you my whole life if you wished me to, just to taste your lips once more," he said as his lips pressed against mine, the taste of him spreading through my bones.

A muffled moan escaped my throat. Warmth filled my insides; I wanted to scream in delight, unable to control the growing desire.

His tongue toyed with mine; the flowers bloomed in reply, wrecking everything in their path.

Francis growled against my lips, deepening our kiss.

My teeth pierced his tongue, allowing his blood to slip into my mouth. A cry escaped me as I melted into his hold.

"Francis," I rasped, breaking our kiss.

"Yes, love," he whispered against my lips.

"I want—" I swallowed, my hands wrapping around his neck. "I need you." I found his dreamy eyes with mine. "Please." I caressed the scar on his jaw. "Please."

"You needn't plead with me, love." His lips planted on my forehead. "There is nothing I would want more in my life than to have you in my arms."

A smile stretched my lips despite the trembling in my hands. My fingers wrapped around his as we walked into the castle, up the stairs, all the way to my room.

Chapter 26. The Taste of Divine.

I closed the door to my room with one hand, the other already working on the buttons of his shirt—with enthusiasm I wasn't expecting from my broken mind.

Our lips crashed against each other as they erupted into a dance.

My trembling hands pulled out my hair pin, freeing the strands. My hair fell down my shoulders; Francis' eyes traveled down its lengths.

I forced air into my lungs, despite my body's protests, as my hands clung onto Francis' wrists. "Please don't pull on my hair," I whispered, searching for his gaze. Searching for anything that would give away his malicious intent—I found nothing, though it only soothed my anxiety slightly.

"I remember." Francis' lips pressed against my chin. "May I touch it?" he whispered.

"Yes." I forced my mind into silence as I freed him from my prison.

Carefully, his hand reached for my strands, putting them behind my ear.

"So soft," he murmured, his lips stretched into a lazy smile.

He pressed a kiss against the corner of my lips as his hand moved further, settling on my collar bone.

Fear rushed through my body, squeezing my heart into its claws; yet before I could let it win, Francis' lips pressed against my own anew, forcing them entrance.

The low sound of satisfaction escaped my mouth as Francis toyed with my lip. His teeth brushed against my skin; I silently begged him to proceed. Yet he did not.

His lips traveled down, leaving a trace along my jaw. "Would you like to continue?" Francis' hands dropped to my lower back.

When I nodded in reply he effortlessly picked me up, carrying me towards the bed.

Silky sheets caressed my skin as Francis laid me on the bed. I closed my eyes as his lips caressed my neck.

Anticipation burned me alive.

His teeth brushed over my skin; a whine erupted through me at his every touch.

His dark chuckle reached my ears.

He was teasing me.

"Francis," I groaned; my hands pulling on his hair.

"Yes, my love?" His eyes met me; his mouth outright abandoned my neck. "Is there something you would like me to do?" Francis crooked his eyebrow, smiling, as though completely oblivious to my needs.

"Francis." I glared at him, fighting my own smile.

"What is it, Cordelia? Tell me." His voice dropped a few octaves as his lips caressed the lobe of my ear. "Just say the words."

A moan escaped me instead. I pulled on the ribbons of my dress, exposing my chest.

Goosebumps traveled down my flesh when his fingers pulled the dress off me, leaving me with nothing but bare skin.

I cared not for my exposure, yet when his eyes traveled down my flesh, my stomach fluttered, my breathing hitched.

A satisfied groan pushed past his lips when they made their way down to my chest, deliberately avoiding its centers.

"Is that what you want, my love?" Francis murmured in between his taunting kisses.

I shook my head, then nodded, then shook my head again. My mind drowned in his touch.

"Ah!" I cried when his lips finally found their place in the middle of my breast.

Francis chuckled, pleased with his work.

"Please, Francis." I pulled on his hair, bringing his lips to my neck.

"Tell me what you want," he teased.

"You know what I want." My voice turned hoarse, filled with frustration and arousal.

"I want to hear you say it." He placed a gentle kiss on the vein of my neck. Too gentle.

Refusing to obey, I bit my lips; my hands ushered him closer.

"I'm patient," Francis whispered into my ear, sending dozens of goosebumps down my flesh; my skin caught aflame.

"Francis—" I whined when his teeth punctured the soft part of my ear. "Taste me," I surrendered.

A low growl escaped from Francis' throat before his teeth sunk into my throat.

Relief washed over me as the pain erupted through my flesh. He sucked onto my open wound; my eyes rolled back in satisfaction.

"Oh!" A cry pushed through my throat; my body shattered underneath his. "Francis—"

His teeth abandoned my neck, to my disappointment, yet I was not able to form a word. His tongue caressed my bleeding wound before he planted a small kiss onto my injury.

His lips traveled down, leaving a trace behind them. Down and down, until they paused for a brief moment on the inside of my thigh.

His knees hit the floor; his lips were aligned with my entrance.

"What are you doing?" My eyes widened as he planted a kiss on my abdomen. My cheeks burned with excitement, even when my heart raced from embarrassment.

"I am tasting you." A wicked smile spread out on Francis' face as he pulled me closer. "Isn't that what you wanted, my love?"

"I—" The words turned into a moan as Francis' lips brushed over the most sensitive part of me.

"Tell me to stop." Francis' hands held onto my thighs, spreading them apart. When only my panting came in reply, Francis kissed down a path from my knees all the way to my bud.

He nibbled on it until my moans turned to cries. His tongue brushed over my flesh; my body jerked forward, begging for more. My hand reached for his hair, forcing him further.

He laughed at my eagerness before his tongue slid inside of me.

"Oh, dear Gods—" Flowers wrapped around my insides, tightening them into a knot. The pressure spread through every ounce of my being, locking me into blissful oblivion.

"You taste divine, my love," he rasped.

My love. The words alone made me burst into flames anew.

My eyelids heavied as I fought for every breath. Francis lay beside me, his soft–as velvet–fingers caressing my cheek.

"Would you say that again?" I whispered as my cheeks warmed. My finger reached for his soft lips. He lay still as I traced down to his throat imagining my teeth in his flesh. I paused at the vein that beat against my finger faster and faster. "Would you call me that again?"

His eyelids closed as he drew a sharp breath in. "My love," he said, his pulse spiraled along with my own.

"Do you mean it?" I asked, almost afraid of the answer.

"I certainly do." He brought my hand to his lips, planting a soft kiss on each knuckle.

The fear I expected to come at his reply remained at bay, and that somehow terrified me more.

"You needn't stress yourself with my feelings, Cordelia." His eyes met mine. "I can keep it to myself if you wish."

"No." I shook my head so slightly. "I don't wish you to."

His brows furrowed slightly at my confession, though he refrained from voicing his questions, and I was grateful—for

I, myself, was unsure what to make of my emotions. Certainly not when I lay bare on the sheets beside him.

My gaze slipped down his trousers as a new wave of excitement awoke my exhausted body.

My trembling hands traveled down his bare chest until they reached their destination. I pulled on the strings of his trousers.

Francis' hand caught mine, denying me entrance. A wave of confusion and embarrassment traveled down my body at such a rejection. "Sorry, I thought—" I forced my lungs to obey, despite only wishing to disappear into the void.

"You needn't feel the obligation to pleasure me." He planted a kiss on my forehead. "I am capable of taking care of it myself. Today is about you."

My brows furrowed in confusion before the realization eased my aching heart. "I want to." I forced my eyes to meet his.

"Are you certain?" His throat throbbed, his voice deepened.

"I am," I said, reaching for his trousers once again. "May I?"

"Of course you may, you needn't ask me, my love."

Blood rushed to my cheeks at the two words that seemed to be the only ones I wished to hear for the rest of my life.

The trousers slipped off. My hands traveled down his length.

I buried my face into the crook of his neck in an attempt to hide my aflame cheeks. A low moan traveled from his throat when my hand squeezed around him.

My thumb caressed his tip as the sound of satisfaction left his lips.

I was too nervous to ask what he would prefer me to do, though he seemed to enjoy my awkward movements despite my inexperience on this particular matter.

I hadn't ever had an opportunity to pleasure another, and quite frankly couldn't imagine it would bring *me* such joy. My only knowledge came from the smuggled books from the Royal's palace's restricted area in the library.

My mouth watered, my teeth ached, as Francis' pulse spiraled against my cheek. My hand wouldn't stop exploring him when my teeth pierced his throat.

His blood filled my mouth, warming my throat, as he hardened against my touch; the flowers inside of me awoke in reply anew. "I want you inside of me," I whispered against his neck, still unable to meet his eyes. "Francis," my voice croaked as I licked every drop of his blood. "I would like to be on top of you."

"As you wish, my love," he purred, pulling me on top of him. When I froze in his arms, his eyes filled with concern. "What is it, Cordelia?" Francis' hand moved a stray strand behind my ear. "It's all right if you've changed your mind."

"No, I just—" I moved a little closer as though this proximity would hide me from the embarrassment threatening to destroy me. "I've never done this before," the truth spilled from me. "But I wish to try." The embarrassment I felt just a moment ago ceased.

"That's all right." A soft smile appeared on Francis' face. "You have nothing to worry about. Take as much time as you need."

I nodded, before gathering all my courage.

My hands fell against Francis' chest before I lowered myself onto him slowly.

I drew a deep breath in before taking him fully; the flowers in me bloomed when the tip of him reached the spot I'd never known of.

"Oh!" I froze as he stretched my insides, my stomach fluttering from the mere thought.

"Just like that," Francis rasped, slowly moving me up and down. "Does that feel good?"

"Yes," was all I was able to say, for his thumb moved onto my bud, stroking my flesh.

It wasn't long before my insides tensed. The room erupted in my screams as my body shattered anew.

"Yes, love—" Francis fell apart underneath me, his fingers digging into my thighs. "Yes, my love—" He moaned, his eyes rolling back.

Our heavy breathings echoed throughout the room as I dropped onto his bare chest. Sweet bliss flowing through our connected bodies.

I could never imagine sex could feel so good, so freeing. So empowering.

Surely, I'd enjoyed some of my previous experiences, though they had often come with a dose of shame for such an outrageous act, and embarrassment for even wishing for it and not merely enduring as I had been told I must.

"Thank you," I whispered against his neck.

"What for?" Francis' chest shook underneath me as he chuckled.

"For treating me with kindness." I planted a kiss on his throat and Francis went quiet.

Silence stretched in between us before Francis cleared his throat, forcing my eyes to meet his. "Don't ever thank me for that, my love."

Chapter 27. Last Dance.

F rancis had left my room, when the sun had set, as he'd done every evening in the last week. We'd spent every given moment in each other's embrace, enjoying the final tranquil nights before the storm.

Tranquilness.

Something I'd used to treasure with my dear life, now felt like a threat.

A whole week had passed since the meeting at the Barren's: a whole week of peace and silence.

The Wurdulacs were quiet: no attacks on human villages, no assaults on the vampire ones either. Yet this unsettling feeling of dread filled the halls of the castle, filled the streets of Faris—something big was coming, something that required the Wurdulacs' proper preparation.

We needed to act now, before the inevitable came—

"Are you ready?" Florence stood at the threshold of my room, leaning against the doorframe. "The ball has already started."

She wore the rich-crimson gown, with golden appliques that twirled up the hem of her skirt. Her hair, usually kept in braids, fell down her shoulders in beautiful coils. Her golden necklace shimmered under the candlelight, complimenting her dark skin.

"You look beautiful," I beamed. "This dress becomes you."

"Thank you, Cordelia!" Her sunshine smile brightened the room. "You look gorgeous as well!" She moved through the room, her features suddenly turning serious. "I have a favor to ask."

"Anything." My brows furrowed at her sudden change as I attached the brooch Florence had gifted me a while ago.

"Please promise me, Cordelia," she started, her hands falling onto my shoulders. "No matter what foolish thing Francis does—or says—you are not going to run away like last time."

My brows flew up at her odd *favor*. "Is there something I should know?"

"Not that I know of!" she blurted, her eyes growing bigger. "But you know..." She shrugged. "With Francis, anything is possible." A small smile appeared on her lips as she sighed. "Promise me you will come to me if anything happens, all right?"

"You are scaring me, Florence." I chuckled at her worried expression.

"Sorry. I don't mean to." Her face turned sour. "I am sure nothing is going to happen." Her voice dropped to a whisper before she added, "He's not worth your tears, Cordelia. No one is."

Florence pulled me through the ballroom filled with dancing bodies. Laughter and joy occupied every inch of the room, accompanied by the beautiful tunes of musicians, despite the hardship that surrounded our minds.

Having a ball in such dark times felt wrong, yet right all the same. If for one night we could forget about the impending danger, it would have been worth it.

And despite my disgust towards the reason for the event, I was delighted to attend. Delighted, for it might have been my last chance to say what I needed to before the end.

"You owe me a dance!" Florence offered me a goblet of wine from the table, taking a sip of her own.

"All right," I laughed; the first drop of wine slipped onto my tongue, the sour filling my mouth. "I will gladly dance with you."

Florence stretched her hand towards me, setting her goblet back onto the table, as the music turned into a faster tune.

"Now?" My brows furrowed, taking another sip of my wine. "I haven't had enough alcohol to dance in front of an audience." I laughed, glancing at the overflowing center of the ballroom.

"Come now, Cordelia, you have nothing to worry about. Your dancing skills are splendid!" Florence beamed, setting my goblet onto the table before dragging me to the center of the room.

"You are too generous," I argued, yet took her hand in mine, the other falling onto her shoulder.

"I am not!" Florence spun us into a dance. "And you still must tutor me, remember?"

"Once the war is over." I nodded, my feet rushing to match her skilled steps.

"Once the war is over." Florence's lips stretched into a small smile.

The music slowed, willing our movement to follow suit; the chords of piano quieted, revealing the delicate notes of violin that complemented the suspenseful cello.

"No matter what happens tomorrow," I started, my voice lowering to reach only Florence. "I wanted to thank you for the kindness you've showed me—"

"No." Florence shook her head, halting our dance. "Don't you dare finish that sentence." Her grip hardened around my hands.

"I want you to know how grateful I am, in case—" I persisted.

"You can tell me when it's over." Florence's gaze darkened into a glare. "Cease allowing such thoughts."

"Florence..." I swallowed the growing lump in my throat as her hands enveloped me in an embrace, my own squeezing her tight.

"Everything will be well," she whispered.

I closed my eyes, pulling her closer, willing my mind to remember this in my last moments. I wished Sandra and I had such an opportunity before the end—

"You do know this part of the room is for dancing, right?" My eyes flew open as Francis' raspy voice reached my ears. "Is it my turn yet?" He met my gaze offering me a hand.

Florence and I broke apart before she nodded, "I should find Roxy." She gave me one last squeeze on my shoulders. "Thank you for the dance!"

Francis and I watched her slip away between the dancing pairs, her crimson dress flowing behind her in beautiful waves.

"Is everything all right?" Francis leaned to whisper into my ear.

"Yes!" I put a smile on my face, taking his hand into mine.

"Don't worry, I will try to not outshine you during our dance." Francis winked as his hand landed on my waist, pulling me closer.

"You couldn't if you tried," I teased, increasing the tempo of our dance. The new piece played, the piano stealing the attention of the ballroom.

Francis' eyes softened under my gaze, his features relaxed. A lazy smile tugged on his lips as his body pressed against mine.

"This is not our last dance," I stated, my nails digging into his blazer.

Francis' brows furrowed as he leaned to whisper into my ear, "Of course it isn't, love." He planted a kiss on my cheek. "I finally got a dancing partner that can sometimes match my skill, I will be stealing dances for centuries to go."

I rolled my eyes, ready to respond with my own remark as his lips landed on mine.

A rush of adrenaline spread through my body in reply.

My hands wrapped around his neck—our dance long forgotten—when I answered his kiss with my own.

The music stopped as everything around us ceased to exist. The back of my eyes prickled as my starving lips found the Moon's paradise.

"The humans are to arrive soon," Francis parted slightly, his lips inches from mine. "Do you wish to go for a walk?"

I nodded, recovering from his kiss.

His fingers wrapped around mine as he lead me through the ballroom—past the musicians that were enchanted by their own creation, past the dancers that were spellbound by their partners—to the back door that led to the depths of the forest: to the door Francis had walked me out through during my very first ball at the Bloodlake Castle.

"I promised Florence I would not go outside today." I laughed, walking through the melting snow. "She was very worried you would upset me and I'd run away again."

Francis put his hand on his heart. "I promise not to upset you on our walk," he chuckled.

The winter's cold spells had loosened their grip over the last couple of days.

The snow had started to melt under the sun's gaze during the day. The creatures of the forest slowly awoke from their rest.

The Moon wandered alongside us as Francis walked me through the night forest's labyrinth.

"I am not going anywhere, you know," Francis whispered into my ear, glancing at my fingers clutching onto his hand in a strong grasp.

"Sorry." I relaxed my hold, despite my every wish. "I am merely wary of tomorrow."

"As I already told you, you needn't go back to the palace." Francis effortlessly picked me up, carrying me through the narrow stream of water that dared to show so early in spring. "Stay with Florence and Ash back in Faris."

"I am going," I whispered against his neck, refusing to let go of our embrace.

Francis sighed, stopping in place: his eyes planted behind me. I followed his gaze until my eyes landed on the Blood lake ahead of us.

"It's glorious." I rushed to my feet, taking a few steps towards it. The Moon reflected in the body of water, the corners of the lake still hidden underneath layers of ice.

I filled my lungs, devouring the view that offered the courage I desperately needed.

"There is something I must tell you," I started, my heart clanging against my rib cage.

"What is it?" Francis pulled me into his embrace, his eyes boring into mine.

My hands fell onto his neck: our skin touched, bringing me safety. "I think—" My voice broke; the claws pierced my lungs. "I'm in love with you, Francis." I nodded at my own words when a hurricane took over my racing mind, leaving nothing but chaos within. "Yes." I filled my lungs, searching Francis' eyes. "I am in love with you, but..." I swallowed as my heart stopped at once. "I don't know what to make of my feelings, and what they entail..." My hands trembled against his neck as I forced more air into my damaged lungs. "My mind is broken in many ways that I am scared to unravel, and you deserve better than to spend your time on someone who cannot promise you—"

"I will wait for as long as you need." Francis palmed my cheeks. "And if one day you want me to leave forever, I will: whatever you need." Francis planted a kiss on my forehead.

"That's not fair," I whispered as tears clouded my vision.

"I am to decide what's fair for me." His hands wrapped around me, shielding me from the world. "Your mere presence is more than I could ever have asked for." He met my gaze, his lips stretching into a lazy smile. "But I am honored by your admission of affection towards me, and apologies for how irresistible I am," he jested and I couldn't even find the annoyance at his unseriousness on the subject.

"I needed you to know before we go." I swallowed the growing anxiety.

"Nothing is going to happen to us, Cordelia." Francis brought me closer, scaring away the worry and dread.

We stood in our embrace with the Moon as our guardian for a long while before Francis pulled away, taking my hand into his, "We must go back before Florence and Rox send out the search party."

"All right." I nodded, following his lead.

The silhouettes of the dancing couples filled the windows of the castle, the music reached us from inside as we made our way towards our home.

Candlelight shone behind the stained windows, life ruled the room.

"Perhaps we should take the main door," Francis pulled me along the perimeter of the castle. "The humans are still there. Unless you wish for another dance..."

"I would rather spend our last hours in private." I gathered all my strength to meet Francis' gaze. "My body is starving for attention," I teased, my cheeks warmed despite the cool weather.

"What a delight to my ears," Francis murmured, leaning me against the stables. "If I could only choose one memory to relive in my last moments, it would be this one." His lips brushed over mine, his teeth teasing my skin—

"And here I thought you wouldn't show." The low timbre swept through the forest as Caleb appeared from the shadows.

Chapter 28.
Selfish.

Caleb took a step from the shadows of the forest that shielded him from unwanted gaze. His face now carried a long scar that reached his lips, the end of his injury still bled.

Adrenaline pumped through my veins when his eyes bored into mine.

"What are you doing here?" Francis unsheathed the Silver dagger from his belt, stepping in front of me.

"Did Cordelia not tell you," Caleb walked towards us, his eyes never leaving mine. "This is where we were going to meet for her part of the bargain."

Francis' fiery gaze landed on me, though he refrained from scolding me as his eyes moved back to Caleb.

I'd completely forgotten Caleb demanded meeting here in the letter. I'd completely forgotten he demanded a meeting at all. "I did not promise you a single thing." I stepped out of Francis' shield. "I agreed to *consider* helping, were you to follow up on my request—nothing more."

Caleb took a step forward, his features sharpened. "Cordelia, I have proven my loyalty to you."

"Bringing a few daggers is hardly any proof." Francis scoffed.

"I risked my life stealing them," Caleb barked, his fist planted on Francis' unmoving figure.

"Risked your life," Francis mocked, returning the gesture as he pushed Caleb away. "How rich."

"Leave this Francis." Caleb's jaw clenched. "It's between me and Cordelia."

"Everything that involves her—involves me." Francis' voice dropped a few octaves as he shoved Caleb backwards.

Caleb staggered before returning the gesture. "Clearly it only goes one way, given she made a bargain without your knowledge." He unsheathed his dagger as it shimmered golden under the Moon's gaze—Royal steel.

I had to do something before they murdered each other.

"Enough!" My heart raced when I moved between the two men. "Enough!" I barked at Caleb before focusing my gaze on Francis. "It's fine, Francis." My hands fell onto his chest, his eyes shone in fury. "Caleb is the only one who can get to the vault, anyway." I crooked my head, begging for Francis to see through my scheme.

"No." He frowned, his hand landing on my forearm.

"You have to trust me." My eyes bored into his. "I trust Caleb with this."

"Cordelia—" Confusion washed over Francis' features as I turned to face Caleb.

"The key to the vault is—" I started, schooling my features.

"Cordelia!" Francis pulled on my arm, his knuckles whitening around the hilt of his dagger.

"Is in the Royal library." I ignored Francis' strong hold that loosened slightly at my words. "Hidden in one of the ancient volumes on Wurdulacs," I finished, silently begging Francis to play along.

"What's it called?" Doubt shone bright across Caleb's eyes.

I offered a small glance at Francis, his stone-like eyes met mine when his voice lowered "You are making a mistake," he bit out.

His words cut through the distance between us, making my body catch aflame. Perhaps he was a better actor than I was.

"I never saw the book with my own eyes," I swallowed. "Mother never allowed me in the restricted area of the library."

"How can you be so sure the key is there then?" Caleb's eyes flickered with suspicion.

"I overheard Mother and Father speaking of it once." The more I talked, the more suspicion Caleb expressed.

Damnation.

"Enough." Francis pulled me towards the main entrance of the castle. "This conversation is over," he spat out as we walked away from the stables.

"How am I supposed to find a book with no title in the biggest library in the Kingdom?" Caleb called after.

"Get out of here," Francis said over his shoulder.

"Not until you tell me the title." Caleb's steps followed after us. "I took you for someone who would keep their word, Cordelia, but I see your Royal upbringing only taught you how to use others for your own gain—"

Francis pushed me behind him as he raised his dagger for a throw—

The dagger spun in the air before landing into Caleb's shoulder as a muffled cry escaped his lips. Anger crossed Caleb's face.

Francis unsheathed his Royal steel dagger in an instant. My heart banged in my chest as my lungs froze.

"One more step and this will land in your heart." He raised the weapon for the throw; Caleb froze in place. "This is your last chance Caleb," Francis seethed. "I should have killed you back in the dungeons, I should have killed you back at the cabin, but I am weak." Francis walked towards the man. "I am weak, for I remember you welcoming me into your family." Francis dug his finger into Caleb's injury, forcing a growl out of him. "I remember your kindness and care when I needed it most.

"But make no mistake, I will kill you in a heartbeat, and not regret it a day in my life, if you as much as look at her one more time." Francis twisted the dagger into his shoulder before freeing it from Caleb's flesh. "This is your last chance. I mean it." Francis let go of Caleb's shoulder, taking a step back. "Leave." He nodded at the forest.

Caleb's jaw twitched when he offered a firm nod. "I am sorry, Francis," he whispered before disappearing back into the shadows.

"Are you all right?" Francis crooked his head, his eyes boring into mine. "Did I hurt you?" He glanced at my forearm, walking towards me.

"No." I shook my head; shock still freezing my mind. "I was worried he would hurt you."

"That bastard can't hurt me." Francis' hand fell onto my waist, ushering me inside the castle. "And you needn't worry yourself with my safety." He planted a gentle kiss on my temple.

The main doors closed behind us; the music reached our ears anew. The ball was in full swing when we walked past the hall, up the stairs.

"I don't want you to kill him on my behalf, Francis," I admitted, stopping in the small corridor between the flights of stairs. "He is not worth it."

Francis sighed, facing me. "Why do you always defend him?" His thumb traveled below my chin, raising it until my eyes met his. "He was the one to put you in danger."

"I don't know," I replied honestly. "We talked in the dungeons and—" I sighed, sitting down on the steps of the stairs, unable to hold Francis' gaze. "Perhaps I saw myself in his words—someone unable to stand against what is expected of you out of fear, someone who tries hard to do what they're told, even if it's the wrong thing to do."

"You are none of those things." Francis shook his head, crouching before me. "You are never scared to go against your own interest. You care not for your own safety—which angers me deeply." A sad smile tugged on the corners of his lips. "If you've committed any wrongs, it was for the ones you love."

"You are wrong," I whispered. "I left my siblings to fend for themselves once I gained freedom. I knew of the horrors Sandra must have endured on my behalf and did nothing until the very end. Her last months of life were spent in suffering because of me, her last moments were spent in an agony inflicted by me." A tear slid down my cheek.

Francis caught my hands, bringing each knuckle to his lips. "You were in a situation that had no right to be forced upon you." Francis wiped the tear off my face. "Sometimes we have to be selfish for the greater good, for if we destroy ourselves over things that cannot be changed, we won't be able to provide help when we are able."

"Perhaps Caleb is doing the same," I offered, earning an annoyed look from Francis. "He did get us the weapons as I asked him to…"

Francis sighed, a small chuckle pushing past his lips. "My dear Cordelia, when will you stop finding trouble?"

I shrugged. "It seems it finds me."

"That it does." Francis brought his lips to mine, planting a tender kiss. "Clearly I cannot leave you alone for even a second."

"Is that a threat?" I smiled against his lips.

"Depends." He got to his feet, offering me a hand. "Come, we need our rest for tomorrow." He walked me through the corridor.

"My room is a level higher." I made no attempt at stopping on our path away from it.

"I told you, I am not leaving you." Francis walked me to his room, opening the door for me to enter. "I also recall someone's body *starving for attention*."

Chapter 29. The Last Night.

Warmth enveloped me whole when my eyes flew open, parting me from my sweet dreams. I closed them again, willing back the peace, yet the dreams did not find me, crashing the dreadful reality upon my mind.

I turned in Francis' arms, willing my mind to remember this very moment in times of hardship.

Francis looked peaceful, deep in his slumber. His features softened; the crease in between his brows ceased.

My thumb journeyed across the scar on his jaw, which I still did not know the origin of. Rough skin met mine as the memories of last night invaded my mind, making my cheeks burst into flames.

The memories of his lips atop the most sensitive parts of me, driving me mad again and again until I had no choice but to give into the delightful bliss.

The memories of our blood mixing into one on our lips and flesh. The memories of my cries against his mouth, and my plea for the pleasure to never stop, his teeth piercing through my skin, and the euphoria drowning us in its paradise.

My thumb moved on to his lips that still carried drops of my blood, then down and down, reaching his bare chest underneath me.

I sighed, enjoying the last moments of peace as my eyes followed the small opening of the curtains in the corner. The sun took on an orange tint—a small line of light fell onto Francis' bookshelf filled with dozens of books—as it slowly disappeared, allowing twilight to take its place.

The room grew darker, bringing the end closer.

I looked around the space, memorizing every detail of it were I to never return here—the place that brought me such peace—until my eyes landed on the side table that carried quill, ink, and dozens of pieces of parchment. At the very top lay a letter: my name curved into the center.

My heart beat faster when I glanced at Francis' peaceful features, listening for his even breathing. My lips turned into a thin line when I moved carefully, so as to not wake him, my hand reaching for the parchment—

"Thief." Francis' hand caught my wrist, stopping it in place. A lazy smile spread on his lips as his eyes stayed closed.

"Go back to sleep, Francis," I groaned, earning a soft chuckle in reply. A sigh of defeat escaped me before I faced him. "What's in the letter Francis?" I demanded. "It has my name on it. I get to read it."

"You aren't the only Cordelia in this Kingdom." Francis' hold hardened when I made another attempt at reaching for the letter; his eyes opened, watching me struggle.

My cheeks warmed at my bare chest atop his as he held my wrist hostage in his grasp. "I know it's for me." I rolled my eyes.

Francis tsked before kissing the corner of my lips. "How arrogant..."

"Francis." I glared into his eyes.

"Let go, or I burn it, and then you will never read it, love." He smirked, moving my hand away.

I sighed in defeat. "I will assume it's a love letter you wrote for me, and are now too embarrassed to show it."

"Perhaps." He shrugged, moving to a seated position, taking me with him. "Perhaps not."

I shook my head, curiosity eating me alive. "Will I ever get to read it?"

"Depends," he purred; a familiar smirk decorated his face.

"Depends on what—" I started, yet he silenced me with a kiss as his lips fell upon mine.

The dried crimson crushed against mine. His teeth scraping against my lower lips, forcing a muffled moan out of me. My stomach fluttered as he licked the dried blood of my flesh, tracing a path down my neck.

"We need to get ready," he rasped against my throat.

"Perhaps in a few minutes..." my voice turned hoarse.

"Mhm," was all I got in reply when Francis moved lower, his mouth atop the center of my breast, his tongue toying with the sensitive spot.

A cry pushed past my lips—

A loud bang on the door froze us in place; Francis sighed, his eyes filling with a silent apology. "The sun has already set, lovebirds." Roxanne slammed on the wood, her voice booming through the closed door. "We must be on our way."

Francis pulled away, sighing. "We will be out in a moment," he told the door.

"Hurry!" Roxanne shouted through the wall before her steps disappeared down the corridor.

"Sorry, love." Francis planted a kiss on my forehead, reaching for the letter. "I will make it up to you." He smirked, charging towards the other end of his room.

The doors to his bathing chambers closed as Francis disappeared behind them, the letter disappearing with him.

Roxanne and Simon stood outside of the stables, their horses saddled and ready when Francis and I made our way outside.

"Where is Florence and Ash?" I asked, pulling out my saddle.

"They left just now, you've missed them." Roxanne glanced at the small opening in the woods—the pathway to Faris.

Claws wrapped around my throat as I nodded, setting the saddle down on Annabelle. At least I got to say my goodbyes to Florence at the ball.

"They will be fine." Simon reached for Roxanne's shoulder, giving it a slight squeeze. "The path to Faris is safe, and they are together," he reassured.

"Yes," Roxanne nodded, her throat bubbling.

"Here." Simon met my gaze, unsheathing three daggers from his belt. "Ash worked all week to get them done. I hope you don't mind that they took a bit of your metal to remold into arrow tips for Roxanne."

Roxanne showed off her new tips, which sparkled golden under the moonlight, before putting them into the quiver with the rest of her arrows.

"Of course. " I nodded at Simon. "And thank you." I tucked one dagger into my belt, offering the other two daggers to my company.

"Those are for you, we have other weapons to fight with." Francis took my daggers, sheathing one into my belt, another onto the belt on my boot.

"But these are Royal steel." I argued when he knelt before me.

"They are yours." Francis got to his feet, mounting his horse in a swift motion.

I glanced at Simon and Roxanne who were armed from head to toe. Two swords strapped to Simon's belt, a bow in Roxanne's hand, the quiver with dozens of arrows peaking from her back.

Royal steel or not, I was the only one incompetent with any kind of weaponry—I was the burden of this trip.

"Let's be on our way, we cannot waste time," Roxanne said, ordering her horse into the woods, away from the castle, away from Faris—towards the inevitable, towards the Royal palace filled with Wurdulacs.

Chapter 30. Ash.

The first snowdrops fought their way through layers of snow, bestowing us with its glory. The melting snow crushed under our horses' hooves, turning to water.

I had never been fond of springs; they had always made me feel as though new beginnings were upon me, and yet my life would turn for the worst. How I wished this spring brought peace—not sorrow.

Francis shot glances in my direction as he rode alongside me, letting Roxanne and Simon take the lead on our journey. I replied to his glances with my own, forcing a soft smile on my face that he certainly saw through—just like I could see through his.

Roxanne and Simon did not pretend to be anything but heartbroken: Simon deep in his thoughts—unlike his usual chatter and joy—Roxanne with cloudy tears in the corners of her eyes that she refused to let loose.

Only nature allowed the music into our silent travels, calming my racing heart so slightly—at least for tonight.

It was agreed to spend the day at the cabin—let ourselves and our horses rest before tomorrow, instead of rushing into the palace with no way of escaping under the sun's powerful rays—only Moon knew in what hurry we would have to flee. Only Moon knew whether we would be able to flee at all.

"Wait," Francis hissed, bringing his horse to a halt before the last turn to the cabin. Simon and Roxanne froze in place before us.

"What's wrong?" I whispered, looking in every direction for danger—I found none. "Francis?" I added when he didn't reply.

His eyes planted onto the ground before us, I followed his gaze, finding nothing unusual.

"Francis?" Roxanne drew one arrow, setting it onto her bow as she glanced around the woods.

"Someone was here." Francis ushered his horse to pass Roxanne and Simon, straight down the path towards the cabin. "Stay here," he threw over his shoulder, disappearing into the woods.

Roxanne rushed after him, Simon and I followed.

The meadow stood silent under the Moon's gaze; the cabin—

A gasp pushed past when my eyes landed on Francis' childhood home.

"Dear Gods..." Roxanne palmed her mouth as her eyes grew bigger.

"Fuck—" Simon let go of the hilt of his sword, dismounting his horse.

Francis froze in place before his home.

The cabin—or rather what was left of it—stood in the center of the meadow, its roof burned to crisp.

The wooden walls blackened with ash; the remains of books lay on the ashy snow, their pages turned into nothingness. And only the metal chimney in the center of the disaster stood untouched.

Francis' cabin was burned to the ground, taking everything with it.

Francis dismounted his horse in silence.

He walked towards the disaster, the snow crunched under his steps, echoing through the frozen meadow. His gaze lowered as he stumbled upon a metal goblet on the ashy snow.

His hands stretched for the surviving object as he studied it before falling down to his knees in the center of the devastation.

His head flew high until his eyes met the Moon.

I swallowed, dismounting Annabelle. My heart rang in my ears as my legs carried me to him.

"Francis," I whispered, not knowing what else to say. My legs met the ground next to where Francis knelt. His face was peaceful, his hands relaxed... his eyes shone with pain.

His glassy eyes watched straight through me as I knelt before him. A single tear slid down his cheek when he caught it before it could reach his coat and the ash.

My hands wrapped around his neck. Tight, I held him in my arms until he accepted my sanctuary.

In silence we sat on the cold soil.

Time passed around us; the cold, wet snow melted into our clothing.

"Francis," Simon appeared by our side eventually, his hand falling on Francis' shoulder. "We must go. The sun is about to come out," he said, his features turning stone cold.

Francis nodded, reluctantly letting go of me. "Yes." He cleared his throat. "We must find shelter." He got to his feet, pulling me with him.

"Issac's friend lives nearby," Roxanne whispered carefully, her eyes still planted on the disaster behind us. "Perhaps we could spend the night there," she added.

Francis merely nodded as he helped me mount Annabelle before charging towards his mare.

In a swift move he turned his horse around, rushing away from the burned down cabin, away from his fallen home.

The dense woods thinned the longer we rode, the familiar spruce turning into naked birch trees.

"Where are we?" I asked Roxanne who rode beside me, trying to remember any markings on the map I had studied prior. Father had often taken Brian and I to ride around the palace, yet he'd always insisted on going west, away from where we were headed now.

"It's a..." She glanced at Francis who strolled before us. "It used to be a Royal warrior village," she whispered for reasons I was not aware of; my heartbeat quickened. "After the war, many stayed there, since they had nowhere else to go." Her lips turned into a thin line. "It's a human village, we aren't exactly welcomed there. It's best if no one sees us."

"Isaac was friends with a human warrior." I thought out loud, keeping my voice low.

"Isaac was friends with everyone who didn't mind his being." A sad smile stretched on Roxanne's face at the memories of her past.

"Follow me." Francis offered over his shoulder, turning his mare towards a narrow path behind a house that was slightly bigger than his cabin.

A small cover on the edge of the forest hid under the birch trees. Four pillars stood at each corner.

Francis dismounted his horse, tightening her reins around the pillar; we followed his lead.

"Are you sure it's safe for us to stay here?" Simon whispered, tying the reins of his horse.

"I have known this man for years, he was a good friend to my brother," Francis' voice cut through the morning twilight, walking around the house to the main entrance.

He banged on the door several times before any sign of life appeared from within. "Have you seen what hour it is!" The voice behind the door exclaimed, followed by heavy steps towards the entrance.

The cold air brushed my hair, letting the stray strands fly over my face. The wet snowflakes kissed my cheeks, melting on my skin in an instant.

The air escaped my lungs when the door flew open.

A young man stood at the threshold of the cottage. His sickly familiar eyes looking over my company.

"Francis?" His brows furrowed when Francis offered him a hand in greeting. "What are you—" His words were lost in the wind when his gaze fell on me. He swallowed, Francis' hand long forgotten. "Lia?" he whispered, his eyes filling with horror.

Chapter 31. Old Friend.

The ground opened up underneath my feet, sucking me into the underworld that awaited my end.

I gasped for air; my mind spiraled, drowning in its own web as I stood in front of the man I'd thought I would never see again.

I took a careful step towards him.

His bronze hair was slightly longer than I remembered—almost reaching his jaw—his green eyes dulled with time. His light skin now wore a slight tan.

His lips were moving, yet no sound reached my ears. Everything spun and blurred as he walked towards me until no distance had separated us.

His hands fell onto my cheeks, his eyes staring into mine, yet only emptiness filled me when I met his gaze. His hands wrapped me into a tight embrace, my face pressed against his shoulder.

His body shook against mine, a muffled sound of laughter coming from his mouth, yet I could not understand a word he said.

My hands hung by my sides, limp. My eyes planted on my company, confusion shone in their eyes.

I sucked in a breath, realization slowly washing over me.

My stomach dropped to my heels as I pushed myself away from the embrace. My hands fell onto his shoulders as though only a touch could be proof I was awake.

"You are alive," I said more to myself than to him, my voice did not belong to me.

A soft smile decorated his face, willing my anger to wake.

My brows furrowed as my hands clenched onto his flesh, my nails digging into his shirt. "You are alive," I seethed through clenched teeth when my fists landed on Gabriel's chest.

Gabriel staggered backwards into the house as my fists kept striking his chest. "How dare you be alive!" I shouted, caring not who heard. "How dare you stand alive before me—" I pushed him further: he did not protest, staggering deeper into his house. "How dare you!"

"I'm—" He put his hands up in surrender as my fists kept finding their place on his chest.

"How dare you!" My palm landed on his cheek, leaving a red mark across his face. "You betrayed me!" My hand reached for the Royal steel dagger at my belt. "You are a disgrace to his memory!" I swung the blade to his throat.

"Whoa—all right," Francis' hand caught my armed one in the air. "All right." He dragged me by my waist, away from Gabriel. "We need him alive, love," he purred into my ear, tightening his grasp around me when I struggled against him.

"Burn in hell!" I yelled at Gabriel as his chest rose and fell. Confusion and hurt crossed his features when he closed his eyes.

"I can explain." Gabriel put his hands down, still shaken from the reaction he certainly had not expected—yet he should have had! His eyes lingered between me and Francis.

I fought against Francis' grasp, in vain. "Let go of me, Francis." I struggled; Francis didn't budge, tightening his grasp. "Let go of me," my voice dropped to a growl.

The door closed behind us as Roxanne and Simon emerged into the house. Their gazes falling onto my raised weapon.

"Let go of the dagger and I will let go of you," Francis' voice was as calm as the morning breeze. He leaned closer to whisper into my ear, though the silence of the house turned his whisper into a shout. "Come now, Princess, it won't be a great look if we wake the whole village up with the sounds of you brutally murdering this man." His eyes landed on Gabriel. "Besides, we might need a fresh meal before tomorrow, in case you do wish him dead, nevertheless."

"Thank you, Francis." Gabriel rolled his eyes before taking a deep breath. "I thought we were friends."

"Drop the dagger for me, love," Francis' voice softened, his breath tickling my ear.

Time passed as the four pairs of eyes watched me: Gabriel's with remorse, Simon's and Roxanne's with confusion, Francis' with... admiration.

I groaned, my eyes closing tight as my fingers loosen their grip around the hilt of my weapon.

The dagger fell onto the wooden floors of Gabriel's house, a dull clang echoed through the silence as Francis kicked the dagger away from my reach, towards Roxanne standing by his side.

She picked up the dagger, sheathing it to an empty scabbard at her belt.

I had two more daggers on my person, though no one seemed to remember that.

"Let go of me," I seethed, pushing against Francis' hand. "That was the deal."

"All right." Francis nodded, loosening his grip slightly. "You have calmed down," he said, though it sounded more like a question.

I drew a deep breath in reply, yet I was far from calm. My heart still banged against my rib, threatening to escape for good; my blood poisoned with rage. "Yes," my voice turned hoarse from shouting.

"All right, then." Francis' hands loosened around my body, reluctantly letting go of me; yet he still stood beside me: our shoulders touching.

My gaze dug into Gabriel's guilty eyes, daring him to speak. He stayed silent, looking at me as though seeing for the first time.

"I am listening for your pathetic excuses." My jaw clenched.

"I had no other choice, Lia—" he started.

"It's Cordelia to you," I seethed through my jaw, my glare burning holes into his flesh.

"Since when?" A choked laugh escaped him.

"Since the moment you disappeared." I walked towards him, forcing him against the wall once again.

"Your mother would have killed me were I to stay, you must realize." Gabriel's voice turned soft—the soft that used to be my salvation and my only peace.

"You could have written to me!" My palm met his cheek again, adding onto the injury. "You could have let me know you were alive." Another slap. My skin cried out in pain, yet my heart was satisfied. "You left me all alone after he died!" *Slap.* "You left me like—" I choked. "Like I didn't mean anything."

"Remind me to never get on her bad side," Roxanne mumbled by the door.

"Brian would never forgive you," I spat out before turning around, storming towards the door. "I'm not staying here." I slammed the door behind me.

The snow caught my steps as I charged towards Annabelle. The door creaked open as expected; Francis walked out of the house, his long steps shortening our distance. "Princess—"

Gabriel stormed out after him, barefoot. "Don't be ridiculous, Li—Cordelia." He rushed after us. "Listen, I'm sorry I haven't written to you, all right? I meant to, but then I heard of the engagement and thought you'd moved on."

My fingers reached for Annabelle's reins as Francis' hands fell atop them. "We have nowhere else to go, love. The sun is soon to rise," he whispered, his soft eyes finding mine.

"I couldn't write to you," Gabriel pleaded when he reached us. "I needed your mother to believe I was dead, or else she'd have ended what she'd started. I barely escaped, Lia." He wouldn't give up, glancing between me and Francis. "She tortured me when she found out about us," Gabriel's voice dropped to a whisper.

The early spring's frost reached my heart; my voice dropped a few octaves, "And whose fault was that?" I willed my gaze to meet his, despite the nausea that brought back the painful memories. "You bragged to the whole Kingdom," I scoffed.

Francis' brows furrowed as he glanced at Gabriel.

"A few guards saw me leaving your room once," Gabriel eyed Francis by my side before continuing, "I had no choice but to confess."

"Spare me your foolish stories." I dropped the reins, facing him. "You knew exactly what you were doing. You hoped Mother would marry me off to you, in the hope of containing the rumor that *you* spread." My hands turned to fists by my side; my abused skin still wailed. "You used my status, and when it was useless you ran."

"That is not fair." Gabriel shook his head. "*You* came to me with that proposition, remember?" He crooked his head, his green eyes boring into mine. "I was the one to hesitate, but you convinced me: were I to be your first, your Mother would cease trying to marry you off to some old duke."

Mother hadn't ceased her attempts even then, only the old duke that was to be my husband turned into a young monster instead. A monster that hid behind a mask of kindness, a young monster that reminded me of my impurity every chance he'd gotten.

"I am sorry for leaving you so abruptly, that was never my intention." Gabriel's lips stretched into a pained smile. "But I am not the only one to blame for how things turned out." Gabriel sighed. "Please come inside, the sun will hurt you."

I glanced at Francis, whose eyes shone with dozens of questions I was unable to answer; his hands squeezed mine, soothing my fury.

Gabriel took a step backwards, his bare feet turning red from the cold. "I have something Brian left for you," he said, turning back towards the house. "Please come inside."

Chapter 32. Old Secrets.

Alone, Francis and I stared at each other, without saying a word, by the pillar of the covering. The first rays of sunshine appeared from the horizon; the snow shone under its touch. I felt nature wake up as the morning enveloped it in its embrace.

Francis' hand fell atop mine; unclenching my fist, he caressed my palm, soothing the throbbing ache. He then planted a tender kiss on my still reddened skin.

"Are you ready to come back inside?" he whispered, breaking our silence.

Annabelle sighed in reply, bringing a small smile to my face. I turned to her, making sure her reins were still tightened around the pillar; when satisfied, I offered her a small pat.

"Yes," I faced Francis, taking his hand into mine before walking back towards the house as the rays of sunshine followed after.

The door screeched open at my push, revealing three pairs of eyes that bored into me.

I walked into the house, ignoring the stares of those within, leaving my boots—covered in dirty snow—at the threshold.

I stepped onto the rug inside the corridor that also served as a kitchenette, taking a seat on the small couch against the wall across the wooden table.

Silent eyes watched my every move until Francis dropped onto the couch beside me with a loud sigh.

"I need a drink," Roxanne mumbled, taking a seat across Simon: at a stool by the table.

Simon took the canteen out of his cloak, offering it to her.

Gabriel leaned against the small set of stairs by the chimney, desperately avoiding my gaze.

Awkward silence fell upon the room as Roxanne chugged the contents of the canteen before returning it to Simon. Her face squirmed when she wiped her lips; her eyes watered.

Gabriel cleared his throat, willing our attention back to him. "Caleb told me you might come." He glanced at Francis, taking a seat on the stairs.

"You saw him." Francis' eyes shimmered with curiosity... and concern.

"He came last week." Gabriel nodded. "He said your cabin was destroyed and you might need a place to stay." He walked across the room, towards a little cabinet attached to the wall. Gabriel looked through it until his hand pulled out a folded piece of parchment. "He asked me to give this to you." He handed it to Francis.

Francis broke the red seal with a Royal stamp on it, unfolding the letter.

"What does it say?" Roxanne pressed, reaching for the parchment.

Francis crushed the parchment in his fist.

"What *did* it say?" Roxanne's brow crooked.

Francis shook his head before raising his gaze to her. "Caleb is behind the burn."

"What?" Roxanne' brows furrowed.

Francis disposed of the letter into the chimney. "Kane learned we've been lingering around the palace, and wanted to send us the message," he said, sitting back on the cushion. "He ordered Caleb to destroy it."

"He didn't think to mention it when we saw him last night?" I seethed.

"He knew that dagger would've been in his heart instead of his shoulder, were he to confess to my face," Francis scoffed. "He didn't know we would come to the palace tonight."

"Why *are you* here?" Gabriel looked around the room, meeting our silent glares.

"What else do you know of Caleb's whereabouts?" Francis asked instead, his eyes darkening.

"Nothing!" Gabriel blurted, putting his hands up in surrender. "I swear, I know nothing. I saw him last week for the first time in years."

"It's safe you don't know," Roxanne insisted. "For us, and for you."

"What if I am able to help?" Gabriel wouldn't give up.

"I doubt it," Roxanne scoffed, leaning against the wall on her stool.

"Try me." Gabriel challenged.

"Don't," I said before anyone could reply. "He is not very good with secrets." I glared at him.

Gabriel laughed, rolling his eyes. "Who would I even tell around here?"

"Apparently you keep Wurdulacs as company." Roxanne shrugged.

"Wurdulacs?" Gabriel's brows furrowed. "I had no idea Caleb was a Wurdulac until he showed up here. And when I confronted him, he reassured me he is working as a spy, to destroy their forces from within," Gabriel protested. "Why are you going to the palace?"

"It matters not if he knows." Simon's words cut through the air as he looked around the room. "Tomorrow we either come out alive and get far away from this place, or we don't."

"I like you, ginger man." Gabriel nodded at Simon, earning an eye roll from me.

Francis and Roxanne glanced at each other, locked in their wordless conversation. Silence fell upon the room before Roxanne offered a barely visible nod.

"We need Royal steel to stand a chance against their army," Francis spoke, meeting Gabriel's gaze. "We are here to break into the palace's vault and find archives on how to make it for our army."

"I've made Royal steel before." Gabriel' brow crooked slightly. "Is that it?"

"No, you have not," I scoffed, shaking my head.

"Brian taught me." Gabriel shrugged.

"Nonsense!" I laughed at his foolishness. "He couldn't have!" My voice cut through the space.

"And yet he did." Gabriel's lips turned into a small smile.

"Do you still remember how to?" Simon asked. "Can you make it?"

"He is lying." My hands shook.

"It hurts that you think the worst of me, Lia." Gabriel sighed. "Brian taught me before our last battle in Vel'mi'. And yes," he turned to Simon. "I still remember how to."

Impossible. My stomach turned upside down as I leaned against the wall. My lungs ached with every breath I took.

"It's quite easy," Gabriel started. "But I still need—" he trailed off, looking over everyone before continuing, "—the golden flint kept in a hidden room behind the Royal forge."

I glanced down at my mother's ring that sat heavy on my ring finger. The symbol of my parents' nonexistent love now decorated my hand deep crimson. The symbol that we took from the grave of my resting mother was now useless.

We disturbed the dead for nothing.

I was going to be sick.

"So we must go to the palace either way." Simon sighed.

"Where is this hidden room you speak of?" I held my breath, already having a great idea where that was. Brian had mentioned the mysterious flint once after scolding me and Sandra for playing hide and seek deep in the dungeons, near the forge.

"Neither of you are allowed here, and you know it!" He'd yelled at us. *"You are lucky I was the one to catch you here, and not our King."*

I swallowed when Gabriel met my gaze. "There is a door behind the chimney."

I nodded as a set of new problems arose: the rooms underneath the palace did not have hidden passages—the only way in and out was through the Royal corridors, and—now guarded—doors.

"Did you tell Caleb?" Francis narrowed his eyes on Gabriel.

"What? No." Gabriel shook his head. "I would never share a secret like that."

"I am glad you can at least keep something to yourself," I mumbled, trying to remember the best path to the forge—I remembered none.

Gabriel sighed. "Here, these are for you." He passed me a small casket decorated with crimson ravens trapped in a black widow's web.

I opened the casket, revealing dozens of letters carefully arranged in order. I closed it in an instant when I saw the name of the sender. *Brian.*

"It is decided then." Francis glanced at the casket in my hands before meeting the eyes of our company. "We are going to the forge with the sunset." He got up from the couch, everyone else followed.

"I am coming with you." Gabriel nodded along, getting up from the stairs.

"You are a human." Francis shook his head. "Breaking into a palace full of Wurdulacs isn't such a great idea as a human."

"I wouldn't say it's a great idea for anyone," Gabriel countered. "But I can take care of myself. And I am the only one who's made Royal steel before. You need me."

Francis sighed, looking over at me; when I offered him a shrug, he relented. "Fine. You will come back with us to Faris, but you are staying to watch over our horses at the palace. It's final," he said.

Gabriel rolled his eyes, but didn't argue.

"Tomorrow is promising to be long." Simon sighed, taking a sip of whatever it was in his canteen.

The dark green curtains of the small room hid me, Francis, and Roxanne from the sunlight.

The room downstairs didn't carry any beds, leaving us to the woolen blankets on the floor. Simon and Gabriel disappeared upstairs to a similar arrangement.

The house seemed rather empty, despite Gabriel claiming he had lived here for the last five years. The walls held wooden shelves that carried anything from articles of clothing to jars of seeds to plant in the spring.

"You can never leave her, Francis," Roxanne's voice traveled through the darkness of the room as all of us lay on the floor by the walls across from each other: Francis and I by one side, Roxanne by the other. "Or she will find and murder you, and I'm afraid I will be far too entertained to stop her."

"I am right here, Roxanne." I rolled my eyes, staring at the ceiling of the tiny room. The corners of the ceiling were covered in spider webs and darkened spots from leaks.

"I know," Roxanne said, I could hear the smirk on her face. "My point still stands."

"I wasn't planning on leaving." Francis' hands pulled me closer in his embrace, fixing the blanket around us. "Now go to sleep, both of you," he said as my eyes closed against his warmth.

Chapter 33. Court Jester.

The sun disappeared from the horizon, announcing our time had come. I wiped the sleep off my eyes, sitting up on the wooden floors.

Surprisingly, I felt refreshed, despite spending the whole day on the hard surface—my body full of strength, my mind full of determination.

I looked around the space, noting that Roxanne had already departed from the room—her woolen blanket splattered on the cold floor.

"How did you sleep?" Francis got to his feet beside me, offering me a hand.

"I slept well." I took his hand as he pulled me upwards. "You?"

"I always sleep well with you in my arms." Francis winked, passing me the cloak I'd left on the stool in the corner. "Come, we must be on our way." His fingers interlocked with mine, walking out of the room.

The strong smell of warm human food floated in the air of the kitchenette. The open curtains revealed the growing Moon and dozens of stars. I sat on the couch, as I had last night, willing my heart to calm before our upcoming trip.

"Breakfast?" Simon asked, offering us the bottle of wine filled with blood. When Francis and I shook our heads, he merely shrugged, taking a sip for himself.

Simon and Gabriel sat at the stools adjacent to the table, a plate of freshly cooked eggs sat before Gabriel.

"Uh—" Gabriel mumbled, mouthful. "Please have some, I don't feel like serving as a meal tonight." He chewed on his eggs, staring at me and Francis.

My palms sweated as my throat ached at the reminder of my growing hunger. Gabriel's presence certainly did not help.

His pulse fastened under my gaze, the smell of his flesh reaching my bothered beast. I bit the inside of my cheek in an attempt to silence it, in vain.

I glanced at Francis as panic slowly clawed at my stomach. How could we not think of my hunger beforehand?

"Don't worry about it," Francis whispered into my ear, squeezing my hand into his as he sat beside me. A soft smile appeared on his face as though it was the answer to all of my silent questions—

The main door to the house flew open, allowing the cold air to sweep through the space, allowing the warm smell of blood to ease. "Did anyone—" Roxanne appeared at the threshold of the house, snowflakes covering her hair. "Oh, good, you are awake." She looked me and Francis up and down. "We still need to figure out our plan before we go." She took off her snowy shoes before stepping onto the rug. "What is the best way to get to the forge?" She faced me.

"There is no path leading to the dungeons, we will have to walk through the other paths closest to it," I replied; my heart beat faster.

"That is far too dangerous," Simon noted, taking another sip of his drink.

"That is not true," Gabriel said, sending another piece of his breakfast—or rather dinner—into his mouth. And annoyance, at his knowledge of the palace exceeding mine, sent another dose of unsettlement into my veins. "There is one path that leads straight to that room, it connects to the King's rooms."

"The King's room doesn't have a passage," I stated confidently, unexplained anger blinking through my vision.

"It does not, but the corridor from the back gates is right next to it." Gabriel shrugged, oblivious to my distress.

"That gate will be guarded," I argued. "The gate is far too big to leave exposed."

"That is the only way," Gabriel insisted. "And it's no more than half a dozen Wurdulacs—at least that was the amount of Royal guards." He averted his gaze to Francis. "Surely you can get past them."

Half a dozen warriors didn't sound like a lot, given my company's profound skills with weaponry, yet we needed to get rid of them without bringing attention to ourselves. This was a horrible plan.

"We will have to figure it out when we are there," Francis replied to my silent question. "If that is the only way, we have no choice but to try."

"It is better than strolling through the whole palace, hoping no one would notice." Gabriel nodded, finishing up his meal before sending the dirty plate into the metal basket that served as a sink.

"Let's not waste time then," Simon corked his bottle before walking outside of the house, waiting for the rest of us to follow.

I doubleknotted the laces of my boots, walking out the door after Francis.

With each passing day, the nature warmed so slightly; the snow at the threshold of the house, that had been present last night, now turned into a puddle that wetted my boots.

"I think there is a better way," I told Francis as we walked towards our horses. "Walking through this gate—" I scoffed. "We might as well scream our exact position to the Wurdulacs."

"I'm sure there is, love, but we have already lost time with the foolish ball, we cannot wait another day in the hope that we will come up with something more clever," Francis sighed. "Everything will be well, all right?" He returned the dagger I had been forced to give up last night, putting it into the empty scabbard at my belt before helping me to mount my horse.

"All right." I nodded, sending Annabelle towards the Royal grounds.

The trip to the palace took an additional hour from where Gabriel resided—no wonder his village was not yet bothered by the Wurdulacs' return: as their village hid in the very depths of the woods, with nothing but the forest's spirits surrounding it.

Gabriel led our way through the woods as we all followed after: Francis by my side, Simon and Roxanne a few yards behind.

My eyes fell onto Gabriel's throat far more often than was appropriate as the growing hunger spun my head into frenzy.

I bit my lip, forcing the air into my lungs: in, out, in—

"For you," Francis' voice reached my ears as he took the canteen out of his inside pocket. His hand stretched out, offering me the drink.

"I can't," I whispered as my heartbeat quickened. It was foolish really: to deny the blood that was already taken and spare the possible disaster. Yet I was determined to manage without either. I starved for weeks before, surely I could survive a night. Though, Gabriel's presence complicated my wish.

"Cordelia." Francis crooked his head, forcing my gaze to his. "Take it," his voice sharpened.

My brows furrowed, eyeing the canteen. I shook my head, not believing Francis would offer me human blood: knowing my feelings on the matter.

"Just try it," he pleaded, looking around at our company. "Trust me," he added.

I filled my lungs, my hands reluctantly stretching for the canteen.

"Trust me." A sinister smile shadowed on his lips when he nodded.

I swallowed the growing lump in my throat, bringing the drink near my lips.

The familiar aroma reached my senses as my stomach fluttered; my eyes flew to Francis, my brows furrowing in confusion. He offered me a swift nod as he winked, sending my cheeks aflame.

The first drop of Francis' blood fell onto my tongue, soothing the growing ache in my throat. The familiar taste brought clarity to my maddened mind.

I drank his blood out of the canteen, trying not to think much of how it found its way into the metal container.

"Thank you," I murmured, finishing the contents before passing the canteen back to him. My cheeks warmed under his gaze anew.

"Any time, love." Francis winked, pocketing the empty canteen back into his cloak.

I offered him a soft smile before glancing back towards our pathway.

Gabriel rode a few yards away, whistling a familiar tune to the birds. His nonchalant mood felt odd within the purpose of this journey.

Though, I supposed that was his character, and the reason my strict, serious, brother valued his company.

Guilt crippled deep in my chest as the last of the fog disappeared from my mind. No longer bothered with his human presence, shame enveloped my heart whole.

I'd threatened to take his life last night, and yet he had been nothing but helpful with our mission. I'd accused him of betrayal, yet forgot everything he had done for me and my brother.

I offered Francis a glance before making Annabelle walk faster, reaching Gabriel, who rode in front.

"I'm sorry about yesterday." I cleared my throat. "And for using you in my schemes."

"Don't be." Gabriel laughed, shrugging. "I knew you never liked me. Not like that. That's what friends are for, I suppose." He offered me his boyish smile.

Ashamed, I looked down at my hands that grasped onto the reins for dear life. "I'm glad you are alive and well," I added, meeting his gaze.

"You too." He nodded. "A vampire, huh?" He looked me up and down. "I thought the rumors of a Royal Princess turned vampire were tales."

I shook my head, sighing. "Caleb turned me for Kane and Mories."

"Mories?" Gabriel's brows furrowed.

"She thought I would be safer this way." I swallowed the growing lump in my throat at the memory of her. Where was she? Was she still alive? "I suppose she was right, after what happened to the rest of my family."

"I'm sorry about your siblings." Gabriel nodded, his lips turning into a thin line as though unsure of what to say next.

"How have you been?" I spared him the awkwardness.

"I've been well." A slow smile stretched his lips. "I help at the local school in the village during winters, and on the fields during summers." He met my eyes before adding, "It's been peaceful."

"A teacher?" I laughed, not believing my own ears. "What could *you* possibly teach those poor children?" My laughter traveled through the night forest.

"Laugh, laugh," Gabriel mocked. "But I am smarter than you think." His bright voice swept through our company. "They chose me as Brain's confidant for my mind." He pointed at his temple.

"I thought they chose you as the prince's personal jester," Roxanne chimed in.

"That too, of course." Gabriel shrugged as the first battlements neared. He ordered his horse to the right, off the pathway, into the depths of the woods. "This way," he told us. "The gate is on this side of the palace."

I caught Francis' worried gaze before he could hide it under a soft smile, taking a turn towards my nightmare.

Chapter 34.
Golden Flint.

Two guards stood adjacent to the wide-open gate, one of them leaned on the wall, his eyes closed.

"There's only two of them," I whispered to Francis as we crouched behind a line of dense spruce. "They can't be that arrogant; something is wrong."

Even Mother knew the importance of guarding this gate from the outside.

"Perhaps Kane ran out of live shields." Roxanne charged the first arrow with a Royal steel tip, pointing it at one of the guards.

"Or they are inside, waiting for someone foolish to take the bait," Francis mumbled. "At least there is no fire surrounding them."

"Can you reach them from here," Simon glanced at Francis and Roxanne.

"Yes," they hissed in unison, their faces crossing with offense.

"I'm merely making sure. You both only have one shot." Simon rolled his eyes before his features turned serious. "If anyone comes running from the outside after your assault, we will still be able to reach Gabriel and our horses from here; if no one does, we will go in." He met each of our gazes.

Roxanne and Francis nodded, gathering to their feet—a charged bow in Roxanne's hand, a Royal steel dagger in Francis'.

They took a small breath in before letting their weapons free.

The arrow cut through the air with a muffled whistle, boring straight through the Wurdulac's warrior attire, finding its place deep inside of his heart.

The dagger spun through the air at the perfect arch, landing inside of another man's throat. Blood spattered as he choked, his hands trying to stop the flow, yet it mattered not—the poison from the blade would reach his heart within minutes.

Both men slid down the wall of the gate; both men stared at the Moon with vacant eyes.

"No one is coming," Simon broke the growing silence. "Let's go." He got to his feet, searching every inch of the tree-line before breaking into a run.

Francis flew after him, leaving me and Roxanne to follow behind.

We ran through the exposed field, towards the wide-open gate, as I counted every step I took. Once I reached thirty two, the gates stood before me, their golden bars shone under the bleak moonlight.

"Wait here," Francis hissed at us as he disappeared behind the entrance.

Simon followed after him, nevertheless.

Roxanne rolled her eyes, yet stayed put by my side.

My heart banged against my rib cage as I waited for Francis to reappear. Minutes passed, yet only silence followed—

The steps grew heavier behind the gate. Roxanne charged another arrow pointing it into the dark tunnel; I unsheathed the Royal steel dagger—

"It's clear," Francis walked out of the shadows, Simon by his side. "Lead the way." Francis nodded at me as I walked through the opening: into the corridor I'd rarely used.

The drops of water dripped off the stoned walls, reminding me of the sound from the dungeons. We weren't far from the place I'd lost my sister, and the memories invaded my mind like never before.

I breathed through my mouth as nausea worked its way up my throat, walking my friends to the heart of the Royal palace.

Two turns to the left, three to the right, down the stairs, through the forge, I recited Gabriel's instructions, though I could find my way around without his assistance.

Francis held my hand, bringing comfort to my crying soul, as our quiet steps journeyed through the tunnel until the rusty, metal stairs appeared on our path.

"I will go first." Francis walked past me, leaving me to follow after as he made his way down the set of stairs.

The metal grinded under our steps, the drops of water fell on our heads from the ceiling.

"The room is empty," Francis whispered, offering me a hand on the last two steps.

The room was empty, indeed. The forge my father cherished now only carried a beaten up chimney in the corner.

The walls that had held swords and daggers years ago now stood bare.

Three pairs of eyes bored into mine.

"The room is behind the chimney." I walked towards the metal door that perfectly matched the stone walls. "It's here—"

The stairs screeched under heavy steps, freezing us in place.

Damnation.

My heart banged in my ears.

Damnation—

We were trapped in a room with only one exist—

Weapons drawn, Francis pushed me behind him, waiting for whoever followed us here to appear.

Roxanne pointed her arrow at the exit, ready to let it fly free.

The tip of Simon's sword faced the nearing shadow—

The shadow stopped: the face of our enemy appeared. Roxanne's arrow glided through the air.

"Dear Gods!" Caleb swung to the side, avoiding the arrow by an inch. "It's me!" He put his hands up in surrender. "It's me!" He walked out of the shadow; no one lowered their weapons.

"What are you doing here?" Francis seethed, his dagger ready to fly.

"What *am I* doing here?" Caleb shook his head. "What *are you* doing here?"

Francis charged towards him, a muffled roar pushed through his throat as he shoved Caleb against the stoned wall. "With the Moon as my witness, I tried to spare your pathetic life." He brought the Royal steel dagger to Caleb's heart.

"We don't have time for this Francis!" Roxanne hissed, her bow still charged with an arrow.

"We can't let him walk away." Francis allowed himself a glance at Roxanne. "He will report us to his leader," Francis spat out.

"Let me help," Caleb swallowed, eyeing the dagger by his heart. "I can help with whatever you are here to do." His breathing heavied the longer Francis held the dagger against his flesh.

"After you burned my house to the ground?" Francis seethed.

"I had to." Caleb shook his head, sweat falling down his forehead. "Kane was suspicious of me, and I needed his trust." Caleb closed his eyes, drawing a small breath in. "I know all of his plans. Please, trust me." He swallowed before adding, "I will kill myself before I betray you again, brother. Please, trust me."

The dagger stood unmoving against Caleb's chest, Francis' hand visibly shook around the hilt.

"Kane is planning an attack on the Barren's estate in a few days," Caleb whispered. "Let me help."

"Let go of him, Francis." Roxanne lowered her bow, her voice echoing through the forge. "We are wasting time, and he might be of use." Roxanne looked Caleb up and down.

Francis glanced at her before lowering his dagger, "If he runs, shoot him," he said, walking back towards the hidden door—with no handle—behind the chimney. "How do we open this?" He asked me.

"There has to be a key hidden behind one of these stones." I felt the stones around the door, pushing at their corners.

"You won't find the key there," Caleb walked towards the door, his hand in the pocket of his cloak. "Because I have it." He passed the silver key with a Royal stamp at the top of it. "I found it a few weeks ago, but the room behind is empty, whatever you are looking for is not there."

"Perhaps you weren't looking well enough." Simon put his sword back into its scabbard.

"The room is empty." Caleb shook his head.

I took the silver key, setting it into the hidden lock as my stomach turned in nausea. If Caleb was right, we were doomed.

The lock opened when I rotated the key, the door opened silently at a slight push. I took a step into the empty room.

"Simon, guard the entrance by the stairs," Francis instructed before following after me. "You guard the entrance to this room," he told Roxanne. "You," he pointed at Caleb. "Better start telling us about Kane's plans before I decide you are useless."

Caleb cleared his throat, joining us in the empty space. "Kane has lost a lot of his support." He looked around the room before meeting Francis' gaze. "After gaining the power of human royalty, many did not want to attack their own."

I walked along the wall, my fingers brushing over the cold stones, searching for entrance. "Gabriel said the flint is behind one of the stones—same as the key."

Francis followed my lead, reaching where I couldn't.

"What do you mean by *their own*?" Francis glanced at Caleb before pushing at every corner of each stone.

"Kane is planning to take over Silverstone and Faris." Caleb began to search for the flint as well. "Not everyone agrees with the latter: many have family and friends in the vampire village."

"Wasn't it obvious all along?" Roxanne's voice echoed through the room as she stood by the entrance: her arrow drawn. "Kane didn't make his wish of bringing the whole Kingdom—including vampires—to their knees a secret."

Caleb shook his head. "While he openly shared his goals with his supporters, not many believed he actually wished for the vampire village to fall." Caleb sighed, moving onto the next row of stones. "Needless to say, now that he is on the throne, he is not very good at sharing his power."

"How much of his army is still by his side," I asked; my lungs squeezing tight from the lack of air in the stone room.

"Majority, but I'm sure given the opportunity, some will run for their dear lives," Caleb's voice lowered. "Just like what happened when the palace was taken and humans fought back. Many in his army aren't warriors, merely lunatics who decided Kane's world is the paradise needed. He has about a thousand people in total."

My finger froze above the stone. *A thousand?* That was far more than what we had: Silverstone and Faris combined. Numbers weren't on our side—that was certain.

"But they don't have many weapons," Caleb continued. "They are saving the Royal steel for the attack on Faris, as there are only about two hundred royal steel weapons in their possession. If we manage to make Royal steel for every person in your army, we stand a chance."

A chance.

"My advice," Caleb sighed. "Is to combine your forces with Barren's."

The room fell into silence, the drops of water from the ceiling echoed down the chambers—

"There." I pointed at the brick that had an odd gap, connecting to the stone next to it. "It must open somehow." I pushed on the stone' every corner.

"Let me." Francis unsheathed his dagger, the blade sliding into the gap like butter. "I feel something." His lips turned into a thin line, his eyes shut close. "Something like a lever."

"Try my dagger," I unsheathed my weapon. "My blade is thinner."

Francis eyed my dagger before taking the offering. "It's stuck," he said, battling with the stone.

Simon rushed into the room, a finger tight to his lips. "I hear steps from the opposite side of the tunnel," he whispered. "We need to hurry."

"Got it," Francis whispered, pushing the dagger upwards.

The stone opened wide, revealing a hidden pocket within. A sparkling golden flint lay atop a wooden board, its sides shone bright even in this lightless room.

Francis held out the flint, crimson stones decorated its every corner—

A loud ringing vibrated through the walls of the forge, the bells from the palace's tower pierced through the air.

My eyes widened as I met my companions' startled expressions—

"What in the Kingdom—" Simon unsheathed his sword: a dagger in his other hand.

"We have to go." Caleb rushed to close the wicked stone, charging towards the door. Roxanne and Simon rushed down the stairs before him.

"Kane knows someone has invaded the palace, he is going to drop the portcullis." He held the door for Francis and I as we hurried out of the forge.

"Portcullis?" I yelled to Caleb as my heart skipped a beat. Francis pushed me up the stairs, his hand tightly holding mine. "They haven't worked ever since the Crimson War!"

"They do now!" Caleb yelled rushing after us. "Run!" He screamed to Simon who stood by the corner at the end of stairs, waiting for us to make it all the way up before breaking into a run.

Chapter 35. You Must Go, Love.

My legs carried me forward, my eyes planted at the turn of the passage Roxanne had disappeared behind. It was at least a hundred yards to the portcullis that I knew of: if the bells signaled for them to drop, we had no chance of making it on time.

I glanced behind me for a split second before taking the first turn of the tunnel; Francis ran behind me, ushering me forward: Caleb and Simon fell into step behind, their weapons drawn.

"Duck!" Caleb yelled, and we all dropped to the ground before the first arrow flew past us. "Run!" his scream echoed through the stone walls as Francis pulled me upwards. "Faster! They are on our trail!"

They are trapping us into the portcullis, like prey—

I swung at the second turn of the passage: two more to go.

We won't make—

More arrows flew past my head when Francis pushed me down to the ground.

"Fire!" Caleb's voice rang through the bells as a hot wave of air hit my back. An agonizing scream followed after.

My own scream ripped through my throat when I glanced behind me—

My legs refused to obey when my eyes planted on the horrid scene. "Simon!" I cried.

"Run!" Francis barked, pushing me forward.

"Simon!" A roar ripped through my throat as the arrow that had planted deep in his chest caught aflame. The black shadow traveled down his skin in every direction, turning it into ash. A silent scream froze on his face when the flame reached it as well.

In a fraction of a second his flesh was no more than ash, falling down on the ground—

"Don't look!" Francis pushed me before him as we reached the third turn.

Roxanne stopped at the next corner, her arrow flying past us.

Francis' hand squeezed mine before dropping it. "Keep going!" He unsheathed his daggers, holding them out for a throw. "Go!" He stopped at the corner, averting his gaze from me.

My lungs cried from pain as my legs carried me away from our followers, away from Francis. I managed a quick glance when the daggers left his hands, flying towards his targets.

"Which way?" Roxanne yelled from ahead of me.

"Left!" I told her, glancing behind me. "Francis!" I screamed, when he ran after me emptyhanded. A second later, Caleb appeared behind him: his sword now carried crimson.

I dropped to the floor, sliding my dagger towards Francis.

"Run!" Francis caught my weapon as a figure in a dark blue cloak appeared behind the corner, a few yards away from Caleb—two swords in their hands.

"Behind!" I yelled to Caleb as my legs carried me towards the fourth—last—corner.

Caleb swung his sword, cutting the waist of the figure in half in one swift move—

Roxanne stood at the entrance to the passage, her arrow drawn, pointing in our direction before it flew above our heads, landing in her target. The only sign of her success was a heavy thud of a body against the stone floors.

"Hurry!" She yelled, looking upwards when—

The shriek of chains against each other reached my ears above me.

The portcullis were about to drop.

"Francis!" I screamed.

"A little more!" His boots hit the stone floor behind me. "I'm right behind you!"

The chains howled, my heart stopped.

I halted right before the golden gate, looking up to where the screeching of chains were coming from.

"Francis!" I screamed, refusing to cross without him.

Roxanne' hand caught mine in an instant as she yanked me forward—

My ears popped at the sound of metal hitting the stones.

My legs stumbled upon themselves when our bodies hit the ground. I lay atop Roxanne when my lungs screamed out in pain—

The banging echoed in my ears—

"Fran—" I rushed to my feet, my head spinning the grounds and the skies together. "Franci—" I turned back to the golden gates. The rusty bars cut through the ground beneath us.

Francis stood behind the portcullis.

"No!" I pulled on the metal, willing it to move—it didn't budge. "No." Hot tears streamed down my face.

"Shh." Francis' hand fell upon mine as he pushed the gilded flint into my palm. "Shh, it's all right, it's all right." He put the dagger I passed him back into my scabbard.

"Francis," a whisper pushed past my lips.

"You must go, love." His finger wiped the tears off my cheeks through the metal grids. "I will be all right, I swear it to you." His eyes landed behind me, offering a quick nod, before his eyes met mine once again. "You must go, love." He took a step backwards, standing beside Caleb. His lips shook into a soft smile as he nodded at me. "Everything will be well."

"No." I shook my head, my hands fighting with unmoving bars. "No!" I bellowed as Roxanne's strong hands wrapped around my waist. "Francis!"

Caleb's throat bubbled when he glanced at me. He unsheathed his dagger before averting his gaze to Francis. "You will have to trust me."

"Francis!" I screamed when Roxanne's hands pulled me away from the bars.

"We must go before Wurdulacs arrive," her voice broke as she dragged me away from Francis.

"Everything will be well, Princess." A soft smile spread across Francis' face before he added, "I love you." He nodded, his eyes filling with a softness that was foreign to me. "Everything will be well," he said before turning to Caleb. "What's the plan?"

"Play along." Caleb walked around Francis, grabbing him by his hair, planting a dagger against his throat.

Caleb's eyes met mine for a split second before he drew a slow breath. "I caught them!" he yelled into the tunnel, walking Francis towards the darkness.

Chapter 36.
Aflame.

"Let go of me!" My voice broke as heavy tears streamed down my cheeks.

"I'm sorry." Roxanne dragged me back towards the woods.

"Let go," I choked on my own tears when another pair of hands grabbed my other side, carrying me away. "Please!" I cried out when Gabriel's palm fell onto my mouth.

"The Wurdulacs will hear us, and then we are all dead!" he hissed before dropping his hands to my waist, effortlessly picking me up before breaking into a run. Roxanne followed after. "Did anyone see you going this direction?" He asked Roxanne.

"No, but I'm sure they will soon realize Francis and Simon weren't the only ones there."

The cold fabric of Gabriel's cloak soaked my tears as he carried me through the woods; my palm fell onto my mouth, muffling the cries that fought for their way out.

"Are you injured?" Gabriel turned his gaze to me.

I shook my head, my eyes shutting closed.

The fire erupted in my mind, the fire that took Simon away. His agonizing scream thundered in my ears. The smell of burnt flesh spun my stomach into nausea.

"Can you ride?" Gabriel released his hold until my feet felt the ground.

My knees weakened as I leaned on the willow tree.

The willow tree, which I'd often climbed as a child, hid us from unwanted view, hid the tunnel Francis disappeared into: away from me.

I took a step out of the sanctuary, towards the open view of the palace grounds.

The dark night skies were peaceful, laughing at the disruption that had occurred under its watch. The snow fell slowly onto the palace's walls as though it was no more than an ordinary night. And nothing but the most damning storm spawned deep within me.

"She will ride." Roxanne caught my arm before I managed another step in the direction of the palace. Her fingers wrapped around my wrist in an unrelenting grasp.

Gabriel untightened the horses' reins, letting Francis' and Simon's free.

"We can't leave him." My voice shook as I met Roxanne's empty gaze. The tears froze in the corners of her brown, glowing eyes. "We can't—"

The cold snow froze my own tears when my eyes caught a figure in a blue cloak running in our direction from the corner of the palace.

"Let me go!" I hissed at Roxanne, fighting with her firm grasp. "Let them take me, it will give you more time to get away." I shoved the flint into her pocket.

"Get on your horse!" she hissed back, shoving me towards Annabelle. "You can't help him, not by yourself and not right now!" She shoved Annabelle's reins into my palms.

"And you cannot help him if you are dead! And if you don't get on this horse right now that is what awaits you." She pushed me into the saddle before mounting her own horse.

"They are going after us!" Gabriel screamed as three figures in dark blue cloaks ran towards where we stood: their bows drawn.

"Go!" Roxanne screamed when Gabriel ordered his horse into the depths of the forest.

I glanced back at the Wurdulacs as they shortened the distance. Their arrows pointed at us.

"Cordelia!" Roxanne drew her own bow, sending the first arrow flying straight into the closest man's chest. The arrow did not stop his run, as he simply broke off the end of a weapon: dropping it onto the snow. "I will kill you myself if you don't start moving right this moment!" She sent another arrow flying in our followers' direction.

The small flame erupted in the Wurdulac's hands as they set the tips of their arrows aflame before letting them free.

"Fuck!" Roxanne ducked, ordering for her horse to run. "Cordelia!" She glanced back, yet all I could see was the fire taking over Simon's flesh—

"Cordelia!" Roxanne yelled, spooking Annabelle into a run: away from the flaming arrows, away from the palace, away from Francis.

I love you. He had told me.

And I hadn't said it back.

Chapter 37. Spare Daggers.

The woods were as quiet as the morning lakes when the Wurdulacs had finally lost our traces. The bare trees froze in place where we stood, allowing our horses a swift break after their sprint.

At least an hour had passed since we'd escaped the palace: at least an hour of Francis being trapped behind the enemies' walls.

"We have to go back." I searched Roxanne's and Gabriel's gazes. "No one is following us now. We have to go back." The tears spilled from my eyes anew as the reality crushed upon me with excruciating speed. The claws scratched from the inside of my rib cage; my hand fell onto my throbbing heart.

"We can't get him out now—not when the palace is filled with Wurdulacs." Roxanne swallowed. "And we need more weapons." She shook her head, lowering her gaze.

"But—" I started.

"Francis is clever, he will be fine. Caleb is with him." Roxanne's gaze hardened. "He knows we will come for him when Kane attacks. We have to warn everyone who resides at the Barren's duchy and prepare our armies."

"They will kill him by then!" I cried. My hands shook at the mere idea of his suffering.

"We have no other choice." Roxanne's throat bubbled. "You can't help him if they throw you in a dungeon, Cordelia. And after our failure today, they will be on high alert for anyone near the palace. We have to wait for a distraction."

"And if Kane doesn't attack in the next few days, what then!" I demanded. "What if Caleb lied! What if—"

"Kane will attack, and you know it. Francis is far from his priority right now," Roxanne sighed, shaking her head. "We just have to hope Francis' mouth doesn't kill him before Kane's attack happens."

I shook my head, my gaze rising to the cruel Moon. *Why do you do this to me?* I wanted to scream at her unfairness. *Have I not paid for my many wrongs yet?* A silent tear slid down my cheek.

"It's just a few days." Roxanne reached for my hand, giving it a squeeze. "And right now, you need to focus on convincing Barren to work with us," her voice sharp as the tip of her blade. "You have to make sure that whatever strategy he chooses for this battle works in our favor, as well as the people in Faris."

"I know nothing of war strategies, and he knows that." I shook my head. "He won't listen to me."

"Make sure he does," Roxanne bit out. "This battle is our last chance at surviving the Wurdulacs and getting Francis out alive."

I wiped my tears, filling my lungs with as much air as possible.

"Do you understand?" Roxanne searched my eyes. "Collect yourself, and do what needs to be done, Cordelia."

"You can do this, Lia." Gabriel's gaze bored into mine.

I managed a small nod in reply, though I felt far from the confidence she wished me to act upon.

"Let's not waste time." Roxanne dropped my hand, ordering her horse to run.

Barren's castle stood quiet under the night skies. The stone courtyard beyond the gate was now cleared of melting snow, the soil of a little garden peaked through the layers of white.

"Haven't been here in ages," Gabriel muttered as we slowed our horses right before the gates.

"I wish I could say the same." I drew a deep breath before dismounting Annabelle and walking towards the guards standing behind the obstacle. They drew their weapons as I neared, their eyes surveying me for threats. "Allow us entry," my voice banged through the courtyard. "We brought His Grace the weaponry he asked for."

The guards glanced at each other before one of them broke into a run towards the main doors. It must have been at least a quarter of an hour before he came back, whispering into another's guard's ear the message William had sent him with.

I rolled my eyes at such theatrics, though I stayed put, awaiting their verdict—they stayed silent.

The sun was about to come up and they knew it as they watched our every move. Were they to not allow our entrance, we were as good as dead—save for Gabriel, who stood by my side, sending furious glares in the guards' direction.

Gabriel's shoulders straightened; his chin held high, despite the disproving gazes of the soldiers that stood by the other side of the gates.

"If Barren doesn't want our help in this war, we will be on our way," Roxanne seethed at guards.

"Let's go." I turned back towards our horses.

"Wait!" One of the guards hurried to open the gate. "His Grace awaits you in his study," he said, walking to the side, freeing our way.

"Barren will pay for the wait," Roxanne said, caring not who heard as we walked through the courtyard.

"If something happens," I whispered to my friends. "Go all the way to the bottom of the stairs, their passages are hidden underneath the castle." I gave Roxanne and Gabriel the same instructions I'd given Francis a few months ago as we walked through the empty corridors, towards the courthall. No warrior accompanied us.

"What good would that do?" Roxanne mumbled. "The sun is about to come up, we are trapped here."

"You both are vampires," Gabriel shook his head. "No matter what they say, they are petrified to death by you."

"Gods, I hope that's enough." Roxanne sighed, her boots squeaking against the marble floors.

"They need us, and they know it," Gabriel argued as we took the last turn towards the courthall.

The closed door of Barren's *study* appeared at the end of the corridor. No guard stood by the entrance.

I swung the door open, without waiting for permission. Barren's head flew in my direction: the crease between his eyebrows deepened.

Roxanne and Gabriel walked by my sides as we made our way through the candlelit room: every curtain drawn closed.

Barren sat at the head of the table, his hands crossed atop of it; despite his freshly brushed hair and well fit attire, his eyes gave away the annoyance of being woken so early.

His personal guard stood a few feet behind, eyeing the weapons at our belts.

"Gather your commanders, we have much to discuss." I sat at the other head of the long table—Roxanne and Gabriel by my sides.

"I thought you had brought me your part of the bargain, yet you seem to be emptyhanded," Barren tsked, looking us up and down. "I told you, Cordelia, no weapons—no army."

"Gabriel knows how to make Royal steel. He will get to work right after we talk through our battle plan." I eyed my opponent. "Given our time is short, and Kane is planning to attack within a few days, I suggest you call for your commanders. Now."

Barren sat unmoving, yet a slight clench of his jaw gave away the concern my words had brought out of him.

"If you want our army to fight alongside yours when the Wurdulacs come, I suggest you do as she says," Roxanne added, leaning back on her chair.

"And why would I believe your tales?" William smirked. "The agreement was: you bring us the weapons, and then we talk—not the other way around."

"You are committing your people to death by wasting our time," Gabriel's low voice bounced off the walls of the courthall.

"Ah! Gabriel, is it?" Barren's eyes squinted. "I remember you running like a puppy after His Highness." He averted his gaze to me. "Cordelia, you seem to exchange lovers more often than dresses." William laughed.

Gabriel's hands turned into fists, but before he managed to reply to William's foul remark, I spoke, "I would wish you luck in the upcoming battle, yet all I can hope for is for your people to have a quick, painless death: for they do not deserve to pay for the mistakes of their incompetent leader." I turned to the guard that stood by Barren's side. "If you want to live, call for all of the commanders that are currently here. Now."

The poor guard with black as night hair glanced between me and Barren—his eyes filling with fear when Barren's lips turned into the ugliest of smiles—yet he stood still by his side, nevertheless.

"You cannot give orders to *my* people, dear Cordelia." Barren smirked, the greasy strand of white hair falling onto his forehead.

"Soon you will have no people to order around." I unsheathed my dagger, averting my gaze back to the guard. "Do as I say, or this dagger finds its place in *His Grace's* heart."

Barren's laughter echoed through the court room, yet it was cut short when I let go of the dagger, sending it flying inches from Barren's ear, piercing straight in between the two stones behind his head.

If I said it was pure skill, I would be lying, for that was the first time I managed to throw a dagger successfully without Francis' presence and advice.

Barren's face turned the shade of his hair, glancing behind him at my successful throw. William swallowed, turning to his guard, who drew his sword in an instant—the guard's hands visibly shook as he held the sword in our direction. None of us batted an eye.

"Summon the commanders." Barren told the guard, who offered him a swift nod before hurrying out of the courthall, his sword still drawn.

"I suggest you listen to me moving forward, William." I smiled. "I have more daggers to spare."

Chapter 38. Her Highness.

The room fell into silence as Tamira, the grayhaired man, and their seconds, took their seats across from each other; their features were unreadable as they awaited their orders.

"Arthur," William addressed the grayhaired man—his personal commander, I guessed. "Tamira," he turned to the commander of the Royal army. "I have summoned you here on such an early morning, for it seems we will be attacked by Wurdulacs. I order you to—" Barren started.

"By our knowledge, Kane and his army will be here within the next couple of days." I interrupted before Barren managed to finish his sentence. His jaw clenched at my boldness, yet he refrained from saying a word: his eyes flickered to the dagger at my waist. "Kane's army is approximately a thousand people, but they don't have enough Royal steel weaponry to supply every warrior. Which means, we can fight on equal grounds once Gabriel produces enough Royal steel for our armies." I pointed at the man by my side. "However, the numbers are still on their side, and we must find a way to eliminate as many as we can before they arrive at Silverstone."

"We must evacuate the residents of Silverstone first." Tamira nodded, glancing at Barren. "Then we can establish our forces around the perimeter of the region."

"The residents can seek shelter at the human village near Faris," Roxanne suggested. "They will be safe there for the time being, as long as we manage to funnel the Wurdulacs here—at the castle, where stone walls can protect our armies from direct attack."

"Agreed," Arthur offered a slight nod, turning to Barren for approval. "Do I have your authority to start the evacuation of the local villages immediately, Your Grace?"

"Are you mad, people? We all must evacuate!" Barren stood up from his chair. "The Wurdulacs are coming here, their army is five times as big as mine—"

"Evacuate where? If we run, we would just prolong our suffering, not be rid of the threat." Roxanne rolled her eyes; her arms crossed at her chest. "They will attack Faris next if they are successful here, it's best to have the battle at this castle: when we are at our strongest."

"Surely you wish for my people to die for your kind," William snickered. "*Have a battle here, so we have time to flee,*" he mocked.

"As I already said, we will retrieve Faris' warriors once the sun is down." I forced a slow breath into my lungs before turning to Arthur and Tamira. "Evacuate everyone who cannot fight to the human village near Faris," I told them.

Arthur looked visibly nervous as he met my gaze. Tamira, however, nodded at my suggestion; before she managed to say anything, Barren slammed his fists against the walnut–wood table. "It is my army; I give out the orders!" he screamed at the top of his lungs, his face reddened. "Hence, *I* decide what is right for them! We are evacuating," he told Arthur and Tamira.

"Where!" I repeated the same question Roxanne had asked through clenched teeth. "They will hunt you anywhere. Only, by then, your army will be tired and without shelter. These walls are stone, they will protect humans while fire erupts!"

"My word was final, Cordelia. You've lost your right to speak on the issues of our people once you turned into the devils' spell," he spat out, pushing the chair out of his way. The chair hit the marble floor with a muffled thud as Barren's *graceful* steps clicked against the marble, walking towards the door.

Arthur got up from his chair, his second—a blond boy that looked barely past eighteen—followed his lead, yet the uncertainty shone bright, deep in their human eyes. Arthur's lips were sealed as his eyes watched William departing from the room, it was Tamira who spoke, "Your Grace, you are making a mistake." She faced William, her shoulders straightened, nothing but determination present in her features. "Her Highness makes a compelling argument."

Silence. William froze at the door before turning on one heel.

I could have blamed fear for Barren's rash decisions and emotionality, yet I knew better.

"*Her Highness,*" he tsked, laughing. "Her highness," he mocked. "Oh, sweet Tamira, you are mistaken: she is no Highness—merely a filthy vampire like the rest of her kind, with no respect for human tradition and value." He put his hands behind his back as he rounded the hall. "Her rich speeches about wanting to help are no more than a ploy you are getting trapped in." He smirked when his eyes burrowed into mine. "We are evacuating."

Tamira stood from her seat, her hands inches from the weapons she kept at her belt. Barren's eyes fell onto the blades as his throat bubbled.

"My army is staying here," Tamira stated at last.

"What did you just say?" Barren seethed, yet took a small step backwards.

"*My army* is staying here." Tamira's chin rose high. "I do not answer to you, duke, I answer to the crown." Her voice dropped a few octaves. "And regardless of the crown's decision, my duty is to do what is best for the warriors I am responsible for. I will never put my people into jeopardy. And what you are offering is madness."

"Your duty is to follow orders of the crown, commander." Barren nodded. "Given that the crown is no longer with us, you are to answer to me." His body shook, the muscle on his temple twitched. "Gather your people, commander, we are leaving these grounds."

"My people will never flee from hardship, we were trained to fight till our last breath, we were trained to protect, not run." Tamira shook her head. "And we are surely not running into the uncertainty you propose. I will not expose my people to more danger than we are already in."

A bright laughter broke through the halls, bouncing off the walls, as Barren's lips stretched into a sneer. "My army is bigger than yours. There will be no man left after *we* evacuate, leaving you behind with only these devils." He shook his head. "Arthur," he called, opening the doors to the hall.

When Arthur didn't move, Barren's voice screeched through the room. "How dare you, bastard!" Saliva splashed out of his mouth as he spoke, "*I* put you in that position, you are to answer to me!"

"Forgive me, Your Grace." Arthur swallowed, his head hanging low. "I cannot order my warriors to run from this battle, not when many of them have lost so much at the hands of Wurdulacs."

"They are *my* warriors." Barren's piercing scream cut through the air. "I don't need you to rule *my* army." With that Barren escaped the hall.

The court hall fell into silence, six pairs of eyes piercing through my flesh.

"What is our plan?" Tamira voiced the question that lingered in the air—the question I did not know the answer to—as she looked at me, her hands locked together on the table.

I'd told Roxanne I knew nothing of strategy, and I hadn't lied. Mother never allowed me into the war room; besides, when the last war ended, I was a seventeen year old girl, still believing in princes from fairytales.

"We must use fire to our advantage," Roxanne began when I glanced at her. "Set our first wave of protection at the perimeter of Silverstone. Our best archers should be there, hiding within the tree lines. Once the Wurdulacs cross the border, our armies should attack from behind: trapping them in." She looked over the table. "We will lure them here, to the castle, where the rest of us will wait, prepared."

"We only have fifty archers currently at the castle, that is not enough." Tamira shook her head.

"Faris will bring a hundred more," Roxanne argued. "They will use fire arrows, giving them a slight advantage against Wurdulacs: vampire flesh burns within seconds."

I drew a breath as Simon burned in my mind, his last screams echoing through my heart.

"Once Wurdulacs have nowhere else to go but here, we will launch our second wave of defense, surrounding them on each side," Roxanne continued. "The Royal steel weaponry will be to our advantage."

"What then?" Arthur sighed. "The numbers remain on their side. Even if we manage to kill half of them before they make it here, what good would it do if we have no one left to fight."

"We need to create a trap," Gabriel's voice boomed through the room; every pair of eyes landed on him, waiting for elaboration. "Oh, I don't have a trap in mind, I am merely stating that is what we need to do." He shrugged, leaning back on his chair.

My gaze met Roxanne's as my lungs squeezed shut. Her eyes narrowed as though the same thought reached her mind. She crooked her head, her brows rose high in question. I offered a small nod, swallowing the growing lump in my throat. "This castle has portcullis as well," I answered her silent question, forcing a sinister smile to spread across Roxanne's lips.

I lost track of time as we sat in this candlelit room. Maps and small figures splattered on the table, covering its every inch. The conversation, the planning, all swept through my head without lingering long enough for me to comprehend.

Arthur and his second had left a while ago to organize the evacuation of the nearby residents, leaving Roxanne and Tamira to plan through each line of defense.

My eyelids fought to stay open as the exhaustion, hunger, and... heartbreak took over every ounce of my being.

What awaited us when we returned to the palace? What kind of suffering had Francis to endure right now, as I sat in this room being utterly useless? Was he strong enough to survive the damage inflicted upon him until I could reach him? Were his last words to me a goodbye...

"His Grace left the estate, along with fifty three of our warriors." Arthur walked back into the hall, pulling me away from the dark thoughts in my mind. "He headed South, as he planned."

Those who followed after the Barren were as good as dead if we failed this battle. All of us were.

"Is the plan complete?" He studied the maps with wooden figures.

"Yes, merely small details left to finalize." Tamira nodded, getting up from her chair.

"I should start on the weaponry, then." Gabriel stretched his open palm to Roxanne. "We mustn't waste time."

"I will go with you." Roxanne got up from the chair, her hand lost in the pocket of her cloak.

"No, you need rest before the trip to Faris. The sun is going down in a couple of hours." Gabriel shook his head. "I can do it myself." His hand was still in the air, waiting for the flint.

Roxanne bit her lower lip as her eyes filled with concern when they lingered to me. If only I knew what to do... With Barren gone, I worried not for our safety in this castle, though the risk was still there: despite Tamira's and Arthur's reasonable minds.

"We can assign a few warriors to your aid. How many do you need?" Tamira turned to Gabriel.

Gabriel looked at me before replying. "The forge of Royal steel is highly secretive. I can do it myself."

"It's fine, Gabriel," I protested. "Take as much help as you need, there is no reason to keep this a secret. Humans are privy to this information, especially in times like these."

Gabriel nodded. "Ten, if possible," he told Tamira.

"Consider it done." She nodded at her second. "Louis, take Gabriel to the forge and find the best smiths among our army for his aid."

Louis—a middle-aged man with long, light-brown hair that reached his waist—nodded, walking out of the hall. Roxanne threw the flint at Gabriel, who effortlessly caught it, hiding it into his pocket.

"Would you like someone to accompany you to a room in the meantime, Your Highness?" Tamira faced me, her hand inclined.

"It's Cordelia," I said as Tamira frowned at my desire to ignore my foolish title—something she no doubt considered insubordination. "And no, I know my way around the castle, thank you." I gave her a swift nod, gesturing for Roxanne to follow after, as I led us to the only room in this castle I could bare: to the room that used to be my sanctuary—most of the time, at least.

Chapter 39. Old Ghosts.

The strong smell of alcohol erupted in the room I used to call mine. The same dark-blue curtains revealed the sun that had burned my flesh; the same dark blue bedding as the last time I'd stayed here.

I averted my gaze from the bedframe as painful memories invaded my weak mind. Timothy's shadow lingered in every corner of the room, yet there was no other room I would rather be in—this had been my only salvation, as he had rarely entered with the guards by my doors. Sometimes he managed to slip in anyway.

Other rooms hadn't granted me such protection, as Timothy would come up with foolish excuses to disallow my guards access to the rest of the castle. Had I protested—more pain would have fallen onto my shoulders... I'd quickly learned to endure it.

Roxanne locked the door behind her, rushing towards the window to draw the curtains. "I still think one of us should have stayed with Gabriel, Moon knows what can happen, and he is our only chance at Royal steel." She threw her cloak on the chair in the corner of the room, revealing her scabbard filled with blades.

"Tamira assigned help and protection to him, and he is right—" I took the woolen blanket out of the drawer when nausea made its way through my stomach: the drawer was filled with my old dresses, cut to shreds. I forced air into my lungs before laying the blanket on the settee by the now covered window.

"And what if one of his *helpers* does something to him?" Roxanne frowned when I lay on the settee.

"We have to learn to trust each other, otherwise death will take us one by one." My eyes closed from fatigue, revealing the fire that took Simon. "He will be fine." I shook my head to get rid of the horrid memory. "At the end of the night, he is human, and most of the guards here fought alongside him in the Crimson War."

Silence followed as Roxanne's steps neared to where I lay. "If you say so." She stood by the settee, willing my gaze to meet hers. "I won't bite," she rolled her eyes, pointing at the bedframe. "This bed is big enough for the both of us."

"I prefer to sleep here." I swallowed the nausea that rose deep within me as the memories of what had happened on that bed flooded my mind. I turned away, facing the wall.

"It doesn't look comfortable," Roxanne argued. When I didn't reply the room fell into silence: the silence that brought Simon's screams, the silence that brought Francis' last words.

"Don't touch me!" I screamed. "Please! Please!" I cried.

His hands wrapped around my hair, forcing me atop the bed.

"Please!" I begged, my nails digging into his face, scratching at the sickly pale—covered in cold soil—skin. "I beg of you, don't do this—"

"The less you resist the easier it will be, Cordelia." Timothy whispered into my ear as blood—his blood—spilled into my mouth, soaking my throat.

"Please!" I choked on his blood as his hands cut through my dress. The tears streamed down my face, soaking the sheets underneath me—

His hands felt my uncovered skin. My stomach dropped to my heels as nausea fought for its way out—

"No! No! Please don't touch me!" I cried. "Please!"

"Wake up, Cordelia!" Strong hands shook my shoulders, scaring the nightmare away. "Wake up!" Roxanne's eyes bored into mine.

I gulped for air as hot tears streamed down my face. "Sorry," I mumbled, wiping away the evidence of my distress. "Sorry."

Roxanne walked to the satchel she'd left on the wooden floor before going to bed. "Here." She offered me a bottle of wine that was filled with a darker shade of crimson. "Take it."

"I'm fine." I shook my head, pushing the bottle away from my lips. The divine smell of blood reached my nostrils, sending my mind into a frenzy. "Put it away, please."

Roxanne's brows furrowed at my refusal, yet she did as I'd asked. Her piercing gaze would not leave my broken figure when she hid the bewildering drink from view.

I sat on the settee, my hands wrapping around my body to keep it from shattering. "Sorry for waking you so early."

"The sun is about to come down," Roxanne said as though that was answer enough. "I should get going: Faris must arrive as soon as possible, given we don't know the exact day Kane will attack, and Florence must be going mad by now." Roxanne glanced at my palms, swallowing.

I followed her gaze. The shadows of my nails dug deep into my palms, bleeding crimson. I wiped my hands against the cloth of my dress. "All right." I filled my lungs with air. The bitter taste of blood still lingered in my mouth.

"Do you wish to come with me?" She asked, putting the satchel over her shoulder.

"I should go and help Gabriel." I shook my head. "I'm sure Tamira and Arthur will also need help before Faris arrives."

"All right." Roxanne walked towards the door. "Stay safe," she offered over her shoulder before closing the door.

I froze on the settee, my lungs still aching for air, silent tears streamed down my cheeks—

My insides turned upside down as I hurried to the bathing chambers. My jaw locked in place as my stomach squeezed tight—

I choked as my empty stomach pushed the remains of blood out.

My head spun into an oblivion I'd desperately tried to avoid. I had no time for such weakness, I had no time for heartache.

Numb tears clouded my eyes as I forced myself to the sink. The cold water streamed down my face, bringing my mind back into reality. I forced the water down my throat. The tasteless liquid filling up my stomach.

Breath in. Breath out.

I could not afford to break into pieces, not now, when so much was at stake. Not when Francis' life depended on my well–being.

I washed my face, meeting my own gaze in the mirror. My eyes glowed darker than usual—determined to deliver the promise I'd given so long ago.

The forge was a lot smaller than the one at the palace. The stone walls had darkened with age, the floors covered in dirt. The strong smell of burning coal forced my eyes to water as I made my way through the room.

The forge, that had been filled with laughter and chatter a moment ago, quieted: five pairs of eyes—including Gabriel's—meet mine. The delightful smell of human flesh invaded my mind, waking the beast, yet I paid it no attention.

"What are you doing here?" Gabriel asked. "I thought you were going to leave with Roxanne."

"I won't be of any use there," I replied, taking another step inside the forge. The men that accompanied Gabriel took a deliberate step back.

"You look horrible," I studied Gabriel, ignoring his company.

Gabriel laughed, nodding. "You too, Your Highness."

I rolled my eyes. "How can I help?"

The men in dirty warrior attire looked at me as though I had lost my mind.

"There is not much to do until the moon is out." Gabriel pointed at all the heated blades that lay inside the chimney. "These swords have been heated with fire spawned from our golden flint. Now we need to quench them in Moon water mixed with a drop of vampire blood."

"We've already set the barrels of water outside to charge." One of Gabriel's friends cleared his throat, meeting my gaze. His skin was covered in ash and coal, the ends of his blonde hair slightly burned.

"We were just contemplating where to get the vampire blood..." said the other that looked identical to the first: same blonde hair split in the middle, same shaped brown eyes, same high cheek bones. Brothers perhaps, maybe even twins.

"How much blood?" I asked, eyeing the swords: their tips turning bright orange under my gaze.

"A drop, maybe a few, per barrel." Gabriel shrugged, watching me with curiosity.

"All right then." I nodded. "Show me your barrels."

"Are you sure?" He frowned. "We can wait for someone from Faris to arrive."

I rolled my eyes when pity filled his eyes. "Show me the barrels, Gabriel."

"All right." He raised his hands in surrender. "If you insist, follow me." He walked past the four men who split to allow me entrance. Their every gaze followed me out of the forge's back door.

Outside, the spring air brought clarity to my still faded mind. Fresh, blooming aroma filled my lungs as I followed Gabriel around the corner of the forge.

A dozen wooden barrels stood side by side along the perimeter of the castle under the Moon's light. The water shimmered under the stars, reflecting each one of them.

"Here." Gabriel pointed at the barrels. "You really don't have to do this, hundreds of vampires are to arrive soon," he said as I pulled up my sleeve.

Dark blue marks scarred my skin, yet no pain followed with it. The burns had healed slowly, no matter the medicine. Perhaps I was meant to carry this scar as a reminder of my own foolishness forever.

"What happened to your arm?" Gabriel's brows furrowed as he glared at my old injury.

"Nothing," I said, walking towards the first barrel.

"I only have Silver blades—" Gabriel trailed off as my teeth pierced my own wrist. "I suppose that works too," he scoffed.

The blood slipped from my wrist, drop by drop, reaching each barrel as I walked past them. The wicked sensation brought an odd calmness to my heart as the memory of Francis' teeth atop my flesh snuck through the strong walls I'd built in my mind—I had no time for such distractions.

I shook my head when I reached the furthest barrel. The last drop of blood fell into the water, drawing circles around it.

"You are not hungry, are you?" Gabriel's eyes narrowed when I walked back. He took a shy step back as I reached him, offering me a clean cloth from his pocket.

"I am, actually." I allowed a small nod, wrapping my wrist in the cloth. Gabriel's eyes grew wide as he took another step back; his terrified expression almost brought a smile to my face. Almost. "Don't worry, I don't fancy humans." The words left me before I could catch them.

Gabriel let out a shrieked laugh, his eyes searching mine for clarity. "You must be the first vampire in the entire Kingdom who doesn't fancy humans," he laughed. "Who do you fancy then, if not humans?"

My heart ached as I dropped beside the barrels. My back met the stone wall as I looked at the Moon, wondering if Francis could see it too.

"Ah." Gabriel took a seat beside me, keeping a reasonable distance: to my amusement. "I'm sorry for what happened. I'm sure you and Francis will soon reunite," he offered.

"If Kane doesn't attack by tomorrow," I whispered. "I am going back to the palace myself. We can't wait longer than that."

"No," Gabriel sighed, and I worried I'd made a mistake sharing my secret plan with him. "You won't go by yourself," he added. "I will go with you."

A soft smile tugged at the corners of my lips, my hand falling atop his. "Thank you, Gabriel."

"Of course, Lia." He smiled back before returning his gaze to the Moon.

Heavy steps emerged from the corner of the forge, two broad shadows appearing before where we sat.

"You've been out here for a long while," one of the twins said, his eyes surveying Gabriel for injuries.

"We just wanted to make sure you were—" The other twin continued.

"Alive?" Gabriel suggested, laughing.

"Uh... well, yes." The twin itched the back of his neck.

I rolled my eyes when both men stared at me.

"Apparently my blood is too filthy for her taste." Gabriel chuckled, giving my shoulder a slight nudge—as he had often done when we were children.

The gesture brought comfort to my mind, as though we were still sitting underneath the willow tree by the palace, listening to one of Brian's lectures.

"I think the water is ready." A man with dark brown hair walked out of the forge. His face crossed with fear when he saw the distance between me and Gabriel.

"It hasn't even been an hour." Gabriel got to his feet; I followed after.

My eyes planted on the barrels, not believing the peculiarity I witnessed. The water shone crimson—the most unnatural crimson I'd ever seen. The blinding color made my eyes water the longer I stared, yet I had no strength to avert my gaze.

"Bring the swords," Gabriel instructed the men; a half smile tugged the corner of his lips upwards.

The men rushed inside, their hands filled with heated swords and daggers when they returned, leather gloves wrapped around each hilt. They all looked at Gabriel for further directions as they stood by the barrels.

"Quench it as you normally would." He shrugged, disappearing into the forge, leaving me alone with the four strange men as they quenched each blade.

"How do we know the Royal steel works?" A random man called after Gabriel before his gaze fell onto me, sending a shiver down my spine. "I'm merely jesting." He offered me a toothless smile.

Gabriel reappeared from the corner moments later, two blades in each hand. "It works." He pushed past me, shielding me from the man's view. "Stop wasting time and get to work." He dipped his sword into the crimson water until the blade took up the golden tint. It sparkled under the Moonlight, reminding me of my old sword.

The men followed his lead, submerging their weapons, turning it into Royal steel. The fear from their eyes, as they looked at me, ceased.

"I think I will go," I whispered to Gabriel, without averting my gaze from the, now armed, men. "Roxanne should return any moment now, I am sure they will need help."

"I will see you later, then." Gabriel nodded, noting my distress as he glared at the men. "Be safe," he offered when I turned the corner, escaping through the forge.

The dark corridors of the castle were empty, as most had spent this time resting. The Barren's walls stood naked from any paintings, the floors black as the darkest of nights.

The usual nauseous smell of coldness slowly turned to spring's freshness: though it did nothing to the sickly aroma of irises that still enveloped this castle whole.

I walked past the library, refusing to go back to my old room, as my plan worked its way through my mind.

Whether or not Kane would attack by tomorrow, I had to act. Alone, or with Roxanne's help—it mattered not. Only Moon knew what had already been done to Francis; I would not wait longer, no matter what Roxanne ordered.

The moment the sun set over the horizon, I would find a way to escape before anyone woke. Perhaps the Wurdulacs would send their forces here before I made my way to the Royal palace. Perhaps I would get lucky and the palace would stand empty at my arrival.

The halls filled with chatter the more steps I took. My brows furrowed as I followed the noise, straight into a citadel of the castle—the place that Wurdulacs would soon be trapped in.

Roxanne and Tamira stood in the center of the citadel, surrounded by hundreds of Faris's warriors.

"Take any room available," Tamira instructed the new-comers. "Return here in half an hour for your orders for this battle," her voice banged through the open space, reaching every ear.

When no one moved at Tamira's command, Roxanne yelled, "You've heard her. Move!" She shook her head as vampires slipped through the doors of the castle, rushing past me.

I stood against the wall, searching for familiar faces in the crowd as the vampires poured into the wide corridors.

When my eyes landed on the two familiar figures walking past me, I rushed after them.

"Florence," I pulled her from the sea of vampires.

The woman turned, her eyes filling with relief as her hands wrapped around my neck. "Cordelia," she breathed, her hands squeezing me tightly.

"I missed you." I returned the gesture. My eyes closed when I brought her closer. The familiar smell of wildflowers and sunshine erupted within my senses, filling my lungs with relief.

We stood in an embrace as the warriors' steps disappeared into the distance. The now empty halls quieted.

"Are you hurt?" Florence pulled away, eyeing my—wrapped in cloth—arm.

"No, it's nothing." I shook my head, surveying her for injuries. When I found none, I continued, "They needed vampire blood for the Royal steel. That's all."

"I was so worried," Florence sighed, her eyes closing when her hands wrapped around me anew.

"Let's go," Roxanne's voice echoed through the hall. "We have much to discuss," she added quieter, searching every direction for unwanted ears.

Chapter 40. No Soul.

The rich smell of irises followed us to my old room, spinning my head into sickness.

We walked through the wooden, beautifully carved, doors when the morning twilight fell upon us.

Florence paced nervously across the room, her eyes studying each corner, while Roxanne surveyed the halls before locking the door behind her.

"Gabriel will accompany us to the palace. I made sure he is stationed at one of the outskirt posts to draw less attention when he escapes." Roxanne's eyes jumped between me and Florence. "The moment the fight breaks out, he is to meet us in the woods, on the west side of Silverstone."

Florence nodded, taking a seat on the settee. The ends of her black trousers were wet from snow, her deep crimson tunic was tucked into a belt that carried five small blades with no visible hilt.

"We must be ready to leave at a moment's notice," Roxanne continued, fixing her undone braid. "The moment the first sounds of battle reach you, head for the stables."

"What if Kane doesn't attack tomorrow?" I voiced my biggest concern, hoping to not have to leave alone when the sun goes down. "We cannot wait any longer." My lips turned into a thin line, waiting for Roxanne's and Florence's replies.

"We must," Roxanne's voice cut through the air; her gaze boring into mine. "We've discussed this: we need as many Wurdulacs as possible out of the palace before we enter."

"They could kill Francis at any moment," I whispered, plea filling my voice.

The room fell into silence. No one dared acknowledge what was so loud in the air. *What if they have already?* A thought I had not allowed myself until this very moment.

I would know if Francis' soul resided with the Moon. I would know, I told myself.

"We have no choice." Roxanne's throat bubbled before she straightened her shoulders. "I must help Tamira get orders to our armies before sunrise. You two—" Roxanne pointed at me and Florence. "Get as much rest as you can." Roxanne's eyes lingered, her head inclined slightly.

"I got this," Florence mouthed, allowing a soft smile to spread her lips.

"I will see you soon." Roxanne threw over her shoulder as she slipped through the door, leaving us alone.

"We cannot wait." I met Florence's gaze, taking a seat beside her.

"I know." Florence nodded, taking her cloak off. "But it will be all right." She took a wine bottle out of her satchel. "We will figure it out." She smiled at me, offering me the bottle. "But no matter what happens, you must stay strong." She forced the bottle into my hands.

The sweet aroma reached my senses, spinning my head into frenzy. I eyed the drink as the beast within me rebelled.

"You must have some," Florence's voice softened.

"I cannot," a whisper escaped me; my eyes were locked on the bewitched drink. "I cannot."

"You must." Florence brought the bottle near my lips.

"I haven't had human blood since..." I swallowed the lump quickly growing in my throat. "I can't." I pushed the bottle away as the memory of Sandra's limp body underneath mine invaded my peace.

"You must." Florence's lips stretched into a sad smile; her hand enveloped mine in a strong hold. "You must be strong to rescue Francis," she said, giving my hand a squeeze. "Do it for him."

I shook my head as the open bottle hypnotized my strong will. "What if this blood makes me mad," I swallowed, searching Florence's eyes "What if I hurt someone." My hands reluctantly reached for the bottle.

"I am the only one in this room, you can't hurt me," Florence reassured. "And I would never let you hurt anyone." She nodded at the drink in my hands. "I swear it to you."

I brought the neck of the bottle to my lips. The beast in me was eager to feast as it imprisoned my mind in its hard grip, silencing every rational thought.

The first drop fell into my mouth, burning on my tongue. The unfamiliar taste turned my stomach upside down, yet the beast cared not for the crimson's owner, cared not for their well-being.

I drank the blood as it soothed my scraping throat, filling my empty stomach. Despite my best wishes to protest—the drink had brought strength to my weakened mind. The drink had brought clarity to my clouded thoughts.

The sour taste had brought peace to the beast, calming its furious waves.

"Better?" Florence took the empty bottle from my hands, a soft smile stretching her lips.

"Yes," I admitted. "Thank you, Florence."

"We will get Francis back." She nodded, giving my hands a squeeze before letting go. "We will, I promise."

I managed a weak nod at her reassurance, yet a small—treacherous—part of me could not believe her words.

"This used to be your room?" Florence got up from the settee, walking towards the drawers filled with jewelry that I'd never worn.

"When I had to stay here overnight." I nodded. "Yes."

Florence's fingers brushed over the golden necklace. "These are gorgeous," she marveled at the stones.

"Timothy used to get them for me every time after he..." I swallowed, meeting her gaze. "Every time after he assaulted me." I'd said the words out loud for the first time in my life.

Florence dropped the bracelets as though they were fire, taking her seat beside me; her head dropped on my shoulder. "You killed him." She stated, as though that was the answer to everything.

"I did," my voice did not belong to me as the memory of his limp, empty body laying in the crimson snow flew through my mind; the thought of his empty eyes staring out in the distance calmed me. "I killed him." The words brought peace to the part of me I'd carried as shadows for so long.

"Good." Florence nodded; approval rang in her voice. "The Moon will refuse his soul for what he did."

"I don't think he had a soul," I chuckled, though it sounded more like a choke.

A corner of Florence' lip rose as she got up from the settee. "Let's get some rest," she sighed. "I fear tomorrow will be long," she added, as an odd feeling of dread spread through my veins, and that feeling was soon validated, for the moment the sun had set, the banging on our door broke free.

Chapter 41. Chaos.

My eyes flew open at the banging sound on our door. Roxanne rushed out of the bed, hurrying towards the entrance.

Racing boots screeched against the marble floor in the hall when Roxanne opened the door. Dozens of voices screamed out commands, their voices ringing through the walls of the castle.

I rushed to my feet, checking every dagger in my scabbard. Florence followed my lead.

"Tamira?" Roxanne's hoarse voice echoed through the room as she looked the woman up and down.

"Our furthest posts have reported an attack," Tamira met my gaze as I reached the women. The skin underneath Tamira's eyes darkened as her exhausted gaze met mine. "Wurdulacs are on their way here, we must prepare."

"The sun just went down." My brows furrowed as I watched the chaos beyond our room. "How could the Wurdulacs possibly manage to get here so fast?"

"They took shelter in one of the deserted villages," Tamira replied before facing Roxanne. "The report says that only half of their army is present: if your estimates were correct. It is safe to assume that the rest of them are still at the Royal palace." She glanced at the parchment in her hands before adding, "Kane is nowhere to be seen."

"Thank you, Tamira," Roxanne said. "I will relay the message to the vampires."

Tamira offered a quick nod before joining the running warriors in the hall.

"We have to go." I rushed to put my boots on once the door shut. My trembling fingers battled with the laces.

Roxanne nodded, yet concern shone bright in her eyes. "Why is half of Kane's army still at the palace?" she thought out loud, throwing a satchel to Florence.

"We will figure it out once we are there." Florence caught the satchel, putting it around her shoulder.

"I will meet you at the stables." Roxanne attached the quiver to her back.

"Where are you going?" Florence glanced up from tying her shoes.

"I have to relay Tamira's report to our army before we go." She opened the door, letting our room fill with the panicked voices from beyond. "I will be quick." She closed the door to the room, muffling the disarray that had erupted within the castle's walls.

"Are you ready?" Florence walked to the door.

"Yes." My trembling hands secured the cloak around my shoulders.

Chaos filled the air as dozens of warriors—human and vampire—sprinted in every direction: nothing but determination filling their features.

"This way." I pulled Florence away from the crowd, gesturing for her to follow after me. "The stables are closer from here." It mattered not to discuss our whereabouts quietly: everyone was too occupied with preparation to pay us any mind.

We ran down the stairs, my feet slipping across the marble before I could catch my balance. The disorder from above quieted the lower we traveled.

Florence caught my free hand, rushing down the steps at my side. "Where to now?" Her brows furrowed when we reached the end of the stairs, standing before a stone wall.

I pulled her behind the staircase, crouching beside a small handle on the floor. "This passage leads straight to the stables." I pulled the heavy door open.

The darkness welcomed us as we moved down the ladder into one of the hidden passages of the castle.

Silence filled the narrow path as we walked through it; drops of water fell from the ceiling onto our heads. "Almost there," my whisper echoed through the tunnel, our boots splattered the water on the stoned floor.

Our short–lived silence was interrupted as I pushed open the heavy door at the end of the passage. Chaos enveloped us once again as the dark stables appeared before us.

Dozens of people moved frantically through the stables, preparing the horses for battle: nobody paid me and Florence any attention as we walked through the space, searching for our horses.

Anxiety corrupted the stables: the unrested horses swayed from side to side in reply to everyone's distress.

"We must wait for Roxanne," Florence said when I saddled my horse. She moved to prepare Roxanne's when more people poured into the stables. "She will be here soon," Florence mumbled under her breath.

When Roxanne's horse was ready, Florence's worried gaze met mine. "Where is she?" The worry shone bright in her eyes as she mounted her mare.

Warriors walked their horses out of the stables, some of them throwing confused glances our way—

"Let's go!" Roxanne ran towards us: her bow drawn.

She mounted her horse in a swift motion, gesturing for us to follow. "We will have to go around Silverstone," she yelled as we ran out of the sanctuary, into the courtyard filled with warriors.

"No!" The wind carried my voice. "It will take far too long!" I protested.

Going around Silverstone would add an additional hour to our travels—if not more...

"Silverstone is an active battleground right now!" Roxanne barked as we passed the gates of Barren's estate. "If you want to reach Francis alive, we must go around!" She ordered her horse north, through the woods, away from Silverstone.

Florence and I had nothing left but to follow.

The cold air struck my face as Annabelle carried me towards the palace.

The naked trees blurred in my vision as we flew through the path of the woods.

"If we miss Silverstone," my voice traveled with the wind. "How will Gabriel meet us?"

"He will figure out the change in our plans!" Roxanne turned, her voice getting lost in the distance. "And meet us at the palace!"

"What if he does not?" Florence forced her horse to run faster.

"We will figure it out, Sunshine!" The wind dropped Roxanne's hood, freeing her red hair. "We just need to get there!"

My feet pushed on Annabelle's sides, willing her faster.

I'd lost track of time long before the first empty villages appeared from the east. The tallest of the buildings still carried the fiery remains, the smoke reaching us from such a distance.

I was too afraid to imagine what Silverstone would look like after the attack, and could only hope no innocent souls suffered the disaster.

"On your right!" Florence yelled, slowing her horse slightly. "Is that one of Faris' warriors?" She asked Roxanne, who had matched Florence's speed.

"I don't think so." Roxanne shook her head, her eyes narrowing on the figure in... a dark blue cloak.

"Wurdulacs!" I screamed, forcing Annabelle back into a sprint.

"Fuck!" Roxanne drew an arrow as four more cloaked figures appeared from the other side.

"They are surrounding us!" I shrieked, unsheathing one of my daggers that stood no chance against figures' long swords.

Panic squeezed my throat as the Wurdulacs shortened their distance between us.

"They are close!" Florence willed her horse to run to the side, passing Annabelle with ease.

I allowed myself a quick glance behind me: Roxanne's arrows flew in every direction, meeting the hearts of our followers—

"Cordelia!" Florence's voice broke through the air, forcing my gaze towards her. "Watch out!"

The air was knocked out of my lungs as my back met the ground—

A broad figure lay atop of me as I gulped for air—

"Were you headed to the palace, lost princess?" The man's lips stretched into an ugly smile. "Kane misses you dearly." He murmured, bringing a blade to my throat—

I had no time to allow fear into my veins, I had no time to allow panic to take over my mind, for the man's eyes grew bigger before freezing forever.

His weight crashed upon me, the grip on his blade loosened as it fell onto the ground: barely missing my flesh by an inch.

My arms screamed in protest as I pushed the man off of myself, gasping for air.

I choked in the silence of the woods, my eyes landing on the small blade buried deep inside of Wurdulac's heart—Florence's blade.

"Are you all right?" Her worried eyes met mine.

I managed a nod, searching for Roxanne, yet nothing but silent bodies lay around us.

"Roxanne went to catch Annabelle." Florence read into my expression, as she pulled me to my feet, before retrieving her Royal steel blade from the man's heart.

I filled my lungs, my eyes jumping from one limp body to another: Royal steel arrows were buried in each of their hearts as they lay in the now peaceful woods.

"They were waiting for us," I croaked, meeting Florence's eyes. "Kane knows we are coming."

Chapter 42. The End.

I wiped the last tip of Roxanne's arrows against the bottom of my cloak, freeing it of Wurdulac's blood, before setting it on the ground by my feet.

"What is taking her so long?" Florence watched the depths of dark woods where Roxanne had disappeared into.

"Should we go after her?" I asked, following Florence's gaze.

"We sh—" she trailed off as the redheaded woman appeared in the distance: no horse followed after her as she rode towards us. "I'm sorry," Florence whispered to me.

"I couldn't catch her, she was too frightened," Roxanne said when she reached us. "Sorry."

I shook my head, passing Roxanne her lost arrows.

"You should ride with me." Florence walked to her horse. "My horse is a lot bigger, she can carry us both."

"It will still slow us down." I followed after her nevertheless.

"We have no other choice." Florence helped me mount her horse. "At least we are not far," she mumbled as I sat behind her, my hands wrapping around her waist when she ordered her horse into a run, towards the palace.

The quiet battlements of the palace appeared in the distance as we slowed our steps. The dark clouds hid the Moon from our view as we neared our end.

"Wait!" Roxanne hissed, bringing her horse to a stop. Florence halted in an instant. "There is someone by the trees," Roxanne pointed towards the spruce that surrounded the palace. "Right there, you see?"

Florence and I followed her gaze.

A figure in a black cloak—with a hood covering their head—stood by the line of dense spruce, their eyes planted on the palace's silent walls.

"Wait here," Roxanne whispered, drawing her bow as she ordered her horse to walk slowly in the direction of her target.

Florence and I froze in place; Roxanne closed the distance between whoever hid behind the bushes—

Roxanne lowered her bow, her shoulders visibly relaxing as she gestured for us to follow.

"Roxanne?" The figure got to his feet, walking towards us as we neared. "I thought I'd lost you," Gabriel looked over at me and Florence. "The outskirt villages are in ashes," he added, lowering his gaze.

"Have you seen anyone leave the palace?" Roxanne dismounted her horse, tying the reins to a nearby tree.

"Not a single soul," he replied. "The palace seems vacant."

"Tamira said half of the army is still here." I jumped off of Florence's horse, before we all made our way into the bushes. "It must be a trap."

Three silent pairs of eyes met mine as I scanned the empty grounds of my old home.

No guards stood at the perimeter of the palace, no Wurdulacs guarded the main gate. No candlelight flickered through the palace's windows: only a withering wind whispered its spells, brushing over my hair.

"It's quiet," Florence whispered.

"Perhaps some of them left, like Caleb had predicted." Hope shone in Roxanne's eyes as she pointed her arrow at every entrance of the palace, searching for possible targets.

"If Kane is still here, he isn't alone; he wouldn't stay without protection." I shook my head. My mind wandering through every possibility—

Damnation.

How did I not think of it earlier?

My heart banged against my rib cage. "I should go by myself." I swallowed as the realization swept through me. "It's a trap for me."

"What do you mean?" Gabriel's eyes met mine.

"Kane wanted me to join him," I explained. "He made me kill Sandra to prove my loyalty." I forced air into my lungs before continuing, "He was mad I wasn't by his side from the very beginning, but Caleb convinced him I didn't know any better." I met Roxanne's and Florence's gazes. "Now that I've openly refused him, he will want retribution for my disloyalty—Francis is my bait." A chill went through me at the words, yet Kane's intentions were clear as day. "I should go alone, give Kane what he wants."

"Are you mad?" Florence caught my hand when I got to my feet, pulling me back down.

"Perhaps he will let Francis go if he has me!" I hissed, fighting with Florence's strong hold.

"No!" Roxanne hissed back. "He will not, and you know it." She lowered her bow, looking around the perimeter of the palace. "Where do you think they are keeping him?"

"Probably the dungeons: same place he'd kept me." I swallowed the growing lump in my throat.

"Then it should be easy enough," Roxanne mumbled, her eyes searching for the small door connecting to the dungeons. "We won't have to go through any obstacles like we did last time."

I prayed to the Moon she was right, despite a small voice telling me the opposite.

"It's time." Gabriel unveiled an unused torch attached to his saddle. "We cannot wait any longer, we must leave the palace before the sun starts to rise. We have an hour, or we will be trapped in there."

I watched the door to the dungeons carefully, as though it would open at any moment, and Francis would walk out unscathed.

"Ready?" Roxanne asked, looking over at all of us. Satisfied with our determined gazes, she took a long breath in before getting to her feet. "Let's go."

We jogged to the palace silently: our cloaks like shadows under the raising sun.

My heart stopped as my legs carried me back towards the place that had stolen everything from me; my lungs froze in place as my legs carried me towards the place that could give me everything.

Roxanne halted right before the entrance to the dungeons, gesturing for us to freeze in place.

Gabriel took the canteen out of the inside pocket of his cloak, pouring the contents onto the tip of his torch. "Let me go first," he whispered to Roxanne, taking the golden flint out of his pocket. "The fire will take whoever is inside off guard." He stroked the flint against his sword, before lighting the torch in one smooth motion.

Roxanne nodded before averting her gaze to me and Florence. "Stay safe," she whispered, disappearing behind the door after Gabriel.

I held my breath, counting every beat of my heart, as utter silence followed from the dungeons.

"Let's go," I told Florence as my eyes captured the last moments of peace before I took a step into the dungeons.

The strong smell of mold reached my nostrils as my eyes watered. The familiar smell of Sandra's blood made my stomach turn upside down.

The dungeons were dark, save for Gabriel's torch, its stoned walls keeping the sun away as we walked through the—

My eyes planted on the splattered blood across the floor. The memories I was so desperate to get rid of overwhelmed my mind anew.

Sandra's empty blood body lay in the middle of the room, her empty eyes staring back at me, thanking me for taking her life. My hands shook as I watched the dry blood stain the stones—

"Francis!" Florence's voice echoed through the dungeons. My head flew in her direction as I ran towards the open cell.

"Francis!" I dropped to the floor in the corner of the cell. "Francis!" My voice echoed through the dungeon when my hands reached his peaceful—too peaceful face.

"Go get the horses!" Roxanne ordered Florence. "We can't carry him all the way there."

Florence offered a quick nod before disappearing behind the door that led outside—

"Put pressure here!" Roxanne pushed my hands against Francis' open wound on his stomach. "It's silver," she mumbled under her breath.

The shining blade had pierced deep into his insides as his closed eyes planted on the ceiling. I held my breath, listening for the only sound that mattered in that very moment—Francis' weak breathing. "Francis," I whispered as a groan escaped his lips, yet he did not move.

"We need *chapizhnik* leaves to burn out the poison." Roxanne rushed to cut the bottom of her cloak.

"*Burn!?*" My crimson hands shook when I met Roxanne's gaze.

"Where is the apothecary in the palace?" She wrapped the fabric around Francis' wound.

"I—" Panic choked me as I glanced back at—unmoving—Francis. Blood splattered around him, soaking my fingers red. "It's—"

"I will take you there," Gabriel's voice banged through the dungeons as he shoved the torch into my bloody hand. "For protection," he threw over his shoulder to me, charging towards the only door that led up to the palace.

"Stay with him, and continue applying pressure!" Roxanne yelled, rushing after Gabriel—Royal steel dagger in her hand.

The undergrounds of the palace quieted, the weak echoes of Francis' slow breathing whispered against the walls. The torch's fire danced on his face, illuminating the dark purple bruises covering his cheekbones, illuminating the blood–painted cuts on his lips.

"Francis," I whispered as tears clouded my vision. My hands fell to his chest, feeling his heart—

A hard surface met my fingers. My brows furrowed, undoing his cloak. Francis' metal canteen shielded his heart from my touch.

My crimson hand wrapped around the full flask, bringing a sad smile to my face.

My eyes never left Francis, as though a mere glance lost would strip him away from me forever.

How long has he been like this for?

"Francis," I whispered when his eyes fluttered open before closing anew. "Please stay with me." Tears rushed down my cheeks—

The sound of boots outside reached my ears when a shadow appeared on the stone walls.

"Florence?" My voice shook as my hold hardened around the shaft of the torch. My other hand pocketed the flask inside of my cloak.

The slow steps neared; the shadow grew bigger.

My heart banged in my chest as I gathered to my feet, moving the torch in the direction of the entrance.

"Florence?" I whispered, praying to all the Gods and Goddesses that would listen—

A broad figure appeared at the threshold; the fire illuminated the familiar features.

"Caleb?" My eyes narrowed on my blood brother.

"I'm not alone," he croaked, taking a step into the dungeons.

With a blade to Caleb's back, Kane walked the man to the middle of the room. "I'm sorry, Cordelia," Caleb met my gaze; his face was covered in bruises and cuts that still bled crimson, a bright silver dagger planted deep in his stomach. His right leg dragged behind him as Kane pushed the man forward.

"And so we meet again, daughter." Kane's lips stretched into an ugly smile as he brought a Royal steel sword to Caleb's throat.

Chapter 43.
Brother's eyes.

Kane's dark brown eyes bored into mine, the fire from the torch flickering in his irises. The tips of his gray, wavy hair wore crimson, a freshly inflicted wound crossed his face. Kane's lips stretched into a grimace as he studied me as though I was prey.

I stood in front of the two men as they stayed unmoving; the Royal steel sword sparkled against Caleb's neck. His tired, empty eyes stared behind me.

I followed his gaze until my eyes landed on Francis' fading away body, before averting my gaze back to Kane's.

The fire shook on the stone walls as my hand held the torch in its firm grasp; an unnatural calmness enveloped my body whole.

"You see, these two bastards thought they could outsmart me." Kane's voice banged through the dungeons as his gaze jumped from Caleb to Francis. My heartbeat quickened in an instant as the realization of his presence settled in my mind.

"Thought they could somehow play me for a fool with their priceless act," Kane continued, his lips stretching into a grin. "Oh, Cordelia, how I wish you could've seen how hard your lover tried to save you from the same fate," he tsked.

"How many lies have spilled from his mouth, trying to spare you from my revenge."

I swallowed the growing terror, taking a step forward: my torch a few yards away from the man that called himself my father.

Spare Francis, dear Moon, take my soul instead. I beg of you.

"But he had forgotten one thing..." Kane sighed, unbothered by the deadly weapon in my hand. "The bastard had forgotten that I knew him well, for I offered my castle to his homeless family, I offered him my meal, and I offered him safety."

"Let him go," I heard myself speak, yet the voice was foreign to my ears. "Let them all go, and take me instead!" I spat out, taking another step forward. The fire was close to the men, close to their end, yet I could not find it in me to let the flames take their lives: not when Caleb was among the ones that would have to pay for my doings.

Spare Francis.

"I cannot." Kane lowered his blade from Caleb's neck slightly, sidestepping from the shield. "You see, daughter," his voice lowered. "I knew *you* would come for Francis, hence why I only planted my blade through his body once the Wurdulacs left the palace for Silverstone." A dark chuckle pushed past his lips. "You think I kept him alive as a bargaining chip? Oh, my dearest Cordelia, he remains for nothing more than my amusement." His lips stretched into the most disturbing smile. "I left it up to fate to decide whether you would see him alive one last time before you pay for your mistakes."

My heart skipped a beat at his words; everything in my body screamed at me to flee, yet my legs refused to obey.

Take my soul instead.

"I always wished for a daughter," Kane spoke again; the fire from my torch danced in his eyes. "After having two sons—one of which did not know of my existence—I dreamed of a daughter," he sighed. "Your mother only allowed me to see you once before she tossed me out of the palace forever. Every night, I thought of you; I thought of how you were growing up within the walls that were lying to you."

I beg of you, dear Moon.

I shortened the distance between us, pushing the torch closer, yet my legs froze when Kane forced Caleb in front of him anew.

Spare my family.

Only a few yards separated me from setting Kane on fire, only a few yards separated me from killing an injured Caleb in the process.

Only a few yards separated me from ending my own life, for if I were to send the torch free, Kane's mere touch would take me with him.

Take me instead.

"I had given you a choice, remember?" Kane crooked his head to one side, forcing his blade against Caleb's side; Caleb's eyes met mine before he glanced at the torch in my hand. "I allowed you a chance—something I don't give out often," Kane continued, unbothered by the fire I had pointed at him. "For Mories, oh dear long–resting Mories, vouched for you. Too bad you couldn't deliver what she had promised, revealing her blatant lies to me."

Please, dear Moon, grant my dying wish.

The strength at which my heart beat could not compare with the strongest of storms; my mind drowned in a hurricane, my mind calmed in the morning breeze.

One last wish.

The fire of my torch slowly started to ease: soon enough it would cease at once.

One last, dying wish.

My hand shook as I studied Caleb's features—the ones that reminded me of Brian. I searched my brother's eyes one last time.

So many things could go wrong, so many—I'd lost count.

The vulnerability I would be forced into once the torch left my hand... I only had one chance.

"The Moon has a humor of her own, doesn't she?" Kane laughed, taking a step closer; the tip of his Royal steel sword pressed against Caleb's side. Kane's hand tightened around Caleb's shoulder, keeping him in place.

Crimson covered every inch of Caleb's face when his lips tugged upwards; his shoulders rose and fell in even rhythm when he offered me a barely visible nod.

Forgive me for the sins.

"The Moon had given me three children that I longed for," Kane continued. "And yet, every single one of you betrayed me in the end. Every single one of you deserve what I—"

I'm sorry, I mouthed to Caleb; my hand ready to let the fire free—

My body stilled. My heart stopped.

The long-forgotten torch—stuck in my grasp, for the blade that sparkled golden pierced Caleb's side, freezing his silent scream for eternity.

Chapter 44.
Poison.

An excruciating scream broke through the dungeons. The gilded blade shone bright as its end carried crimson, boring through Caleb's side—

Kane's dark chuckle erupted throughout the room as he disappeared into the shadows, escaping the dungeon—

"Caleb!" My own scream followed as my legs carried me towards my fallen brother. "Caleb!" My hands shook when my eyes fell onto his bleeding crimson wound. "Oh, dear Gods!"

"Florence," Caleb croaked, freeing himself of the gilded sword. "Florence is in danger." He pressed on his wound: the poison would soon reach his heart. "Go!"

My heart stopped at once. Terror enveloped my body when my eyes landed on the door Kane had disappeared behind—the door that led to my unprotected friend.

"Florence." My legs carried me out of the dungeons: my hand tightly wrapped around the torch. "Florence!" A scream broke through my throat when the dark fog blinded everything around me. "Florence!" I yelled in every direction, caring not who heard me.

My hand reached for the Royal steel dagger at my scabbard. "Florence!"

The fire eased at my torch, only minutes remained before it would die out—

The slow steps neared, yet my vision had betrayed me. The dark chuckle followed after.

"Get away from me!" I swung the torch in every direction, hoping the fire would illuminate the threat.

"Don't be foolish, daughter," Kane's voice whispered from behind. I turned in an instant, yet nothing but fog appeared in front of me. "You cannot win this battle," his voice traveled from the other side; the torch followed his voice, yet was met with nothing. "Embrace your loss, and pay for your betrayal!" Kane roared, as an excruciating pain erupted in my leg—

"Ah!" My cry echoed throughout the courtyard of the palace. The agonizing pain drowned my mind in torture, the piercing pain traveled up my bones. "Show yourself!" A roar broke through my throat. "Show yourself, you coward!" I bellowed as my knees weakened, the torch shaking in my hands—

The cold soil met my body when a new wave of stabbing agony washed over me, sending my mind into insanity.

"Show yourself!" I croaked, forcing myself upwards through the pain; the fire loosened its strength against the melting snow—

"You have lost, daughter," Kane's laughter traveled through the fog. "The fire in your hands is soon to die, and your injury is soon to kill you."

The ground and the sky spun together. My vision blurred as I swung my dagger in every direction. "I will not leave Moon's realm without you," I seethed through the torment.

Every muscle ached from the motion, my thigh went numb within seconds—

"I never wanted for this to happen." Kane's voice neared. His shadow walked towards my weakened body. "This place took everything from me—"

I forced the torch in his direction: the flames fought strong to stay alive. "You will burn in hell!" A roar bursted through my throat when Kane's face appeared from the fog.

My hands trembled as strength left me bit by bit. "You will burn," my voice shook as I lunged forward.

The torch missed Kane's flesh, the fire diminishing from the movement.

I have to get closer.

Kane's laugh traveled through the dark courtyard as he stood yards away from me.

"Don't worry, daughter," Kane murmured, sighing. His eyes filled with a sadness I'd seen in Brian's gaze when we'd said our last goodbyes. "The poison in your wound will soon stop your heart and all of this will be over—"

A battlecry jabbed through the courtyard. Caleb lunged towards Kane: the bleeding, gilded sword in his hand. "You will die alongside me!" He roared, swinging his sword with a determination I'd never seen him possess. "You will!"

Kane easily averted the attack, swaying backwards. "You are mistaken, son," Kane laughed, unsheathing the dagger from his belt. "You are mistaken!" He threw the dagger at Caleb, missing his flesh by a mere inch.

Nausea worked its way through my body, the weakness winning over my strong will. My vision darkened at the sounds of clanging metal, my breathing slowed at the sounds of battlecries.

Strength—

Allow me the strength—

My trembling hands struggled with the material, ripping through the bottom of my cloak, the dark fabric wet from the melting snow.

Just a little strength before you take my soul for eternity—

Caleb swung his sword with no particular strategy as his body faded by the moment. The sword kept missing Kane's flesh, forcing the man to laugh at Caleb's struggles.

Everything spun when I wrapped the fabric around the blade of my dagger.

I needed more time—

As though hearing my thoughts, Caleb threw himself atop Kane, the sword flying away from their fight.

"You—" Caleb shrieked, his fist meeting Kane's jaw.

"You have mere seconds to live, son." Kane deflected Caleb's throw, planting his Royal steel dagger in Caleb's shoulder. "You have done this to yourself!" Kane wrapped his arms around Caleb's neck.

Please, Moon—

My shaking fingers fought with the lid of Francis' canteen, forcing it to open.

"It's all right, son." Kane tightened his hold around Caleb's throat. "It's all right."

Caleb's eyes met mine one last time before they rolled backwards. The wound on his side bled no more.

I poured the contents onto the fabric, bringing the tip of the dagger to my dying torch—

The fire erupted within moments, barely missing my flesh.

Grabbing the hilt of the dagger, I readied it for a throw—

My Royal steel dagger flew through the space; the fire flew through the distance that separated us, erupting on Kane's flesh in an instant.

A silent scream painted his face. His arms let go of Caleb's limp body, which was soon to be turned into ash.

The flames traveled across Kane's coat. The blackened bolts sprinted through his skin, swallowing his muffled cries.

Brian's—Kane's—eyes met mine, the fire illuminated the dark brown.

His mouth moved, yet I heard no sound.

The flames reached his throat, reached his face.

I watched the fire take the last of my blood family until nothing but ash was left.

The ground soaked in the men's ashes, the ground dared me to join.

The last of my family burned on the cold soil by the palace. The last of my family was soon to meet the Moon.

And I was to meet the Moon alongside them, for the poison traveled up my body, nearing my heart.

Chapter 45.
Nothingness.

The wounds on my thigh pulsed as I lay on the freezing ground. My heartbeat slowed; the darkness dragged me into its lonely embrace.

Peace traveled through my body, announcing my fight was over.

The Moon glanced down at me, accompanying me on my last journey. "Please let Francis live," I whispered to her. "Please let him live—" My eyes closed. Fatigue froze my bones in this single moment. "I love you too," I gasped, drawing a small, choking breath. I drew my final breath—

The piercing pain erupted in my knee. My pulse quickened against its touch, yet my mind could no longer struggle, drowning me deep into its peaceful nothingness.

The strong waves of darkness fell apart at someone's strong hold. I wished for them to stop depriving me of peace. I wished for them to allow the Moon to claim my soul.

"Don't you dare die!" Florence's voice echoed through the calm breeze of my dreams. "Don't you dare die, Cordelia!"

I fought for my eyes to open, to see my friend one last time, in vain. My mind slipped away from my grasp, and I had no strength to battle against it.

"Cordelia!"

The cold swept through my numb legs. The wound Kane had inflicted upon me cried anew.

Let me go.

Piercing pain washed over me with new power, forcing a muffled cry to push past my lips.

My heartbeat quickened.

Is this the end?

The blood escaped my poisoned wound. The agony spun my head into oblivion—

I forced my eyes to open.

Florence sat beside me, her mouth planted on the injury across my thigh as she sucked on my blood.

The blood slipped down her dark hair, painting it crimson, every inch of her beautiful skin now carried red.

Is she injured?

"Florence?" I heard myself speak.

More pain followed when my heart skipped a beat. My lungs ached, choking on each breath. I closed my eyes as the darkness presented herself in front of me.

"Take this!" Florence bit out, her hands pulling me upward. "Drink this! Now!" Her voice was so near, yet so far... "Cordelia!" A slapping sound vibrated in my ears.

My eyes flew open when my cheek erupted in pain.

"Drink!" Florence brought the bottle to my lips, forcing the contents down my throat.

The crimson slipped into my mouth, filling my empty stomach. The blood tasted bland compared to its usual delight.

"You will be all right." Florence nodded, wiping off the blood from her lips. "You will be all right, there's no poison left in you." She pulled me to my feet when the last drops of blood reached my throat.

"Everything will be well." She dragged me back towards the dungeons, towards dying Francis. "Just a little further," Florence said when we entered the wicked room.

I leaned on the wall, sliding down when Florence rushed towards my friends.

Roxanne and Gabriel sat beside Francis' limp body. Jars of differently colored medicine covered the floor.

"I've never done this by myself." Roxanne's eyes filled with tears as she pulled the dagger from Francis' wound. "I've never done this by myself," she said again and again when her hands reached for the medicine.

"You can do this!" Florence's voice turned harsh as she passed the jar to her beloved.

A sound I'd never heard Francis make erupted in the room when the medicine met his flesh. His eyes flew open when another roar escaped him—

My eyelids heavied at the sounds of his cries. The emptiness took over my weak mind—

The darkness had won.

My sweet dream shattered at once when my eyes fluttered open.

The familiar space spun as my vision adjusted to the candlelight in the corner of the room in Gabriel's house.

I forced a deep breath in that welcomed the nausea anew. A quiet groan escaped my lips when I willed my body to a seated position from the woolen blankets on the floor. Every bone in my body screamed in protest.

"Princess?" The familiar voice echoed through the small room, forcing my eyes into its direction.

"Francis," I rasped when my eyes landed on the one I'd thought I would never see again. He dropped the book in his hands, rushing to where I sat. "Francis," I mumbled when he sat beside me. His hands reached for my face, his eyes searching mine.

"Francis," I whispered as tears slid down my cheeks. My hands brought him closer until my lips landed atop his.

His lips felt divine against mine; my hands wrapped around him, deepening our connection.

I kissed him with everything I had, praying to all who heard me for this delight to never end. Hot tears streamed down my face as I drowned in his strong hands. The tears didn't stop when I broke away, for my eyes longed for proof of his presence.

"You are alive." I carefully studied his features. "I was so worried," my voice turned hoarse. "I was so worried that I would never see you again." The memories of what had happened slowly returned to me, willing my gaze to Francis' stomach. "Your wound—"

"Shh, it's all right, love. I am all right." He petted my hair, planting a tender kiss on my forehead. "You should lay back down, you are still recovering."

"Don't leave me," I cried at the sound of his voice. "Please, don't leave me." I caught his hand, bringing it to my cheek.

"Never." He brought me closer, enveloping me in his embrace. More tears escaped my eyes.

"I was so worried," I mumbled against his neck; my hands clenched on the collar of his shirt as though my life depended on it.

"Shh." His hands tightened around me, shielding me from the world.

"I love you, Francis." I broke away from the embrace slightly, meeting his gaze. "I love you too."

"I love you," he whispered back, a lazy smile stretching his lips before a sigh pushed past them. "Everything is well now."

I moved closer to him as a dull pain traveled up my thigh. My brows furrowed when my eyes landed on my injury.

"Florence tells me you were stabbed with Royal steel." Francis helped me lay back down. "She arrived moments before the poison reached your heart." Pain crossed Francis' face when he glanced at the bleeding fabric around my thigh.

"Florence saved me." The memories of the last fight invaded my mind. Caleb's dying eyes froze in my thoughts.

"She did." Francis nodded; his eyes filling with relief. "You should rest some more, love. A wound like that takes time to heal." He wrapped his hand around mine. "But you will be all right. And I will be right here with you." Francis wiped the tears off my face.

"I love you, Francis," I whispered, closing my eyes against his touch.

Francis' hand palmed my cheek, his thumb stroking my skin as he whispered, "*For I'm a fool without your presence,*

For I'm a fool without your heart.

Your mere glance—is my essence,

Your mere glance—an arrow's shot." He planted a kiss on my forehead when the door to the room opened.

"Cordelia!" Florence rushed towards us, her hands wrapping around my neck in a tight embrace. "You're alive," she whispered when I returned the gesture.

"Because of you." I tightened my hands around her. "You saved my life."

"You saved all of our lives." Florence pulled away, the sunshine smile was back on her face.

"Are you injured?" The memory of when I'd seen her last came back to me: covered in blood from head to toe, she'd sat beside me, trying to save my life. "Caleb said you were in danger."

"Danger?" She scoffed. "Two Wurdulacs tried to attack me when I left for the horses. One of them was almost able to escape." A soft—dangerous—smile decorated her face.

"What about you?" I glanced at Roxanne, who stood at the threshold of the room. "And Gabriel?"

"We are well, Cordelia." Roxanne walked into the room, settling on the floor beside us. "It's from Gabriel." She offered the piece of parchment to me. At my furrowed brows she added, "He left for Silverstone a few days ago to share the news about Kane." Pride shone in her eyes when she looked at me. "Silverstone still stands. It's over."

I opened the parchment as my eyes scanned the contents.

The portcullis worked. The Wurdulacs no longer live. We won. Gabriel.

"No more war." A slow smile stretched on my lips as I reread the letter again and again, the realization settling deep in my soul.

"No more war," Roxanne nodded, pulling me into her embrace.

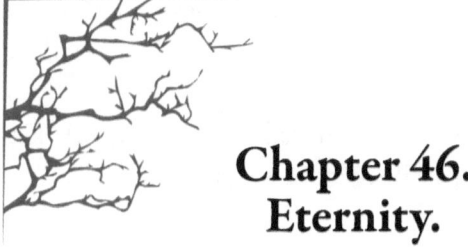

Chapter 46.
Eternity.

Dusk was upon us, the evening sunlight peaked through the small opening of the curtains as Francis and I lay in the corner of the room: his arms keeping me safe.

Two nights had passed since the moment I'd awoken, two nights in Francis' embrace: as he refused to leave me for even a moment.

"Are you certain you don't want to stay another day here?" He whispered against my neck. "You are still healing."

"I'm certain." I turned on the woolen blanket to face him. "I'm sure a lot needs to be done at Silverstone after the attack."

"There are plenty of people there to deal with the aftermath." Francis' thumb brushed over my lower lip. "You needn't worry yourself with it. You did more in the war than anyone could've asked for."

"I want to go," I stated, meeting his gaze. "I'm tired of laying around, being useless."

"So I see, my presence bores you," Francis chuckled. "Very well then, but if you feel ill during our trip, we are stopping for a break."

"If we take breaks we will not make it back to Silverstone before the sun comes up." My brows furrowed. "And I will be fine. I feel a lot better."

"If you say so," Francis murmured, planting a gentle kiss on the corner of my lips. "But before we go, we should attend to another matter..."

"What's wrong?" I pulled away slightly, searching his eyes.

My favorite smirk appeared on his face as his hands pulled me closer. "You need to feed, my love."

A delighted smile stretched my lips at his words. "That I do," I whispered against his neck, my tongue tracing the path on his skin.

"Please, Princess," Francis moaned when my tongue played on his skin. "Please, bite me," he begged, his hands guiding my mouth to his pulsing vein.

My teeth pierced the sensitive spot, forcing a satisfied groan out Francis. His blood filled my mouth, slipping onto my tongue. A moan pushed past my lips as I devoured his blood.

"Oh, how I missed your mouth." His breathing heavied.

His blood melted on my tongue, spinning my head into a frenzy. My eyes rolled back as the flowers bloomed deep within me.

"Francis," I breathed, licking every drop of blood off his skin.

"Take more, take all of it." His hand landed on the back of my neck, holding me against his open injury.

My lips met his soft skin anew, my stomach fluttered at such intimacy—

The knock on our door echoed throughout the room, yet I cared not to move away. I drank his blood with urgency I had not known before.

"If we are to leave tonight, we must go," Roxanne's muffled voice sounded through the door. "The sun has set."

Francis' hold hardened as he visibly fought with his growing moan. I chuckled against his neck before planting my teeth in his flesh once more. "We will leave in a few minutes—" Francis replied, his voice struggling to stay even.

"We will wait for you outside, then." Roxanne's steps disappeared in the distance.

"Aye, Princess, you are taunting me." Francis' laughter turned into a whine.

"You don't seem to mind," I chuckled, pulling away.

"I do not, indeed." His thumb brushed over my lips. "I wish we didn't have to stop so suddenly." Francis brought my mouth to his. His tongue danced across my lips, licking the blood off, forcing a cry out of me. "I suppose we will have plenty of time soon enough." His breath tickled my skin.

"Eternity." I gulped for air at his proximity.

"Eternity," Francis agreed before covering my lips with his once more.

The spring was in her full glory, bestowing us with her blooming aroma and the fresh streams of water, taking away all the horrors this winter had brought upon us. The bare trees were now decorated with their first small buds, ready to leaf out; the first snowdrops bloomed through the melting snow.

I leaned on Francis as he controlled our horse, enjoying his warmth and proximity. My thigh still throbbed at every move of our mare, yet the pain was bearable enough to hide—though, it hadn't not stopped Francis from asking if I wished for a break every so often.

Florence and Roxanne rode alongside us, sharing their stallion.

The trip back to Barren's estate was surprisingly pleasant: was it Francis' presence or the spring's powerful waves, I did not know—perhaps both.

No matter the horrors we'd witnessed as we'd passed the outskirt villages near Silverstone, everyone's faces were decorated with soft smiles.

"Do you wish for a break?" Francis met my gaze, slowing our horse down slightly.

"You asked me a few minutes ago, Francis." I rolled my eyes, yet could not hide the bright smile that fought its way onto my lips.

"And yet?" He wouldn't give up.

"We are almost there." I shook my head as my eyes watched past him. "You can see the castle from here." I pointed into the depths of dense spruce, at the merlons that peeked through the trees.

"Fine." Francis forced my gaze back to him. "But once we are inside, you are going to rest." His brows flew up, daring me to argue.

I merely rolled my eyes in reply.

"Cordelia," his voice became stern.

"Fine," I sighed, laughing at his sudden tone.

Satisfied with my answer, Francis smiled, turning our horse towards the open gates of the castle, following after Florence and Roxanne.

I closed my eyes, enjoying the last moments in Francis' arms before we arrived. The smell of jasmine and wine hit my senses, bringing calmness to my mind—

"Your Highness!" Tamira ran across the court-yard—filled with dozens of warriors: vampire and human—once we crossed the gates. A man and a woman ran after her. "Roxanne." Tamira stopped before my friends, a small, prideful smile appearing on her lips.

Francis brought our horse to a halt beside them, jumping off the saddle in a swift move. "Rest, remember?" His hands wrapped around my waist as he effortlessly picked me up from the horse, setting my feet on the bleeding soil.

The walls that separated the castle from unwanted guests now carried ash. The soil underneath my feet was painted crimson as every inch of it was covered in—I hoped—Wur-dulacs' blood.

"Your Highness." Tamira took a step towards us, lower-ing her head. Several small scars painted her skin red, her hands covered in bruises. "I am delighted to know you sur-vived the attack, I hear a lot fell onto your shoulders." She glanced at my thigh.

My eyes scanned her body for any major injuries. "It's Cordelia." I smiled when I found nothing besides bruises and small cuts. "And I am very happy you have survived the assault that erupted here." I leaned on Francis when my thigh ached from fatigue, my eyes scanning the courtyard: warriors carried the remaining bodies of the fallen.

"How many have we lost?" Roxanne followed my gaze, holding Florence's hand in hers.

"We had minimal losses, despite the attack taking our armies off guard and unprepared." Tamira sighed before continuing, "Arthur—the commander of Barren's army—did not make it."

"Where is Barren?" Francis crooked his brow, looking around the courtyard.

"He still hasn't shown. Nobody knows of his whereabouts." Tamira shrugged, glancing at me. "Some say his ship is no longer at the dock. But it's merely speculation." Tamira's lips turned into a thin line as her gaze jumped between me and Francis. "May I have a word with you, Your High—" she trailed off, correcting herself. "Cordelia?"

"Of course!" I let go of Francis' hand, ignoring his irritated gaze at my back. "I will rest after," I threw over my shoulder, following Tamira into the castle.

The halls of the castle chimed with chatter and laughter—something this place had never heard before—bringing a small smile to my face.

The human warriors walked side by side with the ones from Faris, their conversations echoed through the walls.

"I am sorry for such urgency." Tamira glanced at my limping leg as we walked towards the doors of the courthall. "If you would rather rest first—"

"I am well." I shook my head, opening the door for her, ushering for her to enter. "Rest can wait." I entered the courthall after her, dropping on the nearest chair.

"I hear it was you who killed Kane." Tamira sat beside me. "I wanted to personally thank you for your bravery."

"It was Caleb who sacrificed the most." A sad smile appeared on my face as the memories of his dying eyes invaded my mind. "I merely got lucky."

"Of course it was more than just luck," Tamira protested. "Thank you. Without you, none of this would've been possible."

"That is hardly true," I laughed. "It was your brave warriors that fought against the Wurdulacs—"

"Your High—Cordelia, you needn't be modest" Tamira smiled—the first real smile I'd seen her wear. "Though, I suppose that is what makes a great ruler," she cleared her throat. "That is why I summoned you here," Tamira's voice turned serious. "Our Kingdom has lost their leader, and with no leader there will soon be many unsettlements throughout the villages. We need a ruler who will care for their people, a ruler who will lead with grace in times of hardship—"

"I am none of those things, Tamira," I interrupted her, knowing well where this conversation was headed. "You are mistaken, I am not worthy of the crown."

"You are the last of the Royal family," Tamira argued. "Warriors trust you to lead with the same fairness that your mother had."

I almost laughed at her statement, for Mother was anything but fair.

"I am no leader." I shook my head. "I never was." Before she had a chance to dispute, I added, "You are."

Tamira's brows furrowed, her dark brown eyes bored into mine as the realization of what I'd suggested settled in her mind. "I am not of Royal blood," she said at last.

"It's not right for a vampire to rule over humans." I shrugged. "The people trust you, and so do I."

"The differences between vampires and humans are settled, at least for now. People trust you to rule fairly over both," Tamira wouldn't give up as she palmed the wooden table.

"No," my voice echoed through the silent room.

"No?" Tamira looked at me as though I had lost my mind. "You are—you are rejecting the crown?"

"I am." I nodded, my voice turning soft. "I never wished for the throne, and I would never make a good ruler." I straightened my back, filling my lungs before continuing, "As the last of Royal blood, I am to decide to whom the crown, I inherited by blood, is given." A bright smile stretched my lips as I met Tamira's growing eyes. "I trust you will bring many wonderful things to this Kingdom, Your Majesty."

"That is not right—" Tamira whispered, her eyes growing bigger.

"The coronation usually takes place during the full Moon," I added. "Though, as the new ruler, you are to decide on the occasion, Your Majesty."

"You cannot be serious." Tamira shook her head, getting up from her chair.

"I am." I stood up before her. "You will make a great ruler, Tamira." My hand fell onto her shoulder. "Do you accept the crown?"

"I—" She glanced in every direction as though the answer was written on the walls. "I do," her stern voice bounced off the walls when she nodded. "I do."

"I wish you all the strength in the Moon's realm, Your Majesty." I bowed before her as low as my injured thigh allowed.

"May I ask for a favor?" Tamira's brows furrowed at my gesture as she quickly collected herself.

"Anything." I nodded, ready for the first order from my new Queen.

"Would you be the one to coronate me?" Her voice was barely a whisper when she asked.

"It would be an honor." A prideful smile tugged on my lips.

Tamira returned the gesture as her face lit up with a beam of her own. "I want for the coronation to take place at the next full moon, as customs require."

"It is my utter privilege to attend, Your Majesty." I bowed before her before taking my leave.

Chapter 47. The Queen.

One Moon Later.

The Royal palace buzzed with joy and laughter. The halls filled with chatter and excitement.

I walked through familiar corridors to the chambers I'd once called mine: a bright yellow dress in my hands.

"Is that for me?" Charlotte beamed as I walked into the Royal room that all of us had stayed in for the day before the coronation. "It's glorious!" She jumped up and down when I showed her the dress that once belonged to Eleanor.

"Do you like it?" I offered her Eleanor's favorite gown.

"Yes!" Charlotte palmed her mouth, unable to contain her excitement. "Yes, I do!" Her eyes sparkled with joy.

"Well, put it on then!" I ushered her into the smaller room, connected to the living space in the chambers.

"You are going to spoil her." Roxanne shook her head, trying on one of the gowns from my old closet; though she allowed a delighted smile, glancing at the door Charlotte had disappeared behind.

My friends and I had traveled all day long to the palace, to witness the biggest coronation in history of our Kingdom, along with many residents of Faris. Tamira granted the vampires any chambers of our choosings for the day, insisting the vampire population must be part of the event.

"I will not see her for a whole year," I argued with Roxanne. "I get to spoil her before you depart."

"A year for a vampire is not a long time." Florence sat on the settee by the fireplace, her dark purple gown splattered on the cushion in beautiful waves. "You won't even have time to miss us." A mischievous smile spread across her lips when her eyes met mine. "Besides, you and Francis will be far too occupied with each other to remember anyone else."

I rolled my eyes, letting out a small chuckle. "Just promise you will write to us at least once a month."

After the coronation, Florence and Roxanne decided they'd travel across the neighboring Kingdoms like they had always dreamed of, taking Charlotte with them as promised.

Charlotte was thrilled to finally leave the orphanage, thrilled to see the realm that had robbed her of so much.

I'd never seen her more happy than in the last Moon when she'd stayed at the Bloodlake castle with us, only visiting Faris once a week to see her friends from the orphanage: that each had a home of their own. The orphanage now stood empty.

"You should try this one, Sunshine." Roxanne brought out the dress I was to wear for the next Crimson War celebration. I'd always found it incredibly foolish to plan the attire years ahead, yet at that moment I couldn't be happier, for Florence jumped off the settee as the sunshine smile glowed on her face.

"It is absolutely gorgeous!" She gasped. "What if I ruin it?" She looked at me for permission, as though I had any say in it.

"The gown will be fine," I laughed at her worried expression. "You should keep it for the balls at Faris!" I nodded.

The door to the living space of our chambers opened, revealing Francis and Ash at its threshold. Francis wore the same black and gold vest I'd judged him for wearing at the Crimson War celebration last year.

Ash—in similar attire—wore a golden vest, their long hair left loose. "Cordelia, you are a fool for exchanging this palace for the Bloodlake castle," they laughed. "I wish Simon was here to witness it."

"He will forever be here with all of us." Francis patted Ash's shoulder. "We must be on our way, the coronation is soon to begin." Francis' eyes traveled to me. "You look delightful, Princess," he murmured.

Roxanne rolled her eyes, fixing the sleeves of her gown. "They cannot start the coronation without her." She pointed at me. "We can take as much time as we want."

"One day at the palace, and you are already acting like a spoiled royal, Rox," Francis laughed, holding the door for us.

"As a matter of fact, I was never late to any events," I threw over my shoulder, holding Charlotte's hand as we walked through the corridors towards the Royal ballroom.

"I look like a princess!" Charlotte skipped, overjoyed with the event.

"That you do!" The brightest of smiles filled my face when we passed the walls that were decorated with dozens of wildflowers.

The golden crown, decorated with many differently colored stones, clanged at my touch when I raised it from the crimson cushion.

Dozens of eyes planted on me, smiles painted every face in the ballroom.

"By the honor of the Moon's realm." I stood before a kneeling Tamira in the center of the hall; Gabriel—her second in command—stood by her side. "By the honor of the Queen of our Kingdom, it is my privilege to grace our Ruler with this crown."

Dozens of braids decorated her hair, each strand carried a golden trinket, sparkling under the Moonlight, peeking through the windows and the candlelight that filled the ballroom.

Her light grey dress carried many crimson beads, emerging into beautiful flowers and spirals.

"Rule with grace, Rule with kindness." I set the crown on Tamira's head. "Rule with praise, Rule with brightness." I took a step backwards as Tamira rose. "Rule with honor, Rule with fairness to all." I met her smile with my own. "By the honor of the Moon's realm, I shall pronounce you the Queen of the Crimson Kingdom, Your Majesty." I bowed before the Queen.

Every person in attendance: vampire and human, followed my lead before the ballroom erupted in celebration.

UNKINDNESS OF CRIMSON QUEEN

Three nights had passed since the coronation, three nights filled with festivity and mirth. Her Majesty had urged us to stay for longer, yet it was time for Roxanne, Florence, and Charlotte to depart for their journey. It was time for me and Francis to finally go home.

"You are always welcome here, Cordelia," the Queen had told me at last before we took our leave. "Always."

"Thank you, Your Majesty." I'd bowed to her one last time before walking out of the palace's gates, towards the garden. The Royal garden that had changed my life forever.

The Moon smiled down at me when I reached my found family. The five of them stood by the cherry tree that had often served as my refuge, excitement written on each of their faces.

"I will write to you!" Charlotte wrapped her hand around me, skipping towards the small horse–drawn carriage filled with three wooden caskets.

Florence and Roxanne laughed, averting their gaze from the child. "Behave, both of you!" Roxanne pointed her finger from me to Francis before enveloping us into a quick embrace.

"We will try," Francis winked at her. "Travel safely," he offered to the women.

"I will write to you, promise." Florence nodded, when my hands wrapped around her, before following after Roxanne and Charlotte, towards the carriage.

The Moon shone brighter as Francis and I watched the carriage depart, dozens of stars lightened the skies, illuminating their path.

"Are you ready to go home, love?" Francis took his hand in mine as we walked through the garden where we'd first met, towards the stables.

"Yes." A soft smile tugged on my lips when I met his gaze, leaving behind the Royal palace forever.

Francis' letter to Cordelia.

I wish to beg for your permission
  To grant me an eternity with you.
As though it is my lifelong mission,
I'm desperate, for my soul is due.
And when my being drowns in beauty
Of your forbidden, longing soul,
It shall become my utter duty
To beg for mercy, for I'm a fool.
For I'm a fool without your presence,
For I'm a fool without your heart.
Your mere glance—is my essence,
Your mere glance—an arrow's shot.
And for the rest of my poor being,
When I am left with no more pain...
I'll beg the Moon when my end is nearing
To let my last word be your name.
                              The End.

Acknowledgments

F irst and foremost, I would love to thank every reader who made it here! None of this would be possible without your support.

Thank you to my life partner, Bradley, who spent months listening to my rants about my characters and then weeks more editing the disaster this book was in its early stages. Thank you for believing in me, even when I don't!

I would like to thank my editor, and best friend, Lennon. Your kind words of encouragement, and additional commas, always keep me going! Thank you for your utmost support, funny comments, and for catching every time I misspelled the word 'apparently'...

Thank you to my father, Sergei, who is easily the most excited person in my life when it comes to my books: despite being unable to read them. There hasn't been a single day when you haven't asked about my writing and celebrated my wins. Your support means more than you know.

As always, I have to thank my cat, Silver! Despite you disagreeing with my word choices and adding your own every time I leave my computer unsupervised, I am so grateful for your existence and your love!

And last but not least, thank you to all who don't agree with my career choices! Spite is the greatest tool at my disposal!

About the Author

A rya was born in the middle of a horrific snowstorm on a dark, gloomy night in Siberia; scientists claim it was merely a coincidence, yet there hasn't been another snowstorm of that scale, in her hometown, since she moved to the States.

Her whole life Arya used writing to process and express her feelings in the form of poetry and short stories. She's had a passion for literature ever since she was young; there was nothing she dreamed of more than becoming an author one day.

Even after completing a degree in Mathematics, Arya couldn't help but to return to her peculiar worlds.

When not writing, Arya spends most of her time figure skating, reading spooky books, and collecting dry flowers!

ARYA SLOANE

Learn more on:
Instagram @aryasloaneauthor
TikTok @aryasloaneauthor